Government of
Western A...

STATE L...

Item

THE STRONGBOW SAGA,
BOOK THREE

THE ROAD
TO
VENGEANCE

THE STRONGBOW SAGA,

VIKING WARRIOR
DRAGONS FROM THE SEA

THE STRONGBOW SAGA,
BOOK THREE

THE ROAD
TO
VENGEANCE

WESTERN FRANKIA
SPRING AND SUMMER
A.D. 845

JUDSON ROBERTS

HARPER TEEN
AN IMPRINT OF HARPERCOLLINS PUBLISHERS

HARPERTEEN IS AN IMPRINT OF HARPERCOLLINS PUBLISHERS.

THE STRONGBOW SAGA, BOOK THREE:
THE ROAD TO VENGEANCE
TEXT COPYRIGHT © 2008 BY JUDSON ROBERTS
ALL RIGHTS RESERVED.
PRINTED IN THE UNITED STATES OF AMERICA.
NO PART OF THIS BOOK MAY BE USED OR REPRODUCED
IN ANY MANNER WHATSOEVER WITHOUT WRITTEN
PERMISSION EXCEPT IN THE CASE OF BRIEF QUOTATIONS
EMBODIED IN CRITICAL ARTICLES AND REVIEWS.
FOR INFORMATION ADDRESS HARPERCOLLINS CHILDREN'S
BOOKS, A DIVISION OF HARPERCOLLINS PUBLISHERS,
1350 AVENUE OF THE AMERICAS, NEW YORK, NY 10019.
WWW.HARPERTEEN.COM

LIBRARY OF CONGRESS CATALOGING-IN-PUBLICATION DATA
ROBERTS, JUDSON.
THE ROAD TO VENGEANCE : WESTERN FRANKIA SPRING AND
SUMMER A.D. 845 / JUDSON ROBERTS. — 1ST ED.
P. CM. — (THE STRONGBOW SAGA ; BK. 3)
SUMMARY: HALFDAN'S TRAINING AS A VIKING WARRIOR LEADS
HIM TO FIGHT IN BLOODY BATTLES BETWEEN NATIONS—AND
GIVES HIM CONFLICTED FEELINGS ABOUT HIS KILLER INSTINCTS.
ISBN 978-0-06-081304-8 (TRADE BDG.)
ISBN 978-0-06-081306-2 (LIB. BDG.)
1. VIKINGS—JUVENILE FICTION. [1. VIKINGS—FICTION. 2. WAR—
FICTION. 3. FRANCE—HISTORY—TO 987—FICTION.] I. TITLE.
PZ7.R54324RO 2008   2007036729
[FIC]—DC22   CIP
                                                         AC

TYPOGRAPHY BY ALISON DONALTY
1 2 3 4 5 6 7 8 9 10
❖
FIRST EDITION

For Jeanette,
and our journey.

CONTENTS

1

WHAT IS HIS PLAN?

An arrow whispered out of the dark and thudded into something solid. The sound startled me awake, and I reached out, frantically searching for my weapons. My hand hit something—I could not tell what—that fell over with a loud clatter.

"Hush!" a voice nearby said. "They cannot see us, but they are shooting at sounds."

The voice—it was Tore's—pulled me the rest of the way from my sleep, and I remembered where I was.

The *Gull*, the longship of Hastein, my captain, and the *Bear*, Ivar the Boneless's ship, were anchored, lashed side by side, in the middle of the Seine River. We were deep in the heart of Frankia.

Dusk had been falling when they'd plucked me from the riverbank, where Frankish warriors had surrounded me. Deciding it was too dangerous to try to navigate the unfamiliar waters of the Seine in the dark, Hastein and Ivar had decided to wait the night out in the middle of the river, as far as possible from Frankish archers lurking along the shore.

Tore and Odd were crouched nearby, their bows strung with arrows nocked and ready, peering between the shields lashed along the side of the *Gull*.

"Do you see anything?" Tore whispered.

Odd shook his head. "No," he answered. "The shoreline is too far, and the shadows from the trees along it hide too much. He is somewhere over there, though," he added, pointing slightly upstream with his free hand, "judging from the angle of the last arrow that hit the side."

I was lucky to be alive; lucky to have returned unharmed from the dangerous scouting mission our army's leaders had sent me on. I could still feel the fear of knowing that the time of my death was upon me. Yet once more, against all odds, I had survived. Once more, for reasons known only to them, the Norns had chosen not to cut the threads of my life, but instead had kept me alive and a part of the great pattern of fate they were weaving; the fate of all men and of the world itself. I had survived, but my death had felt so near and so certain that I could not shake its grasp from my heart.

Late the following afternoon, we reached Ruda, the Frankish town along the river that our army had captured and made its base. I did not want to return to the home of Wulf, the gruff Frankish sea captain, where I had been billeted before being sent out on the scouting mission. If I'd been alone, I would have gone to the palace, where the rest of the *Gull*'s crew had made their quarters. But I was not alone. I had a prisoner.

When I pushed the door of his house open and stepped inside, Wulf, who was seated at the table in the main room, scrambled to his feet. For a moment he was speechless with surprise. Perhaps he'd thought—or even hoped—that I was dead. Quickly enough, though, he recovered both his wits and his voice, and began protesting loudly.

"I was not expecting you to return here. The town is calm now, and at peace. We no longer need your protection."

What he said was true. Most of our army was encamped on an island in the river just upstream from Ruda, rather than in the town itself, and Ragnar, the army's war-king, had forbidden our men from harassing the town's citizens. Soon enough we might be facing the main Frankish army. Ragnar did not want a hostile populace at our backs to deal with, in addition to a besieging force, if we had to defend ourselves from behind Ruda's walls.

"Why have you come back here?" Wulf continued. "Why do you not stay with the rest of your captain's men in the count's palace?"

Bertrada, Wulf's wife, was standing behind him, wringing her hands, an anxious expression on her face. I knew she could not understand what he was saying—Wulf was speaking to me in my own tongue, rather than the version of Latin spoken by the Franks. But his anger was obvious from the tone of his voice. No doubt she feared I might take offense. In truth, I was beginning to.

I pointed behind me. "I have come back to your home because of her. She is my prisoner. I need quarters where she will be safe." Surely Wulf could understand that. A woman—particularly one as young and comely as my captive—could not be housed in a hall filled with hardened warriors.

"You are concerned for her safety?" he exclaimed, and rolled his eyes—an insolent gesture which angered me. "Is this not a woman you stole? If her well-being worries you so, why did you take her? Surely she would have been safe if you'd left her with her own folk!

"I am running low on food," Wulf continued.

"So long as your fleet is on the river, and our land is under attack by your army, I am unable to take my ship out—I am unable to trade. I can earn nothing with which to buy food for my own family. I cannot afford to feed two extra mouths. She is your problem. She is not my concern."

Genevieve, my prisoner, was standing just inside the doorway, slumped back against the wall, staring at us dully. She had stumbled from fatigue several times during the short walk from the river to Wulf's home, and looked as though she might fall asleep on her feet at any moment.

I felt almost as weary as Genevieve looked. I had been close to exhaustion before Hastein and Ivar had rescued me, and had slept little since. The Franks had been angry at losing Genevieve when they'd believed her rescue was assured. The archers they'd sent creeping to the river's edge had kept up a steady, if ineffectual, fire at us during the night. No one on board either ship had been hit, but after having been hunted for several days by the Franks, the occasional whistle of an arrow passing over-head, unseen in the dark, or the thud of a low shot striking the side of the ship had been enough to keep my nerves on edge, and had made sound sleep impossible.

"We will discuss the question of food at a later time," I told Wulf. "For now, I must rest, and so must she. You will provide us both with food and drink, and a place to sleep." He opened his mouth as if to protest further, but I cut him off. "I am not asking you, Wulf," I snapped. "Do as you are told."

I slept the rest of the afternoon and through the entire night. When I awoke early the next morning, I was ravenous. Even the thin barley porridge Bertrada had cooked to break the night's fast tasted delicious to me. I quickly finished one bowlful and handed the empty dish back to Bertrada to refill. She glanced at Wulf, and when he nodded, she stepped to the hearth, ladled out another serving from the pot hanging over the low fire, and handed it back to me.

Genevieve stepped through the doorway leading to the back room, and stood for a moment, blinking her eyes and looking confused. The night before I had told Wulf and Bertrada to prepare a pallet for her in the back room, where they and their children slept. I thought she would feel safer, and hopefully comforted, being among her own people again. Wulf and Bertrada had looked surprised. I suppose they'd thought I'd taken her captive at least in part to have the pleasure of a woman in my bed.

Wulf noticed me looking toward the back room, and turned and saw Genevieve.

"She is a nun," he said, turning back to me. Apparently he was still annoyed that I had returned, and was inclined to argue about it. "Did you realize that? Do you know what that means?"

"She told me," I said.

"She is a holy woman. Why did you take her? What will you do with her?" he demanded.

"I intend to sell her."

Wulf's eyes widened, and he turned his head and looked at Genevieve again. "You cannot," he said in a softer voice. "She is so young. And she has dedicated her life to serving God."

Which meant more to Wulf, I wondered—her age or that she was a priestess of the White Christ? He'd told me his first wife and their two daughters had been taken by Northmen when Ruda had been sacked several years ago. Did seeing Genevieve call to his mind painful memories of that loss?

"I intend to sell her back to her family," I explained. "Besides being a priestess, she is of noble blood. She says her father is a count. He will pay well to get her back unharmed." Or so I hoped.

The light in the room dimmed suddenly. I turned to see Torvald standing just inside the open doorway. He could move quietly for such a large man.

"You are to come," he told me. "Ragnar is

7

holding a war council with Hastein, Ivar, and Bjorn. They wish to speak with each of the scouts and question them about what they observed."

As I pushed my seat back and stood, Torvald added, "You are to bring your prisoner, also. And you," he said, pointing at Wulf, "Hastein said you are to come, too."

Ragnar was holding his council in the great hall of the count's palace. I was glad that for once I'd been summoned to appear there before him for a reason other than to answer for some misdeed. As we entered the hall, Torvald pointed to a bench against one wall near the doorway.

"You and the woman wait here," he told Wulf.

Ragnar and his sons Ivar the Boneless and Bjorn Ironsides were seated behind a long table. Hastein was pacing in front of it. Four warriors—I recognized them all as scouts from our journey upriver—stood nearby. Einar, my comrade, was among them. Hastein had told me he'd returned safely from the scouting mission, but we'd had no chance to speak, for he'd been retrieved by Ivar's ship, rather than the *Gull*. Einar nodded when he saw me, and stared at Genevieve curiously.

Hastein glanced at Torvald and me as we approached, then said, "Ah, here is Halfdan. He is the last of them."

"Three of the scouts did not return?" Ragnar asked. Eight of us had been sent out on the mission to find the Frankish army.

Hastein nodded. "Two from the south bank and one from the north."

"And it was a close thing with this one," Ivar added, pointing at me. "When we found him, he was surrounded by Frankish warriors. He had killed four of them, and was holding the rest at bay when we reached him. There were close to thirty of them. He is lucky to be alive, for he was much farther upstream than we'd planned to venture. But just when we were preparing to turn and head back to Ruda, we saw smoke rising from up ahead, along the line of the river, and Hastein insisted we investigate on the chance it might be from a signal fire."

"You lit a signal fire?" Ragnar asked me, a scornful expression on his face. It was a look I'd come to expect when appearing before him. "Did you not think that might draw the Franks to your position? Is that how they discovered you?"

Apparently my past sins had not been forgotten, or forgiven. I could feel my temper rising. It had not been my fault I'd been forced to kill one of our own warriors, and had brawled with another. But Ragnar had thought it was, and he clearly expected me to have behaved foolishly

9

again when out scouting.

"The Franks had already found me, and trapped me against the riverbank," I answered through gritted teeth. "There was nothing to lose at that point by lighting a fire." I saw no reason to volunteer that I actually had not intended the fire to be a signal. My fylgja—my guardian spirit—may have guided my hand when I lit it, but my wits had not. In truth, Ivar was right. I was lucky to be alive.

My resourcefulness—or my luck—had clearly impressed Ivar. Now Bjorn, too, stared at me with a new look of approval on his face. Ragnar looked considerably less impressed. At least he was not talking about hanging me, though.

"Show the scouts what you are making," Ragnar told Hastein.

Hastein beckoned us to approach the table. A scroll of parchment had been partially unrolled, and a section as long as my forearm had been cut from it. I suspected it had been looted from some church or monastery, for it was covered on one side with Latin writing. Hastein had drawn a crude map on the back of the piece of parchment. So far there was not much to it—it was little more than a single wavy line running diagonally across the sheet. Nearby on the table was a squat glass bottle with a small brush in it, and a short length of board with a shallow groove, similar in shape to the line painted on the parchment, cut into its surface.

"While Ivar and I were on the river searching for you," Hastein said, addressing all of the scouts, "I took note of the course of the river, of its bends and twists, and marked them on this board. I have copied it onto this map."

"Here is Ruda," he explained, pointing to a circle painted at one end of the line near the top of the sheet of parchment. "And this is the course of the River Seine upstream from Ruda, where you scouted."

"Do all of you understand what this shows?" Ragnar asked. We nodded, and a few of the scouts grunted in assent.

"I want each of you to tell us about any Frankish troops you saw—how many, and what type—and show us where along the river you saw them," he ordered. "And if you located towns, or roads, and can mark their location for us, do that also."

It was a clever idea. Although Ragnar had explained it to us, I suspected Hastein had thought of it. Unfortunately, most of the men had never seen even a simple map before. Captains of ships and leaders of armies, like Hastein and Ragnar, have uses for such things, but carls—simple freeman and farmers—do not. As a result, they had difficulty relating the locations where they had scouted in the Frankish countryside to the mostly blank piece of parchment lying on the table before them.

One by one, the scouts stepped forward and told their tales of what they'd seen. All, on both sides of the river, had seen patrols of Frankish cavalry. Determining exactly where they'd seen them, though, was a different matter. As each man spoke, Hastein became visibly more and more frustrated. In most cases they could only roughly estimate where each sighting of Frankish troops had been, and even that was based primarily on Hastein and Ivar knowing where along the river each scout had been put ashore.

Finally only Einar and I were left. Einar stepped forward and touched his finger to the map. "There is a large town about here, to the south of Ruda," he said, pointing to an area below the line of the river. "I found a road running across country from north to south, which I believe is the same road that leads south from Ruda. I followed it, and it led me to the town I saw here. Many Frankish warriors are in it, and it is protected by a high wall. I watched the town for more than a day. Patrols of mounted warriors rode in and out frequently."

"Are you sure the town is here?" Hastein asked, tapping his finger on the spot Einar had pointed to. After his experiences with the other scouts, he sounded skeptical.

Einar shrugged. "I cannot say for certain. It is not easy to compare the distances I traveled to this," he said, gesturing at the parchment. Hastein sighed. "But if I am correct that the road I saw is the same road that runs due south from Ruda, then the town I saw also lies to the south, and I believe it would be about there."

"Einar is right," I volunteered. "There is a Frankish town somewhere in that area. I myself did not see it, but the prisoner I captured told me of it. She called it Evreux." I pronounced the strange Frankish name with difficulty. "And she said it is on the road leading south from Ruda. I, too, traveled on that road for a time, though I was to the south of the town. And the same road also eventually leads to another town, even farther to the south, which she called Dreux. I think Dreux would be about here," I added, pointing at the map, below the spot Einar had indicated.

"Here? You are certain? And there is a road running north to south that connects these two towns and Ruda?" Hastein asked. I nodded.

Using the small brush and bottle of dark liquid, he leaned over the table and drew a line running down the map from the circle marking Ruda's location, then marked the line with two more circles where Einar and I had indicated the two towns lay. He straightened up, looking pleased.

Ivar put his hands behind his head and slouched back in his chair. "What good does this do us?" he said to no one in particular. I wondered the same thing. Hastein ignored him, and addressed me again.

"Earlier, aboard the *Gull*, you told me you saw a large number of Frankish troops at a fort. Where was the fort?"

"Over here. There is another road that runs east from this second town, from Dreux," I explained, tracing the line with my finger. "My prisoner told me that this road leads eventually to a large town the Franks call Paris. It is larger even than Ruda. I found the Frankish army here, just off the road leading from Dreux to Paris." I tapped my finger on the map where I estimated I'd seen the huge Frankish fort.

Hastein stared at the map, frowning. "You say you saw them here?" he asked. I nodded. "Are you certain you traveled this far south? It is a long way from the river. I put you ashore far to the north of this area."

"Yes," I told him. The more I studied the map and thought about where I had traveled, the more confident I felt. "It was there. And I am certain it was the main Frankish army that I saw."

"You say *you* found the main Frankish army?" Ragnar interjected. From the tone of his voice, he was clearly skeptical. I wondered if he'd have been so quick to doubt had the fort been seen by a scout other than me. "Why do you believe that?" he continued. "All of the scouts, on both sides of the river, saw Frankish troops."

"They mostly saw patrols of mounted warriors. I saw those, too. But the warriors I saw here were building a fort," I explained, pointing again to the area of the map I'd previously indicated. "A huge fort, to enclose their encampment. Many, many men were working on it. Its walls, when they are finished, will be as tall and as strong as those that surround Hedeby, and they will enclose almost as large an area. It was a fort being built to hold an army—a very big army."

Ivar and Bjorn exchanged glances. "How many warriors did you see there?" Ivar asked.

"I did not even try to count them," I told him. "They were far too numerous. But I saw many, many more than we fought here at Ruda. There were units of mounted warriors constantly on the move throughout this entire area, and I also saw foot soldiers marching toward the fort—a column of them, two abreast, that stretched so far down the road I could not see its end."

"Which direction were the foot soldiers coming from?" Ragnar asked. As he spoke, Hastein painted a square on the map where I'd said I saw the fort. It appeared I had convinced him, at least, of the fort's location.

"From the east, from farther inland," I answered. "From the direction of Paris."

"If he saw that many Frankish foot soldiers, it may well be that Halfdan did find the main muster of the Frankish army," Hastein said to Ragnar, who leaned back in his chair with a deep frown on his face. He looked as though he hated to admit that the main Frankish army might have been found by me.

Ragnar was silent for a time, tugging at his beard as he thought. Finally he spoke.

"By now the Frank's king will have summoned them all: the nobles and their retainers—they will be mostly cavalry—as well as troops from the garrisons of those towns beyond threat of attack by us. Those were probably the foot soldiers he saw. And now they all are gathering, in answer to their king's command. The fortified encampment he found south of the river may well be where they are to meet." He shook his head and sighed. "Yet other scouts saw mounted warriors, many, many of them, on the north bank of the Seine, too. What is the Franks' king doing? What is his plan?"

"It sounds to me as though the Frankish king has divided his army," Hastein suggested. "It appears he has placed large forces on both sides of the Seine."

"Hmm . . ." Ivar grunted. "If he has, their king

is playing a slow and cautious game, but a clever one. He aims to cut us off from obtaining provisions. He is using his mounted troops, who can move quickly across country, to tighten a noose around Ruda. If our raiding parties continue to ride out, one by one he will catch them and kill them. And if we can no longer raid, we will eventually run out of food. We will grow weaker while his army gathers and grows stronger. Then, once he is at his maximum strength, no doubt he will march on Ruda. If we do not take ship and retreat downriver before he puts the town under siege, we will be trapped here."

"I, for one, have no wish to fight from behind these walls," Bjorn said. Until now he had been silent. "I see no profit in it. This is a Frankish town. We will leave it eventually anyway. Why waste lives defending it?"

"Bjorn is right," Ivar said. "I am sick of this stinking town. Men were not meant to live this way, so many so close together. I feel as though every breath I take has already been breathed by ten other men."

"So the two of you counsel that we should take what we've won and sail downriver to the sea?" Ragnar asked. Ivar and Bjorn nodded. "My sons," Ragnar said, shaking his head, "have lived in Ireland too long. They speak like true cattle

17

raiders." Ivar glared at him, but said nothing.

Ivar's words made me recall something I'd forgotten to tell Hastein yesterday, in my fatigue and relief at being rescued.

"I found one of our raiding parties when I was scouting," I said. "The Franks caught them out on the plain. I saw where they died."

"You see, Father? It is as I said," Ivar snapped. "It has already begun. So far, three of our raiding parties have not returned. No doubt they have all been caught and killed by Frankish cavalry. It is time for us to negotiate ransoms for those of our prisoners the Franks are willing to buy back, and make our plans to depart. We came to raid their lands, not to settle on them."

"Or be buried under them," Bjorn added.

I thought Ivar's suggestion was a good one. I hoped we could quickly ransom our prisoners and leave Frankia. I looked forward to being rid of Genevieve. And I was tired of this war, of seeing so much death. I was tired of killing men I had no quarrel with.

"I see a danger in the Frankish king's plan," Hastein said.

"That is what I have been saying," Ivar agreed, nodding his head vigorously and nudging Bjorn with his elbow. "Hastein agrees with us, Father. We need to make plans now to leave this town."

Hastein shook his head. "No! I see a danger for the Franks. You are correct, Ivar. By dividing their forces, the Franks can stop our raiding for now. But if he should need to, how quickly can their king reunite his army?"

"The same thought occurred to me," Ragnar said.

Hastein continued. "I have had the Frankish sea captain whose ship I captured brought here. He may be able to answer that question." Turning to Torvald, he said, "Bring Wulf here."

Wulf looked nervous as Torvald brought him to stand in front of the table, and seemed not to know what to do with his hands. He finally tucked them in his belt, behind his back, then took a deep breath and let it out slowly.

"How far upriver, above Ruda, have you traveled?" Hastein asked him.

"As far as Paris," Wulf replied. "I have taken my ship, the *Swallow*, to Paris to sell cargos there."

"How far upriver is Paris?" Ragnar asked.

"In the *Swallow*? She is not a fast ship, especially if she has to be rowed. And there's usually much rowing to be done on that journey. The Seine is a twisting serpent of a river, for sure."

"How *long* does it take you to travel upriver from Ruda to Paris?" Ragnar said, sounding impatient.

"Seven days, more or less, in the *Swallow*," Wulf answered. "It's faster to travel over land, if it's speed you're after. But easier to carry cargo by ship. Of course," he added, "your ships are much faster than mine. I'd wager you could make the journey in half that time."

"Are there any river crossings?" Hastein asked. "Any fords or bridges?"

"No fords at all," Wulf answered, shaking his head. "The river's too wide and deep. And the first bridges across her are at Paris. There are no crossings at all downstream from there, save for a ferryboat or two at villages along the river."

Wulf's words seemed to please Hastein and Ragnar, though I did not understand why. They looked at each other and smiled.

"That is all for now," Hastein told Wulf, waving his hand at him. "You may go."

"What are you and Hastein plotting, Father?" Ivar asked. "I have seen that look in your eyes before."

"Nothing, as of yet," Ragnar answered. "And you are right, Ivar," he added grudgingly. "We should go ahead and parley with the Franks and begin negotiating ransoms for our prisoners. It will encourage our men to know that soon they can trade their captives for silver. And you are also correct that we cannot continue sending out raiding parties. We will lose too many men to the Franks."

"And after the prisoners are ransomed," Bjorn asked, "will we leave?"

"Perhaps," Ragnar answered. "Perhaps not. But all of the men should use this time, while they are waiting in camp and cannot raid, to care for their weapons and repair their armor, if needed. And all archers," he added, glancing at me, "should make certain they have a plentiful supply of arrows. Perhaps, after the ransoms are paid, we shall leave. But we must make certain the army is prepared for war."

2

A PEACE OVERTURE

Wulf had taken Hastein's dismissal literally, and had left the palace to return to his home, leaving Genevieve sitting alone on the bench.

"We are through here," I told her, speaking to her in her own tongue. *"We will return to Wulf's house now."*

"Why was I brought here?" she asked. I wondered the same thing. Certainly she had not been needed at the war council. *"I do not know,"* I answered.

The tone of my voice was gruff and unfriendly. I still could not purge from my mind the way I'd felt there by the river, knowing I was going to die, waiting for the Franks to attack me. When danger threatens, it can be a bad thing to

22

have too much time to think.

No one can escape his fate, and it is perhaps the truest measure of a man—or so my brother, Harald, once told me—how bravely he meets a certain death. Harald himself had shown no fear when he'd met his own end. The fear I'd felt there by the river, and the chill from it that still lingered in my heart, left me feeling shamed. I was not fit to be Harald's brother. How could I hope to avenge his death?

Genevieve had alerted the Franks to our presence there by the river. But for her, I would not be feeling this shame. Unfairly, I blamed her for it. Clearly she'd heard the hostility in my voice, for she quickly averted her eyes and turned her head aside.

"Do not leave yet," a voice said from behind me. It was Hastein. "Let us go to my quarters. I would talk to you and to your prisoner. And I told Cullain to prepare a special meal. It is the least I could do, after what you have achieved. I expect you have not eaten well for some days."

As we walked behind Hastein and Torvald through the halls of the palace, Genevieve asked me in a quiet voice, *"Who are these two men?"*

"He is my captain," I told her, pointing at Hastein. *"His name is Hastein. He is a very powerful leader among the Danes. He is a . . . Jarl."* The last word I said in my own tongue. I could think of

no word in Latin with the same meaning.

Genevieve frowned. *"He is what?"* she asked.

I thought of the Count of Ruda, who'd ruled over this town before we had taken it from him. And Genevieve had said her father was the count of several towns and the lands around them.

"Your said your father is the Count of Paris?" I asked her.

She nodded her head. *"Paris is one of his counties,"* she said. *"There are other towns, also."*

"Does he rule those towns for the King of the Franks?"

"He is the king's administrator for them."

"A Jarl is much the same. He rules a large district in our lands, in the name of our king."

"And the other man?"

"His name is Torvald. He is Hastein's helmsman on his ship, and is his second in command."

"He is a giant," she said, with awe in her voice. *"I have heard tales of such, but never thought to actually see one with my own eyes."*

I wondered if all Franks knew as little as she about the world outside their own lands. Torvald was a very tall man to be sure, and sturdily built, but he was not a true giant. Everyone among my people knew that real giants were much larger than Torvald. They live far from the haunts of men, in Niflheim, the distant, frozen lands that are always covered with ice and snow, or in their distant and hidden mountain kingdom, Jotunheim.

We entered Hastein's quarters, where my eyes beheld a wondrous sight. My captain had indeed undertaken to reward me, for a veritable feast had been prepared. Cullain had rigged a spit in the massive fireplace located on one wall of the room. A huge goose, its skin brown and glistening with dripping fat, was roasting on it. An iron pot was nestled in a bed of coals that had been raked to one side of the hearth, and the savory steam rising from it added the smell of stewing onions and other vegetables to the mouthwatering aroma of the roasting bird. Two loaves of fresh bread lay on the table beside a sizable block of cheese. Most welcome of all, though, was a large pottery pitcher that was filled to the brim with rich, brown ale.

By the time the goose was ready, and Cullain had carved it and served us, we were well into a second pitcher of ale, and I was feeling quite mellow. Even Genevieve, who'd been as skittish as a cat carried into a room full of hounds when we'd first entered Hastein's quarters, appeared to have relaxed somewhat, after drinking a cup of wine. Hastein had thought to offer it to her, correctly suspecting that ale might not be to her taste. She'd seemed disturbed, though, by the large, ornate silver cup Cullain had served her wine in.

"This is a chalice!" she'd protested. *"It is intended to hold only the sanctified blood of Christ."*

"They are pagans, my Lady," Cullain responded. *"They do not understand. My master admires this cup only for the beauty of its crafting, and the fact that it is made of solid silver. He wished to honor you by serving your wine in such a fine cup."*

Cullain's words disturbed me. I wondered why Hastein wished to honor Genevieve. It seemed a strange thing. For that matter, why had he invited her to dine with us? He did not usually treat prisoners so.

"Your prisoner was a rich catch," Torvald said to me. "I heard her father is a count. If true, you should get much silver for her. And she appears to be a pretty thing, too, though she hides her looks under that drab hood and gown. If her father is rich, why does she dress so plainly?"

"She is a priestess," I told him. "It is what they wear."

"She is a nun," Hastein said, correcting me.

"Yes," I agreed. "That is what she called herself."

"They are like the monks in the monasteries we have looted, here and in Ireland," Hastein explained to Torvald. "Only they are women.

"What is your prisoner's name?" Hastein asked.

"Genevieve," I told him. She looked up at the sound of her name, realizing we were speaking about her.

"And is she truly the daughter of a count? Are you certain of that?"

"Yes," I answered. "And from what she has said, I believe he is a powerful one. He rules more than one town."

Hastein looked at Genevieve appraisingly. Being the center of attention seemed to frighten Genevieve, and she lowered her gaze.

"Ask her which towns her father rules."

"My father is the Count of Angers, and Tours, and Blois, and Nevers, and Autun, and Auxerre, and Paris," she said, when I translated Hastein's question for her. I was surprised by her answer. I had not realized her father ruled over so many towns. Hastein looked surprised, too.

"Ask her her father's name," he said.

"Robert," she responded when I asked her. *"And he is called Robert the Strong, for he is one of King Charles's greatest warriors, and a leader of his armies. He fears no man. He will not fear you—he will try to kill you, and all of your men,"* she added defiantly.

Torvald grinned at her answer. He, too, was called the Strong, although his name was due to his great personal strength.

"She is quite a rich prize," Hastein said. "You should do very well by this. Very well indeed. Tell her she will need to write a message to be delivered to her father. Can she write?" he added.

I asked her. Genevieve nodded. *"Of course,"* she said.

"I will tell you what she should write," Hastein continued. "You will explain it to her. We want her to assure her father she is safe, and unharmed . . ." He paused and looked at me. "Is she unharmed?"

I blushed and nodded my head. I was not expecting such a question. Torvald laughed at my reaction.

"A wise choice, when dealing with women of their nobility. It will bring you a richer ransom," Hastein said. "She will tell her father she is unharmed, but if he does not pay a ransom promptly, she fears her captors will take their pleasure of her. That will encourage him to pay a high price—and pay it swiftly."

"What is he saying?" Genevieve asked, looking from Hastein to me.

"He wishes you to write a message that we will have delivered to your father," I told her. *"So we can arrange for your ransom to be paid."*

"What shall I tell him?" she asked. She looked hopeful and eager at the news.

I did not wish to repeat Hastein's words to her. *"We will discuss it later,"* I told her.

When we'd returned to Hastein's quarters from Ragnar's council, he had brought with him the map he'd drawn, as well as the scroll, small brush, and bottle of ink. Hastein unrolled the scroll now, and with his knife sliced another length of parchment from it. Genevieve gasped. He handed the piece of parchment to me, with the brush and bottle.

"You write Latin as well as speak it, do you not?" he asked. I nodded. "Help her write the message and bring it back to me when it is finished. I also plan to have the bishop we captured here in Ruda write one to send to the other high priests of the Christians in these lands. I plan to have him list all of the priests and monks we now hold as prisoners, and to say that we shall sell them all into slavery if they are not ransomed. And we will burn all of the monasteries and churches between here and the sea, unless the Franks pay us to spare them."

Hastein grinned. "I enjoy this part of it," he said. "I enjoy squeezing the silver out of them."

The sun was dropping toward the horizon by the time Genevieve and I made our way back to Wulf's house from the palace. I was carrying a large sack of root vegetables, a smaller one of barley, and a fresh ham from a recently slaughtered pig, wrapped in cloth. I'd been given them by Cullain, after telling Hastein of Wulf's protest that he was running low on food.

"I have never known a merchant who did not keep a store of silver secreted somewhere," Hastein had replied. "And most have several hoards hidden in different places. It is how they protect themselves against unexpected troubles. I suspect Wulf could buy more food if he was truly desperate. He just does not wish to reveal that he has wealth hidden away which we do not know about. But we can share some of our stores with him. You should not suffer meager rations due to Wulf's stinginess, nor should your prisoner."

As we walked, I felt puzzled again that Hastein had invited Genevieve to eat with us. Several times during the meal, he had remarked how pleasing he found her looks, and once had even asked me to translate his words to her. I felt very awkward doing so. She, on the other hand, had blushed, but had not looked displeased.

"I spoke with Wulf while he and I were waiting at the palace," Genevieve said, interrupting my thoughts. *"I asked him why you were living in his home."*

I suspected that question had made Wulf uncomfortable. He would not want any Frank, much less a count's daughter, to know he had helped our army gain entrance to Ruda.

"*He told me he and his ship were captured by Northmen who used it in a ruse to get their warriors close to the city and in through the river gate. He said your captain was the pirate leader who had captured him, and he ordered you to protect Wulf and his family, because the folk of Ruda might have mistakenly believed he had actually helped the Northmen win the city.*"

It was a cleverer lie than I would have expected from Wulf. Perhaps Hastein was right. Maybe he did have a hidden hoard of silver.

"*That was a kindness I would not have expected from your people,*" she said. I supposed not. Genevieve had told me more than once that she considered us murderers and pirates.

"*Wulf told me you saved his wife's life, the night that Ruda fell. You killed one of your own warriors to save her,*" she said. I was surprised Wulf had volunteered that information.

She was quiet for a long time, then finally continued. "*I wish you to know that I am grateful for how you have treated me. For what . . . for what you have not done. I was very afraid, but you have acted with honor toward me.*"

I did not answer. I did not want her gratitude. I wanted only the silver that she would bring—and to be rid of her.

❖   ❖   ❖

The next morning, I left Wulf's house early in the morning, as soon as I awoke, before the rest of the household began stirring. I was tired of being in the cramped, stuffy structure, but more than that, I did not wish to see Genevieve. Besides, Ragnar had said at the council that all archers should use this period to replenish their stock of arrows, and my own supply was by now woefully low.

I broke my night's fast in the Count of Ruda's palace, with the *Gull*'s crew. Tore, as captain of the archers on Hastein's ship, had already begun acting on Ragnar's command.

"I found a room here in the palace where the count's warriors stored extra weapons and gear," he told me. "There are many bundles of arrows there. I'll show you where it is. Odd and I and the rest of the men in our crew with bows have already filled our quivers from them."

The room Tore led me to was much more than the simple storeroom I'd expected from his words. It was true that many extra weapons, including bundles of arrows, were stored there. But the large, open chamber also contained everything needed to make or repair weapons and armor, too. There was a forge, an anvil, and smithing tools.

"The arrows are over here," Tore said, walking over to the corner of the room where tied bundles of arrows were stacked.

"What do you think of them?" I asked. He shrugged his shoulders.

"I have seen better, but I have seen worse, too. They will do."

I picked up a bundle and examined the arrows in it. They were not as long as I made arrows for myself—that would affect how far they could be drawn, and the force with which they would shoot. And their shafts were thinner, too.

"Have you shot any?" I asked. Tore shot a longbow, as I did, and it was a strong one. Our bows were too strong for the other archers on the ship to draw easily.

"Aye," he answered. "They are a bit light. They whip coming off my bow. They no doubt will do the same off yours. But it will be better to have these than to run out in the midst of a battle."

"Do you think there will be a battle? Another one?" I was hoping we'd do as Ivar wished and leave Frankia before that occurred.

"Ragnar is the army's war-king," Tore replied, as if that answered my question. It did not.

I untied the cord securing two of the bundles and began stuffing arrows into one of my quivers. As I did, I noticed beyond the stacked bundles of arrows, lengths of drying timber that had not yet been split and cut into shafts. I walked over and picked one up.

"There is a big sack filled with goose feathers for fletching here, too, and many unmounted arrowheads," Tore volunteered.

This was better. I used the Franks' arrows to fill one quiver—the spare one I'd taken from a dead man. But I would make enough new arrows, matched in length and weight to my draw and the power of my bow, to fill my main quiver—the one that contained my remaining supply of the arrows I'd brought with me on this voyage. I had more confidence in arrows that I made myself, more certainty that they would shoot where I aimed.

The work took almost four days of long and tedious toil. I spent one entire day, and part of another, splitting the lengths of lumber, shaping the splits into shafts that I straightened over the heat of a low fire, and cutting nocks in one end of each shaft and tapering the other to take the socket of an iron head. It took another full day to split feathers into pieces for fletching, and attach them to my new shafts with pitch and bindings of fine thread. Last of all, I used more pitch to mount the metal points, then sharpened them.

I finished on the evening of the fourth day, and celebrated with Tore, Odd, and the other members of the *Gull*'s crew, by sharing more than a few rounds of rich, heady ale from a cask Tore said had been looted from a monastery. The priests of the White Christ did not scrimp when it came to brewing ale.

While I'd been working on my new arrows, I'd stayed each night at the palace with the crew. The night after we'd returned from Ragnar's council, I'd explained to Wulf that I would not be staying every night in his home. After all, he was right— the town was secure now. I did not think Genevieve would dare leave his house, given that Ruda was occupied by our army. But I told Wulf that whenever I was away I would be holding him responsible for ensuring she did not wander away or come to any harm.

After being gone for four full days and nights, though, I thought it prudent to check in on my prisoner. It was late and the sky had long been dark by the time I made my way somewhat unsteadily back to Wulf's house, carrying my two quivers that were now chock-full with arrows.

By the time I reached Wulf's home and entered as quietly as I could, the fire had been banked for the night in the hearth and all had taken themselves off to bed. From behind the closed door to the back room, Wulf's snores resounded like the unsteady roar of distant thunder. I stirred the embers until they flared enough to give me a dim light to see by, and leaned my well-stuffed quivers against the wall beside my sea chest.

My body felt sticky and dirty. Longingly I remembered the bathhouse in my father's long-house. I recalled the day, after a successful hunting trip, when Harald and I had sat soaking in the big wooden tub, up to our necks in hot water, while our sister Sigrid had served us hot mulled wine. That had been a happy time. It seemed so long ago.

On impulse, I stripped off my tunic and trousers and stepped outside to the wooden barrel beside the door where Wulf stored the water he and Bertrada carried from the common well down the street. Scooping handfuls of cold water, I rinsed my face and body as best I could, then hurried back inside to escape the chill of the night air. As I was searching in the dim light for my cloak to dry myself with, a shiver shook me and I sneezed.

"What? Who is there?" a sleepy voice mumbled from the far side of the room.

Startled, I turned to see who had spoken. Genevieve was lying on a makeshift pallet in a corner, and had raised herself up on one elbow, looking bleary-eyed in my direction.

She gasped. *"Where are your clothes?"* she asked, now fully awake.

I snatched up my cloak and wrapped it around me.

"What are you doing out here?" I demanded.

"I cannot sleep in the back room any longer," she

said. *"There is too much noise. I have been sleeping out here the past two nights."*

"Wulf's snoring disturbs you?" It was, in truth, very loud.

"That, and . . . there are other noises, also," she said, then cleared her throat while she brushed one hand distractedly through her hair.

It took me a moment to realize what she was speaking of. Wulf and Bertrada acted reserved around each other during the day, but the affection they shared in the dark was loud and enthusiastic. Having grown up in a longhouse, where many people live close together with little privacy, I had learned to ignore such sounds. Apparently, within the palaces of Frankish nobility, conditions were not the same.

"Ah," I said. And after a moment, added, *"So you plan to sleep out here now?"*

"If you do not object," she answered.

"I do not care. It does not matter to me what you do," I told her. She sighed.

"You are still angry at me. You have been angry at me ever since that day, by the river. I can see it in your face whenever you look at me, and hear it in your voice whenever you speak."

I did not say anything in reply. She was right.

"I am sorry for what I did," she said, in a voice that was little more than a whisper.

"You are sorry you tried to escape?" I asked. I did not believe her and did not try to conceal it.

"No," she said, shaking her head. *"Not for trying to escape, but for what my actions caused. I am sorry for the men whose lives I cost. I am sorry for their families. I feel responsible for their deaths. Had I not called out, they would be alive today. I caused their deaths, just as surely as you did."* Then she covered her face with her hands and began weeping.

So she was sorry for those men's deaths. I was glad to hear it. I had come to think that she thought of no one but herself.

In truth, I was sorry for the Frankish warriors' deaths, too. They'd been brave men. They had been trying to rescue Genevieve and help their wounded comrade. There had been nothing personal between us. If not for the war between our two peoples, we would not have been enemies at all, and they would not have died.

"It does no good for you to blame yourself," I told Genevieve. *"What happened was fate. Those warriors' fates, your fate, and mine. The Norns chose to weave the threads of all of our lives together. I do not know why. No mortal can understand why they weave the patterns they do. But it was our fate that those warriors and I should meet as enemies, and it was thanks to my good fortune that I prevailed."* That, and my bow.

"I do not understand," she said, shaking her head. *"Do you believe your Gods cause all things to happen?"*

"The Norns are not Gods," I said. *"They are the weavers of fate—of all that happens in the world, of the paths that all men's lives follow. Even the Gods are ruled by fate."*

"It is a strange belief," she said, shaking her head and frowning.

I thought it stranger that one would *not* believe in fate. How could a man face life if he did not trust that things happened for a reason—that the path his life was following was being woven by the Norns? Without that, would he not always look back, as Genevieve did now, and wonder if everything that had happened around him, everything that lay behind him on his path, might somehow have been changed had he acted differently?

"It is not a belief," I told her. *"It is the way of things."*

I laid down on my pallet, wrapped my cloak tightly around me, and soon was asleep.

In the morning, when I awoke, I found my anger toward Genevieve had passed.

3

PREPARATIONS

The following day I stayed at Wulf's home, using the time to polish and oil my mail brynie and sharpen the edges of the sword and spear I'd acquired on my scouting mission. I was surprised to discover that in the few days I'd been away, working to replenish my supply of arrows, Genevieve had become an accepted member of the household. She even helped Bertrada prepare the meals, although she obviously had little experience at cooking. Bertrada had to guide her through the simplest tasks. Between meals, she busied herself playing with the baby, Alise, and trying to teach the two older children the rudiments of their letters.

"You should not waste your time, my Lady," Wulf

told her. Despite her insistence that they address her merely as "Genevieve," neither Bertrada nor Wulf were able to keep from showing deference to her rank. *"God willing, Carloman will take over my ship and my trade some day, and Adela will be taken as wife by a decent man."*

"But you are a merchant, Wulf," Genevieve said. *"Do you not know how to read and write? Will Carloman not also need such knowledge?"*

He shook his head. *"I know my numbers,"* he said, *"and weights and measures. You cannot trade without knowing such. But I have no use for letters. They are for priests, not for folk who work for living."* He blushed and looked down. *"Meaning no offense, my Lady,"* he added. *"You being a holy sister and all."*

As I worked on my weapons and armor, I often found my gaze wandering across the room to wherever Genevieve was. I noticed that although she kept her hands busy, she frequently had a distant and sad expression in her eyes, as if her mind was elsewhere. And during the afternoon, while she was bouncing Alise on her knee, she suddenly began weeping. Genevieve handed the child to a startled Wulf, then hurried through the door and out into the street. I followed her.

"Why do you weep?" I asked.

"It is nothing," she said, wiping her eyes with

her sleeve. *"It is no concern of yours."*

"Do you weep for the dead?" I guessed, remembering her remarks from the previous night.

She nodded, then covered her face with her hands. Her shoulders shook with silent sobs. I did not know what to do, so I did nothing at all. It made me feel foolish.

Finally she stopped weeping, wiped her eyes again with her sleeve, took a deep breath, and spoke. As she did, she looked away into the distance, although nothing was there save the blank wall of a house across the street.

"For the dead," she said, belatedly answering my question, *"and for the living. Captain Marcus—one of the men you killed—was one of my uncle's favorite officers. He was often in my uncle's home, and I have met his family. He has a young daughter about the same age as Alise. She will grow up not knowing her father. And I worry for my uncle and my aunt Therese. Leonidas was their oldest son. What pain they must be feeling now in their hearts."*

I did not like to hear about the families of men I had killed. I did not like to see the pain in Genevieve's face, either.

"I am sorry," I said, *"For the pain I have brought into your life."* As soon as I spoke, I thought my words sounded weak and foolish. I wished I could take them back. She was a Frank, I a Dane. She was

a prisoner and I her captor. Torvald, or Tore, or any other member of the *Gull*'s crew would have laughed out loud had they heard me. Yet though I wished I had not uttered such words aloud, in my heart I knew they were true. I did regret the sorrow I'd caused her.

"The worst of it is that they died for me. They gave their lives trying to help me." She began sobbing again. *"It is something you could not understand."*

I should not have cared what she thought of me, but her words stung.

"Something I could not understand?" I repeated, and gave a bitter laugh. *"Because I am a killer, too ruthless and cruel to have feelings? Just a pirate and a murderer—what could such a man understand? Or is it because you think it impossible that anyone could ever choose to give their life for me?"*

"Because you are a warrior, as you so proudly told me," she retorted. *"And yes, because you are a pirate, and a killer, too. I have seen you fight. You are ruthless. I have seen how easily you kill. I'm sure you have been fighting and killing all your life. Is that not the way of your people?"*

My flaring temper began to frame an angry response. But suddenly as I looked down at Genevieve's tear-streaked face, her eyes staring defiantly up at me, in my mind the face I saw was my mother's—when she was young, when she was Genevieve's age.

She had seen her father and her betrothed both slain before her eyes when they'd attempted to rescue her from the raiding Northmen who'd captured her. She had been torn from her home and carried away to a strange and distant land. Had she not felt feelings similar to those Genevieve was feeling now? Had she not, at least for a time, been terrified of my father? Had she not despised him? I felt my anger draining away.

"*Perhaps you are correct about my people,*" I told Genevieve in a low voice. "*Some of us, at least. Some Danes are pirates. Some are cruel, and killers. And I am a Dane. But just a year ago, I was not even a warrior. I had never fought and never killed. I did not choose to become the killer you believe I am. It was my fate that made me what I am today, and no man can escape his fate.*" I turned away and headed back into the house. At the doorway I paused and said over my shoulder, "*And you are wrong—I can understand the pain you are feeling. My mother and my brother both gave their lives for me.*"

Later that day, Hastein paid a surprise visit to Wulf's home. It was the first time he had come there. "I wished to see with my own eyes where you have been staying in Ruda," he explained, as he looked around the small house while Wulf watched nervously.

It seemed unlikely to me that Hastein would care enough about the nature of my quarters to have ventured out to inspect them. I wondered if he was actually hoping to spot where Wulf might have hidden a secret store of silver. His examination did not take long. There was not much house to see.

Genevieve was slicing vegetables for a stew Bertrada had begun for the evening meal. She had not been wearing her hood and mantle all day, and her dark, lustrous brown hair was pulled back and loosely secured behind her neck with a short length of cord.

Hastein commented on it. "She does not wear her nun's hood today," he said, and asked me to translate his words.

"My mantle is soiled," she explained, sounding flustered by the question. *"And when I am working near the fire, it is also very warm to wear."*

"She should never wear it. Her hair is far too beautiful to cover," Hastein said. "Tell her I said so."

Why would he wish to say such a thing to her? She was just a prisoner. *My* prisoner. And why did *I* have to tell her his words? It made me feel uncomfortable.

Hastein's words seemed to make Genevieve uncomfortable, too. I felt glad that she did not seem pleased by his attention, as she had that day in his quarters. She blushed and looked down at her hands when I translated his words for her. *"I am a woman of God,"* she murmured. *"Does your captain not understand that?"*

Hastein laughed when I told him her reply. "Aye," he said. "And that is a great waste of a beautiful woman. If the Franks do not ransom her, I will be sorely tempted to buy her from you myself. You and I could both profit that way."

I had given no thought to what I would do if no ransom was paid for Genevieve. I would not have bothered to capture her—to risk the danger of trying to escape across country with her—had I not believed it would bring me great profit for my trouble. Now that Hastein raised the prospect that perhaps no ransom would be paid, I found it disturbing. What would I do with her if her father refused to pay?

"When the two of you dined with me several days ago, I told you I needed your prisoner to write a message to be delivered to her family. Has she written it yet?"

I shook my head. "No," I said. Hastein looked annoyed.

"I have spent the past four days making arrows," I explained. "Ragnar said all archers should replenish their supplies." My answer did not seem to appease Hastein's irritation.

"And I said you should have her write a message to send to her father. It would not have taken you long to do so. Do it now," Hastein ordered, "and bring the parchment to me as soon as it is completed. On the morrow we will take the *Gull* upriver to seek a parley with the Franks. We will deliver her message then, as well as that written by the Bishop of Ruda, and begin our negotiations for our prisoners' ransoms. You will come, to speak for me to the Franks."

Genevieve addressed her message *"To my most honorable and revered father, Robert."* She wielded the little brush with precision, painting the letters in neat, even strokes. Putting words on a page was clearly a task that was familiar to her.

She told her father she had been taken prisoner by the Northmen—something he would have been well aware of by now. She also insisted on telling him—though I told her it was not necessary, for the Franks undoubtedly had found the body—that her cousin Leonidas, his brother's eldest son, had been slain trying to protect her. *"Please convey to my uncle and to Aunt Therese my deepest sorrow at his death, and assure them he fought bravely,"* she wrote, then let out her breath with a quavering sigh.

"Were you and your cousin close?" I asked. I

wondered how deeply his death grieved her.

She was silent for a time before finally answering. *"No. In truth we were not. But he did not deserve to die. He was but a young man. And his parents are good folk, and do not deserve the suffering his death has undoubtedly brought them."*

Genevieve did not hesitate when I told her to write that she was unharmed. But her face flushed bright red, then turned completely white, when I told her to warn her father that if a ransom was not paid soon for her, she feared her captors would take their pleasure of her. She dropped the brush, making a stain of black ink on the parchment, and looked at me with fright-filled eyes.

"I have already given you my promise that you have nothing to fear, that you will not be harmed," I assured her. *"Those words are Jarl Hastein's, not mine. He told me your message should say that, to spur your father not to delay or consider trying to pay less than we demand. You must trust me. You are my prisoner, and I will honor my word to you."*

That seemed to calm her. *"How much will you ask my father to pay to ransom me?"* she asked.

I answered truthfully. *"I do not know. That is something Hastein will decide. I have never ransomed any prisoner before. And you are not just any prisoner—as the daughter of a count, you are without question worth more than most."*

"Are you truly only recently a warrior?" she asked. I nodded.

"What were you before?"

I did not wish to tell her. She stared at me, waiting for my answer. I did not wish to lie, either.

"I was a slave," I said in a quiet voice. I did not want Wulf or Bertrada to overhear.

"Oh," she said, looking startled. She dropped her gaze to the parchment in front of her. *"I am sorry."*

I thought it a strange thing for her to say. I wondered what she was sorry for.

By the time I reached the Count of Ruda's palace with the message Genevieve had written for her father, dusk was falling. Within the palace, the cold stone corridors were dark and gloomy. They made me think of the low tunnels and dark halls carved beneath the roots of mountains where dwarves are said to dwell.

Hastein was bathing. A large copper tub had been placed in the center of the floor in his quarters, and he was seated in it. As I entered the room, Cullain dumped a pot of steaming water over his head.

"Aahh!" he exclaimed as the water sluiced down over him. "That feels wonderful." He opened his eyes as I drew nearer. "Do you have the message?"

I held the parchment up. "I do."

"Good," he said. "We will depart just after dawn tomorrow, as soon as there is enough light to see the river. You should probably stay here with the crew tonight."

"I will fetch my weapons and gear from Wulf's house, and return," I told him.

"It is good you have acquired a mail brynie and a sword. You did very well when you were sent out scouting. Others—Ivar and Bjorn—took notice. You found the Frank's army, won a fine weapon and armor, and look to gain a tidy sum of silver for the prisoner you captured. That is for her, by the way."

Hastein pointed at a bundle of cloth on the nearby table. "They are some women's gowns," he explained. "They were in one of those large chests when I took over these rooms for my quarters. The nun's robe your prisoner is wearing is filthy. As the daughter of a count, she will not be used to that. Give her these, so she will have clean clothing to wear. Tell her they are a gift from me," he added.

Now Hastein was giving Genevieve gifts. He seemed far too taken with her. More than ever, I worried about what would happen if her father refused to pay a ransom.

Hastein stopped talking for a few moments while he rubbed a block of soap into his hair. "Cullain, where is that girl?" he grumbled. Cullain did not answer. As he straightened from where he had been bending over the fire, pouring more water into the pot suspended over the flames, he glared in Hastein's direction. Then he disappeared through a narrow doorway opposite the main one I had entered through. A few moments later, a young woman entered the room through the same door.

Hastein waved the soap over his head. "Come here. Wash my hair," he said to her. To me, he added, "It is inconvenient that she cannot understand what I say."

The woman stepped over to the tub, took the soap from his hand, and began washing Hastein's hair. She was barefoot and was wearing only a thin white shift that looked like an under-gown.

"What do you think of her?" Hastein asked.

She was pretty enough, or would have been, had her features not looked so drawn and filled with sorrow. What has she lost, I wondered. Her freedom? Her family? Hope?

"She looks unhappy," I said.

Hastein nodded. "She does seem to have a melancholy temperament. I meant what I said, by the way, back at Wulf's house."

I thought I knew what he was referring to, but I willed my features to show no reaction—to hide the growing sense of alarm I was beginning to feel.

"If your prisoner's father should refuse to pay a ransom for her, I will buy her from you," he explained.

If Hastein wished to have Genevieve, did I dare refuse? He was my leader, my chieftain, and I did not wish to anger him. It was the greatest of good fortune that he had taken me into the crew of the *Gull*, and I owed him my loyalty. Even more, I needed the support and help he could give if I truly hoped to fulfill my quest and bring down Toke and all of his men. But I had promised Genevieve she would not be harmed. She was under my protection, and I had given her my word. I looked again at the face of the woman who was bathing Hastein, and knew I could not allow Genevieve to become someone like her.

"If she is not ransomed, I will not sell her," I said, shaking my head.

Hastein raised his eyebrows. "You will keep her for yourself, instead of selling her to me?" There was a tone in his voice I could not decipher. Was it anger, or merely surprise?

"I have given her my word she will not be harmed. I will not break my word," I said. I hoped he would not push this.

"She is just a Frank and a prisoner," he said. His expression was still inscrutable, but he was watching me closely now.

"Wulf was just a Frank and a prisoner," I replied, "but you felt honor-bound to keep your word to him."

Silence hung between us for an uncomfortably long time before Hastein spoke again. "Some chieftains take great offense if their wishes are countered—particularly by one of their own men." He stared at me, trying to make me drop my gaze before his. But I would not. The woman and Cullain both were still now, watching the two of us.

"I myself," he finally said, "think it is good to see a man stand up for what he believes is right. I find it easier to trust a man when I know he values honor above all else—even his life."

I did not know whether to feel relieved by these last remarks or threatened. I suspected that was Hastein's intention—he wished me to feel uncertain—for he stared at me for a few moments longer. Then, with a small smile he looked away and settled deeper into the tub. "Tell her to rinse the soap out now and comb my hair," he said to me, indicating the sad-faced woman. "And tell her to be gentle if she finds any tangles."

I passed his instructions on to the Frankish woman and turned to take my leave. Hastein called after me. "Do not worry," he said. "I feel certain her father will pay." I hoped he was right.

✦ ✦ ✦

Wulf, his family, and Genevieve had already finished their evening meal by the time I returned to their home.

"Did you eat at the palace?" Genevieve asked. I shook my head. She ladled leftover stew into a pottery bowl and set it on the table. *"It is still warm,"* she said.

"I will be gone for a day or two, perhaps more," I announced as I set the bundle of clothing on the table and sat down to eat. *"I have returned only to collect my weapons and gear."* I nodded at the bundle and said to Genevieve, *"That is for you."*

"What is it?" she asked.

"It is clothing. Women's gowns. Jarl Hastein found them in the palace. He noticed your clothing is soiled and thought you would enjoy clean garments to wear." I said it matter-of-factly between spoonfuls of stew. I hoped she would think it was merely a casual courtesy on Hastein's part, and not a gift.

She sighed and nodded. *"It is true. My habit is so filthy it is stiff from the dirt."*

Genevieve unfolded the bundle and gasped with pleasure. The outer garment that had been wrapped around the contents was a short cloak of soft wool, dyed a deep black. Folded within were two under-shifts of fine white linen and two richly colored gowns—one a deep red, the other a brilliant blue.

Genevieve pulled out the gowns and held them up so she could see them clearly in the low light from the hearth.

"Look at these colors!" she said. *"They are so brilliant. I have so missed colors since I joined the Convent of St. Genevieve. No doubt it is a sin that I still long for them so much."*

She looked at me. *"Your captain is a very kind man,"* she exclaimed. *"My heart is touched by this kindness he has shown me."*

I did not think she would be so pleased if she knew Hastein wanted to buy her for himself. And I found myself thinking her judgment was unfair. If Hastein had captured Genevieve, instead of me, what would have happened? I had not harmed her in any way. I had treated her with honor. But because Hastein had given her these clothes, he was now a kind man in her eyes.

"I am glad you feel that way about him," I said. *"He has told me that if your father does not agree to pay a ransom for your release, he wishes to buy you from me."*

The stricken look on her face crushed the momentary pleasure my remark had brought me.

"If my father will not pay a ransom?" she whispered. *"Does your captain intend to demand so much that my father will not pay?"*

That was a possibility I had not thought of. *"I*

am certain your father will buy your freedom," I assured her.

"What will become of me if he does not?" she asked, and looked at me with frightened eyes. "What will you do? What will your captain do?"

I should have kept my mouth shut. "I have told Jarl Hastein I will not sell you," I told her.

"But he is your captain."

"You are my prisoner, not his. Your fate is for me to decide." Me, and the Norns.

The *Gull* headed upstream from Ruda while shreds of early morning mist still drifted over the river. An extra passenger I had not expected—Ragnar—was aboard. We rowed hard. Hastein rotated extra crewmen at the oars throughout the day, giving us all periods of rest in turn, while keeping the ship surging steadily ahead.

"Bend your backs, my men," he directed us. "It is good for you. We have been idle too long. And Ragnar and I wish to see how swiftly our ships can travel up this river."

We saw the first signs of the Frankish army at midday. A ten-man cavalry patrol, its riders silhouetted against the sky across the crest of a hill overlooking the river, sat motionless on their horses. They watched as the *Gull* passed below them. A single rider turned and rode away while the rest shadowed us as we continued upriver.

"They want us to know they are there," Tore said, staring at them over his shoulder as he pulled on his oar. "They want us to know they are watching."

As the afternoon wore on, more riders joined the initial patrol, and others took up the pursuit along the opposite bank, until at least thirty mounted warriors followed our passage along each side of the river. Hastein smiled grimly as he watched them, but said nothing. I wondered why he did not stop and deliver our messages to the Franks now.

We anchored for the night in the middle of the river and continued on upstream early the next morning. In mid-afternoon, as the *Gull* rounded yet another bend in the river, Hastein called out from the bow, where he and Ragnar had been standing most of the day. "Torvald, there is an island ahead. Slow the pace and take us along its north side."

It proved to be two islands, separated by a narrow channel. A small village was situated back from the river's north bank, just upstream from the gap between the islands. Flocks of sheep grazed along the grassy slopes of a curving ridge that overlooked the village. At the sight of our ship, the frightened shepherds keeping watch over them drove their charges toward the tree line just below the ridge's crest.

The thirty or so Frankish cavalrymen who'd been following the progress of the *Gull* on this side of the river since yesterday rode closer to the river-bank and formed a line between us and the village, ready to fight if necessary.

"Torvald, hold the ship steady here. Halfdan, come forward to the bow," Hastein called. At Torvald's command, the rowers switched to a slow stroke, just enough to maintain the ship's position in the sluggish current. I relinquished my oar to another member of the crew and joined Hastein and Ragnar in the bow.

Hastein was tying a large square of white linen to the shaft of a spear. It looked as though it might have been cut from a woman's under-gown. When he finished, he raised the makeshift flag overhead and began waving it back and forth.

"Call out to them," he commanded. "Tell them I wish to speak with the officer who leads them."

"Halloo!" I called in Latin to the watching Franks. *"Our captain wishes to speak with the officer who commands you."*

A rider in the center of the line with a red pennant attached to the end of his long spear rode forward almost to the water's edge. His shield was raised in front of him, and he watched us warily over its top rim.

"*I command these men,*" he said. "*What is it that you wish?*"

Hastein gave me his instructions in a low voice, and I called across the narrow stretch of water separating the ship from the bank.

"*We have messages from captives who are being held by our army. They concern terms for their release. May we land and deliver the messages to you? We give our word that this day, we have come in peace.*"

"*Your ship may pull in to shore,*" the Frank said. "*But only one man may disembark.*"

I looked at Hastein. He nodded. "You shall go," he said. "I will tell you what to say."

While Torvald swung the ship in against the shore, Hastein explained what he wished me to tell the Frank, and gave me the parchment messages to deliver. As soon as he was done, I trotted aft and retrieved my helm, sword, and small axe from my sea chest. Like the other members of the crew, I was already wearing my mail brynie. Tore unlashed my shield from the shield rack along the ship's side and handed it to me.

"Stay close to the river's edge," he told me as I headed back toward the front of the ship. "Odd and I will cover you with our bows."

The Frankish officer had withdrawn a short distance from the water's edge and sat waiting atop

59

his horse there with an impatient expression on his face. His men remained arrayed in a line behind him, less than a bowshot away. Before I climbed down from the ship to the bank, I called to him.

"I am ready to come ashore. Do I have your word that I may do so safely?"

"You have my word," he said. Tore and Odd appeared behind me, both carrying strung bows. *"And have I yours, that your men will not attack me?"*

"So long as you honor your promise of peace, we will honor ours," I told him.

I approached him cautiously, watching his eyes and his hands as I did. He held his shield so it covered him from chin to thigh, and had turned his horse at an angle so I was facing his protected side. He held his spear upright in his right hand and stared at me with a haughty expression on his face. When I was just three paces away, he flipped the spear suddenly in his hand, so the sharpened head was pointed down. I crouched and swung my shield higher in front of me when he did.

The Frank gave an unpleasant laugh. *"Do not be afraid, Northman,"* he said. *"I gave you my word you will be safe."* He stabbed the spear's point into the ground so its shaft stood upright beside him, then released it and held his now-empty hand out toward me. *"Where are the messages you spoke of?"*

I pulled the folded parchments from where I'd tucked them in my belt and extended them up to him. He stared into my eyes for a moment with a gaze he seemed to think was fierce and intimidating, then snatched the papers from my hand.

"There are three," I explained. *"One was written by the Bishop of Ruda—of Rouen—and concerns the priests we have captured, and your temples and monasteries. Can you see that it is delivered to the high priests of your church?"*

The Frank nodded. *"I will give it to my commander. He will see that all of the messages reach whomever they need to,"* he said.

"The second message is a list of all other prisoners we hold," I continued. *"We are giving it to you so your leaders can decide if they wish to pay ransom to free any of these folk."* Hastein had explained to me that he had directed Cullain to prepare this list. Those named on it were mostly soldiers and a few lesser members of the nobility we had taken at Ruda or in raids on villas in the countryside. "They may have no one who is willing to pay for their release," he'd said. "But we will try."

"The last parchment," I continued, *"was written by the daughter of one of your leaders, Count Robert. Her name is Genevieve."*

The Frank's eyes flared and he sucked in his breath with a low gasp. *"I know the lady's name,*

Northman," he growled. *"She is my sister. My name is Drogo. I am the eldest son of Count Robert."*

"Then you and your father will be glad to receive her message and learn that she is well," I told him.

"Do not presume, Northman, to tell me of my own feelings, or those of my father." He unfolded each of the three parchments in turn and scanned them quickly until he identified the letter written by Genevieve, which he read completely. When his face turned a dark, angry red, I suspected he had just read the threat Hastein had insisted be included in Genevieve's message.

"There is no ransom specified in my sister's letter," he said.

"Nor in the other messages," I added. *"The amounts of the ransoms are to be negotiated. Our army's leaders wish to meet with your father, Count Robert, the high priests of your church, and any other of your leaders with authority to agree on terms. Ten days hence, your leaders should come prepared to negotiate and prepared to pay. They will need to bring silver. Much silver. After the amounts of the ransoms have been agreed upon and paid, we will release our prisoners to you."*

"And until then? The prisoners?"

"They will remain safe in Ruda—in Rouen— until then."

"Ten days hence? That is not much time to secure

enough silver to pay ransoms for so many."

"Yours is a rich land, and a rich people," I replied. "I am sure you will manage." Hastein was certain they could, at any rate.

"When and where," the Frank asked, "do your leaders wish to meet for this negotiation?"

"Downstream from here," I told the Frank. "Earlier this day, our ship passed a point where a long, straight stretch of the river ended. Do you know the place I speak of?" The Seine so rarely ran straight, Hastein thought it should be an easy place to identify. He was right.

The Frank nodded. "I know it."

"In the first bend of the river, just upstream from that straight run, there is an island. On the river's north bank, opposite the island, the land is low and flat and mostly open. Ten days from now we will come to that island with five ships. Our ships, the warriors they carry, and the prisoners will all remain on the island during the negotiations—unless there is treachery, that is. Then you can be assured our warriors will cross to the shore. We will land just five men on the north bank, opposite the island: the leaders of our army, and me. I will be there to speak for them."

"Ah yes," the Frank said, with a sneer. "You will translate for your leaders. It is quite amazing to see a Northman who speaks the language of civilized men. Your own tongue sounds like the growling of dogs."

Ignoring his insult, I continued.

"*We will meet and parley at the water's edge. No more than five of your leaders shall come. The rest of your men—however many your leaders choose to bring—must remain at a distance. None of the ten who meet to parley—Frank or Dane—shall wear armor or bear weapons of any kind.*"

"*I will deliver your message,*" the Frank said. "*We will be there. And I suppose that after we have paid the ransoms to free your prisoners, you will all flee down the Seine to the sea and sail back to the dung heap you came from? You Northmen are fierce when you attack farmers and undefended villages and priests. But you will not stand and fight against our army, will you? That is not to your liking.*"

This Frank was someone I could enjoy killing. "*I was not aware,*" I told him, "*that the walls of Ruda were defended by farmers and priests. The Franks I killed, when our army took the town, all bore arms and wore armor and looked to be warriors. Though in truth, judging from the way they fought, perhaps they were not. And their leader certainly fled the town without a fight. He, too, was a count, like your father. Perhaps he is of your family?*"

The Frank jerked his spear free from the ground and began backing his horse away. "*Get back to your ship, Northman.*" he barked. "*You have delivered your messages. I see no reason to allow you to remain upon our soil any longer."*

I inclined my head in a mocking bow—keeping my eyes on the Frank the entire time—and began backing away. After a few steps I turned, showing him my back—all the while hoping that Tore and Odd would keep it safe—and began walking toward the ship.

Suddenly the Frank spurred his horse forward. At the sound, I spun, raising my shield as I did, and reached for my sword's hilt. From the corner of my eye I saw Tore and Odd raise their bows.

The Frank pulled his horse up less than a pace away. I had to step back to avoid being knocked aside by its shoulder. *"The sword you wear, Northman,"* he demanded, *"how came you by it?"*

"I took it from a Frank I killed," I answered. *"I took this mail brynie from him, too. They suit me well, and he was not man enough to keep them. I suspect you know whom I speak of. Your sister told me his name was Leonidas."*

"I will remember you, Northman," the Frank said. *"And God willing, someday I will kill you."*

4

OLD ENEMIES AND
NEW FRIENDS

By the time I walked again down the narrow street leading to Wulf's house in Ruda, it was the afternoon of the fourth day since we'd departed the town. Hastein had set a more leisurely pace on our return journey, but we still made good time, for we were traveling with the current rather than rowing against it.

The door to the house was closed, despite the fact that it was a warm, pleasant spring day. As I approached, though, Wulf flung it open and stepped out to greet me.

"I am glad you have returned," he exclaimed. "Yesterday men were watching the house."

I was weary. Save for my brief encounter with Genevieve's brother, I had not set foot on solid ground for four days. I pushed past him and carried my sea chest and gear over to the corner of the front room that I had made my own.

"What are you saying?" I muttered distractedly as I set the chest holding my armor and weapons on the floor and leaned my bow and shield against the wall in the corner. Bertrada was standing beside the hearth, wringing her hands nervously. Genevieve and the children were not in sight, but I could hear her voice coming from the back room.

"Two men," Wulf explained. "They were in the street in front of the house yesterday."

There were often people in the street. I could not understand Wulf's agitation. "Do you have any ale?" I asked without much hope.

"One of them was the man who was here in my home the night Ruda was taken," Wulf continued. "The man who left, before you killed the other one."

Now Wulf had my attention. "Do you mean Stenkil?" I asked.

"I do not know his name," Wulf answered. "But I am certain it was the man who was here that night and left. The one who came back the following morning with other men."

Surely Stenkil would not be so foolish as to ignore Ragnar's warning and break the peace in Ruda. But why else would he have come back to Wulf's home?

"Did he try to come into your house?" I asked. Wulf shook his head.

"Did he say anything to you?"

Again Wulf shook his head. "No," he said. "He and the other man just stood in the street in front of the house, watching it and talking together. Bertrada noticed them first and called to me. I went to the door to see who they were. It was as if that was what they wished, for when I did—when they saw that I was looking back at them—the other man smiled and then they both walked away."

I frowned. This made no sense. "What did the other man look like?" I asked.

"He was a big man, tall, with black hair and a black beard. He had a deep scar across his face from here to here," Wulf said, waving his hand at an angle across his own face. "And one of his eyes was solid white."

It is never a good thing when your enemies join forces against you. The man Wulf had described was Snorre, Toke's second in command who had followed me here to Frankia. I was certain of it.

I walked to the table, pulled out a chair, and sat down heavily. "Do you have any ale?" I asked again, distractedly. Wulf nodded and spoke to Bertrada. She went into the back room carrying a cup. She returned a few moments later and handed it to me. I took a sip and realized this was a far better brew than the watery stuff she had served me previously. I suspected Hastein was right. If Wulf would hide his good ale, he probably had a secret store of silver hidden somewhere, too.

"You know the other man?" Wulf asked. No doubt the expression on my face when he had described Snorre to me had given that away.

"Yes," I answered. "I do. He is an enemy of mine. I have sworn to kill him, and he has sworn to kill me."

Genevieve stepped into view in the back room, holding Alise on her shoulder. The child's eyes were closed. She stared at me for a moment, then turned and moved out of my sight again.

"I do not think you need worry," I told Wulf, speaking in Latin so Bertrada and Genevieve could understand, too. *"These men's quarrel is with me alone, not with you. And I do not believe they will dare break the peace while we are here in Ruda. Ragnar, our war-king, has forbidden it. You and your family are safe."*

I said the words to comfort Wulf, not because I believed them. Snorre had aided Toke in the attack up on the Limfjord that had led to my brother's death. They had not scrupled then about killing innocent women and children to accomplish their end.

69

I hoped Snorre and Stenkil would not do any-thing foolish now. I did not wish to have to watch my back constantly while we were in Frankia. And if they should attack me and I survived, I did not wish to be brought before Ragnar once again for fighting other warriors in our army.

Having put the baby down, Genevieve came out of the back room and sat across from me at the table. I noticed she was still wearing her soiled robe, rather than one of the gowns Hastein had given her.

"*Do you know anything more about my ransom?*" she asked. "*About when it will be paid, and when I will be freed?*"

"*We merely delivered the written messages to a Frankish officer,*" I explained. "*But it has been agreed that there will be a parley between the leaders of our army and leaders of your people. Your father no doubt will be there. The ransoms for you and for all of the prisoners to be freed will be negotiated then. The parley will occur in eight days. That is when the ransoms, including yours, will be paid and you will be freed.*" And that is when I shall be free of you—and a much wealthier man, I thought.

She sighed. "*I wonder if my message will have reached my father yet, and if my family knows I am safe.*"

"*I feel certain your father knows by now,*" I said.

"I was the one who delivered the messages, because I speak your people's tongue. The Frankish officer who received them was your brother."

Her face brightened. *"Drogo?"* she asked. I nodded. *"I am relieved my family now knows I am alive and unharmed,"* she sighed.

"I am certain they are pleased and will gladly pay a ransom to bring you back safely to them," I lied. I could not forget her brother's words when I had suggested he and her father would be glad to receive news of her. *"Do not presume to tell me of my own feelings, or those of my father,"* he had said. Was there some reason they would not wish for Genevieve's return?

Genevieve was staring at me intently now. *"What is it?"* she asked. *"There is something you are not telling me. I can see it in your eyes."*

"I was just remembering my meeting with your brother," I answered. *"He told me he hopes to kill me someday. I am growing weary of men saying that."*

She stared at me silently for a moment, her expression inscrutable. Then she spoke. *"Those two men Wulf told you of. The ones who were watching the house. What is their quarrel with you?"*

"They each have different reasons," I answered. *"One was here looting in Wulf's house the night Ruda fell. His comrade was the man I killed to save Bertrada's life. He wishes to avenge his friend's death."*

"And the other man?" she asked.

"He is one of the warriors who helped kill my brother. I have sworn to kill all the men involved. Their leader—his name is Toke—wishes me dead, for I am the only survivor of the murders he committed, the only person who might reveal his treachery. I am a threat to him and to his good name, as long as I live. This man—the man Wulf saw— is one of Toke's most trusted warriors. He came here looking for me, to kill me."

She shuddered. *"Your life is so filled with violence and death."*

I did not respond. What she said was true. At Jul of this year, the feast of the midwinter solstice, I had still been a slave. Now it was but spring. I had been a free man and a warrior for only a few months, but already I had lost count of how many men I had killed. And I felt in danger of losing count of how many now wished me dead.

"You told me your brother gave his life for you," she said. I looked up. She was still staring at me.

"He did," I answered.

"What happened?" she asked. I noticed that Wulf and Bertrada were listening to our conversation, looking fascinated.

I did not wish to go back there. I did not wish to revisit that night in my mind. I do not know why I felt compelled to answer Genevieve's question.

"My brother's name was Harald," I began. *"He was a great warrior, a great swordsman. Our father, Hrorik, was also a great warrior and a great chieftain among the Danes."*

Genevieve frowned. *"I thought you said you were a slave,"* she said.

"You were a slave?" Wulf asked, an astonished expression on his face. He stepped over to the table, pulled out a chair, and sat down beside Genevieve, across from me. *"Bertrada,"* he said, *"bring me ale. And refill Halfdan's cup, also."*

I sighed. I had not wished this to become known. I should not have mentioned it to her.

"I was," I said. *"My mother was a slave in my father's household, although in her own land, in Ireland, she had been the daughter of a king. My father stole her in a raid. She became his concubine."*

"And you were born of their union?" Genevieve asked.

Union? I would not have called it that, when a master comes to a slave's bed and demands access to her body. Perhaps though, when I was conceived—before my father married Gunhild—there had been a union between them, of heart as well as body.

I nodded.

"You were born a slave?" Wulf asked.

I nodded again. *"And a slave I remained, until*

73

earlier this year, when on his deathbed my father freed me."

Wulf took a long swallow of ale and shook his head wonderingly. *"This is a tale!"* he exclaimed.

"What of your brother?" Genevieve asked.

"After I was freed, after my father died, Harald trained me in the ways of a warrior. Later, we traveled together with a few of Harald's men to inspect a small estate my father had left me in the north of our people's lands. Toke, who hated Harald, followed us there and attacked the estate during the night. All who lived there—men, women, and children—were slain. Only I survived. In the final fight, Harald was killed while cutting a passage clear for me to escape. He told me someone must live to avenge all who had died. I have sworn that I will bring vengeance down upon Toke and all of his men for their murder of Harald and the others." As I said those words, I wondered when, if ever, I would have a chance to fulfill my oath.

"Who is this Toke?" Wulf asked.

"He is Harald's foster brother," I answered. *"Harald's, and mine. After Harald's mother died, my father married a rich widow. Toke was her son by her first husband."*

"Why did Toke wish to kill your brother?" Genevieve asked.

"He is . . ." I searched for a word in their tongue

that would convey the meaning of "berserk." *"It is as if he is possessed by an evil spirit. His heart is filled with darkness and with anger at the world and at all who are in it. But he held a special hatred for Harald. Harald is the only person, besides our father, who has ever bested Toke."*

"So you say this man who was in the street, this Snorre, is one of Toke's men?" Wulf asked.

I nodded. *"He is Toke's second in command. He discovered Hastein had taken me into the crew of his ship and followed us here."*

"Huh," Wulf said. *"This is a tale indeed. I thought you nothing more that just another wolf among a bloodthirsty pack. There is far more to you than meets the eye. I had wondered why your captain places so much trust in one so young."*

I had not wished to tell Wulf or Genevieve I had been a slave. I feared what Hastein had warned me of—that anyone who learned of my past would look down upon me because of it. The knowledge did seem to change Wulf's manner toward me, but in an unexpected way. From that evening on, he no longer treated me with distrust or fear. He and Bertrada made me feel welcome in their home.

That night as we all dined together, Wulf told tales of his own about the trading voyages he had made north to Quentovic and Dorestad, south to

Nantes, and on a few occasions across the sea to England. His stories were not remarkable, but Genevieve seemed to find them fascinating, and asked him many questions about the different folk and lands he had seen. Wulf seemed pleased to tell her, and Bertrada beamed with pride that a noble lady like Genevieve should be so interested in the doings of her husband.

As Bertrada reached across the table to collect our empty platters and cups, Wulf placed a hand upon her rump and squeezed it. She glanced back into his face and smiled knowingly.

"I have enjoyed this night greatly," Wulf said to Genevieve. *"But now I think it is time for bed. I will tell you more stories tomorrow night, if you wish. I will tell you about the time I saw a sea monster, a great fish larger than this room."*

Wulf's words reminded me of something I had forgotten in the shock of hearing about Snorre and Stenkil.

"Genevieve and I will not be eating here tomorrow night," I told him. *"My captain, Hastein, has requested that we dine with him."*

Genevieve looked alarmed. *"Why does he wish me to be there?"* she asked.

I had wondered the same when Hastein first told me. I had thought—or at least hoped—the issue of Genevieve had been resolved between us.

When I'd asked him, he'd looked at me for a while with an unreadable expression, then answered, "She is from Paris, is she not? It is a town I have not seen. I wish to learn more of it."

"*Do not be concerned,*" I told Genevieve. "*I will be there. You will be safe.*"

She did not look convinced. I didn't blame her. It did not seem believable to me that Hastein would invite her to dine, merely to learn more about some distant Frankish town. I felt uneasy, but did not want her to know.

"*There is something you should understand about my people,*" I told her. "*There is nothing we value more highly than our honor. I have sworn to follow Hastein, to give him my loyalty, to fight for him, and even die for him if necessary. But as my captain, he must also be loyal and act with honor toward me. Men would not wish to follow him if he could not be trusted. Until you are freed, you belong to me. And I have already told Hastein I will not give you up. He would dishonor himself if he tried to take you without my consent.*"

I believed in my heart what I told her. I truly did. Hastein was an honorable man. But he was also a jarl and used to being obeyed. My mind, like a disloyal comrade, kept whispering thoughts I tried to ignore. Hastein had already sent me once on a dangerous mission that I had barely survived. If I were to die, there would be no dishonor in his taking Genevieve for himself.

After Wulf and Bertrada had retired for the night, while Genevieve and I were preparing our pallets for sleep on opposite sides of the front room, I told her, *"You should wear one of the gowns Hastein gave you when we go to eat at his quarters tomorrow night. I think it would give offense to him if you rejected his gift."*

"If it is your request, I will."

"Thank you," I said. I had much to be grateful for to Hastein, and valued his good will. If possible, I did not wish Genevieve to cause a rift between us.

"I have a request to make of you," Genevieve said.

"What is it?"

"I would dearly love to bathe. I have had no opportunity to since you captured me. I have never been this filthy in my life."

Her request surprised me. The Danes as a people are much given to cleanliness. In the home I grew up in, my father had built a small bathhouse attached to the main hall of his longhouse. Judging from the appearance—not to mention the smell— of Wulf and Bertrada and their children, though, I had come to believe that bathing was not a practice

78

regularly observed among the Franks. But at Genevieve's words, I recalled that Hastein had apparently found a tub for bathing somewhere in the count's palace. Perhaps the Frankish nobility were more given to cleanliness than their common folk.

But where could Genevieve bathe? Although Hastein had a bathing tub, given the interest he'd been expressing in her, I certainly did not feel comfortable with the thought of her going to his quarters to bathe.

"I will see if I can borrow two horses in the morning," I told her. *"If I am able to, we will ride downstream from Ruda and find a place where you can bathe in the river."*

"Bathe outdoors?" she asked, as if she had never heard of such a thing.

"It is where most folk in my land bathe," I told her. *"During the warmer months, at least. They bathe or swim in rivers and streams. There are few who can afford to build a bathhouse. If you do not wish to bathe in the river, I do not know where else you can."*

"I cannot swim," she said. There seemed much she could not do. Almost all Danes can swim, for the seas are our roadways.

"I will find a location where you do not need to," I told her.

79

✦ ✦ ✦

I had no difficulty borrowing two horses, for our army was no longer sending mounted raiding parties out from Ruda. Upstream from the town it had become too dangerous, due to the ever increasing presence of Frankish patrols. There was no point in sending raiding parties downstream-—our army had already scoured the land bare in that direction. The stolen herd of horses that once had provided mounts for our men now was gradually being slaughtered to provide them meat.

It was a glorious day. The sun warmed the air and sparkled on the river, and the stretches of open grassland we traversed along the riverbank were blanketed with tiny blue and white flowers. After the close confines of Wulf's house, where every breath was flavored with smoke from the fire and the stale aroma of unwashed bodies, each lungful of clean air I drew tasted as sweet as a drink of cold spring water on a hot day. Ivar was right. Men were not meant to live in towns like Ruda.

The fresh air and sunshine seemed to have boosted Genevieve's spirits, too. The melancholy expression that had so often clouded her features of late vanished.

"*Tell me of your mother,*" she asked suddenly, turning to face me. "*You said that she, like your brother, died for you.*"

I was surprised and somewhat taken aback by her request. Some things—especially those memories that are painful to recall—are not meant to be the subject of casual conversation.

"Why do you ask about my mother?" I demanded. *"Why did you ask about my brother last night? Why do you wish to know these things about me?"*

She looked startled by the tone in my voice. *"I did not mean to give offense by my questions,"* she explained. *"If I have, I ask you to forgive me."*

I shrugged my shoulders and looked away. I wished she would not look at me so. Her demeanor was so serious and her eyes projected concern, as if my feelings actually mattered to her. I did not see how they could.

"There is nothing to forgive," I said. *"I just do not understand your interest."*

"I have never met anyone like you," she explained. *"You are so different from the men of my people—from my father, from my brother, from anyone I have known. You are very fierce—even savage—when you fight. I have seen what you are capable of and it frightens me. Yet there is also a side of you which is very kind. And though you appear young—I suspect that in years we are close to the same age—you have done and seen so much in your life. I have seen so little in mine."*

I shrugged my shoulders again. *"I am what my*

fate has made me," I said. Yet her words caused me to ponder what she'd said. The only kindness I had known in my own life was the love and care shown me by my mother. If there was any kindness in my nature, surely it came from her. My skill at fighting I owed primarily to my brother, Harald, who had taught me well. And if there was savagery in me, as Genevieve said, what was its origin? The fierce warrior's blood of my father that flowed in my veins? Or was it born of the anger and hatred that burned in my heart because of Toke? When and if I finally killed him, would my heart become free of anger and feel at peace?

I sighed. *"What is it you wish to know?"* I asked her. It would be simpler to talk of events past than to ponder such things. And so I told her of my mother—of the home she'd had in Ireland, how my father had stolen her in a raid, how her father and betrothed had tried to rescue her and had been slain. I told her how, over time and against all odds, my mother and father had come to love each other, and how my mother had dreamed of becoming his bride. I told her how my father's ambition had led him to wed Gunhild instead, dooming my mother to a life of slavery.

And I told her how my mother had died, and with her death, had purchased my freedom. She asked many questions then—questions about my father's funeral. The answers I gave clearly shocked her. An expression of horror filled her face.

"How can you not hate your brother, Harald? He killed your mother!"

Her words—and the intensity with which she spoke them—surprised me. *"Harald was not responsible for my mother's death,"* I told her. *"It was her decision, one she made freely. Harald merely made her passing from this world to the next as swift and painless as possible. It was a kindness he showed her, one I am grateful for."*

Mother had been afraid that day, very afraid, and rightly so. She had asked Harald to help her, and he had agreed because of the fondness and respect he'd felt for her. Genevieve was a Frank and a Christian. There was no way she could understand these things.

"If anyone was to blame, it is my father, for asking Mother to accompany him on his death voyage to the next world," I added.

"Do you hate him for it? Do you hate your father?"

At one time I'd thought I did. Not just because of my mother's death, but also because of how he'd treated me. I was his son, yet to him I'd been merely property, a slave. But as I turned Genevieve's question over in my mind and wondered how to answer it, I realized my anger toward Hrorik had faded. I shook my head slowly.

"He was never a father to me. He was my master, and I was one of his slaves. My heart never held any love for him, and the day I learned my mother was to die on his death ship, and for a long time afterward I could not think of him without feeling anger. Now, though . . ." I shrugged my shoulders. *"It is all in the past. There is no point in regretting what has already happened and cannot be changed. My mother's death was part of her fate, and mine, and my father's."*

I wondered if Genevieve regretted asking me about the circumstances of my mother's death. It was, in truth, a strange and terrible tale. To one not of our people, it must have sounded even worse. I glanced over at her. To my surprise, I saw that tears had wet her cheeks.

"Your mother loved you very much," Genevieve said, a catch in her voice. *"So much that she was willing to face a horrible death."*

Horrible? My mother's death had been brave and generous beyond measure, for she had given up the rest of her life to buy a better one for me. But it had been a quick and almost painless passing, thanks to Harald. I did not think her death was horrible. And I could not understand why the tale of a stranger's death, whether she thought it horrible or not, should affect Genevieve so.

Suddenly Genevieve began sobbing. She covered

her face with her hand. Was she such a tender-hearted girl to feel so strongly about the death of someone she had not known?

"Why do you weep?" I asked her.

"We are so different," she said. *"In your life, when you were a slave, you had nothing at all—nothing except the love of your mother. In my life, I have had everything. Everything except my parents' love."*

"What do you mean?" I asked, but she would not answer or even look at me. She merely shook her head, but kept her face covered with her hand, and sobbed quietly to herself. I kicked my horse and moved ahead of her to allow her privacy for her grief.

We came to a copse of trees along the river-bank that had a sunny clearing in its center. It was far enough downstream from Ruda for the water to be clear of refuse from the town and the army's island camp. We were far enough, too, I judged, to be safe from any chance meeting with wandering warriors from our army or folk from the town.

"We will stop here," I told Genevieve. *"The trees will conceal us and our horses from view while you bathe at the river's edge."*

"Where will you be?" she asked, a dubious expression on her face.

"I will stand watch at the edge of these trees, to

make certain no one comes. Do not worry. I will not be able to see you."

My words did not seem to allay her concerns. "*I think I will keep my shift on while I bathe,*" she said. "*I brought a clean one, from the gowns your captain gave me, to wear when I am finished bathing.*"

I said nothing. It was her affair if she wished to bathe while wearing clothing, though it seemed foolish to me.

We found a place along the bank where the tangled roots of a willow growing at the water's edge trailed off into the river. "*You can use these roots as steps and handholds to climb down to the water,*" I told her. "*But be careful and do not venture out far from the shore, since you cannot swim. It looks as though the river bottom drops off fairly steeply here.*"

I left her and walked to the far edge of the clearing, just inside the ring of trees. The grass was thick here, and looked soft and inviting. I laid my bow and quiver on the ground, unstrapped the belt that held my sword and axe, and stretched myself out on the soft, sweet-smelling turf. Although I had told Genevieve I would be standing guard, I did not really expect anyone might come upon us here. In times of war, most folk do not lightly venture far afield from places of safety. We had seen no one else since leaving Ruda.

I was close enough to be able to hear Genevieve gasp when she first entered the river. It would still be some months before the winter's chill was gone from the water. I could hear sounds of splashing, too, as she bathed.

"I am going to get out now," she called. *"Where are you?"*

"I am across the clearing. I cannot see you," I assured her.

Suddenly I heard a shriek, followed by a loud splash. *"Help!"* she cried, in a strangled voice. Then there was nothing.

I ran to the water's edge, but could see her nowhere. Widening rings of ripples were spreading from a point a few feet out from where the willow roots entered the water. As I watched, bubbles of air broke the surface in the center of the rings.

I kicked off my shoes, stripped off my tunic, and jumped into the river. Holding my breath, I ducked my head beneath the surface and began searching for her in the murky water.

Fortunately, the current had not carried her away. The string of air bubbles escaping from her mouth led me to her. She was thrashing wildly, but ineffectively. When I reached her, she locked her arms tightly around my neck, and for a moment I feared she would drown me, too. I swept my left arm around her legs to keep them clear of my own, and held her body pinned tightly against my chest while I kicked my legs and pulled with my right arm, fighting my way back to the surface.

Genevieve coughed until her lungs were clear, then rested her head against my cheek with her eyes closed. I kept us afloat with steady kicks, but did not try to swim to shore. It was as though I could not force my mind to focus on what needed to be done now that she was safe. Perhaps it was because her shift concealed little now that it was soaked through, or because her body felt so warm against mine where I held her tightly against me.

After a time, Genevieve opened her eyes and raised her head. She looked about her, startled. *"Why do you not swim to shore?"* she asked.

Her face was right next to mine. I could feel her breath on my cheek.

"Halfdan?" she asked. It was the first time she had ever spoken my name.

Without a word, I paddled in and helped Genevieve find handholds on the roots extending into the water. As she prepared to pull herself up, Genevieve turned her head toward me and said in little more than a whisper, *"My shift exposes me. I beg you, do not watch me climb from the river."*

I turned and swam upstream to the point where the tree line at the edge of the grove met the riverbank. Pushing off from the shore, I swam hard across the river and back, letting the cold water tire my muscles and calm my body and mind. When I returned to my starting point, I saw that Genevieve had set my tunic and shoes out for me on the edge of the bank. I climbed from the river, dried myself as best I could with my tunic, and dressed. Genevieve was seated across the clearing, close to where the horses were tied, her back to the river and me.

She turned when she heard me approach. Our eyes met, and we both looked away.

"Thank you," she said, in a quiet voice. *"I would have died had you not saved me."*

I did not know what to say. My thoughts were confused. I kept recalling how her body had looked through the transparent gown, and how it had felt pressed against mine.

"I am glad I was there," I told her.

She nodded her head vigorously. *"Yes,"* she said. *"I am glad, too. You saved me."*

I had, but that was not what I meant.

A FEAST
AND A DANCE

We were both quiet for most of the ride back to Ruda. When the walls of the town came into view in the distance, I finally broke the silence.

"Why did you choose to become a priestess—a nun?" I asked her.

She looked startled by my question. "What do you mean?" she asked.

"Why are you not betrothed? Why are you not wed?"

"I am to be a bride of Christ," she said. "There is no finer husband a Christian woman could have."

"I cannot believe a dead God is the finest husband you could have," I told her. Or would wish for, either, I thought, but did not say. It was no business of mine. Then I said it anyway. *"Do you truly believe that is so? I have seen the way you hold Alise. Have you truly never wished for a living husband who could warm your bed at night and give you children of your own?"*

Genevieve scowled at me and retorted, *"You should not say such things! Why do you ask me such questions?"*

I could not help myself. I laughed at her indignation.

"It is just that I have never met anyone like you," I told her, grinning. *"You are so different from the women of my people. Is it wrong that I wish to understand?"*

She blushed, scowled again, and looked away. In a moment she glanced back at me. I saw that now she, too, was grinning.

"It is unfair to use my own words against me," she said. Then she sighed and a serious expression replaced the humor that had briefly lit her face.

"It is true. Once I did dream of having a husband—a real husband, who would lie beside me at night and whom I would awaken beside every morn. And I dreamed of having children of my own. It was the life I expected to lead and I looked forward to it."

"What happened?" I asked. *"Why is your life now pledged to your God?"*

"It is not a choice I made. The decision was made for me."

"Who made the decision, if you did not?"

"My father. I am the youngest of four children in my family," she explained. "I have two brothers—you have met Drogo, the eldest—and one sister. My father values his sons. They are both warriors, captains in his scara of cavalry. And they ensure that my father's line and name will continue after his death.

"Father views his daughters differently, however. To him, we are nothing more than a commodity to be spent carefully, to gain for him some advantage. Daughters of the nobility are an expensive burden, for a dowry must be paid to their husbands when they are wed. My father is unwilling to part with any of his wealth without gaining something for himself in return.

"My sister was fortunate. Though she had no say in the matter of her marriage, at least the husband Father chose for her was not distasteful. The same was not true for me.

"There is an elderly nobleman who lives on a large estate adjacent to some lands my father owns. Though in poor health now, he has outlived all the rest of his family, including three sons and two wives. My father hoped to acquire his lands for our family through marriage—my marriage. He reasoned that because my husband-to-be had no heirs, if I could give

92

him a child, then after he died—something everyone believes will be no more than a few years at most in coming, given his age and the state of his health—my father, as the closest male relative of the infant heir, would by right control the lands until my child reached its majority.

"It was essential, my father stressed to me, that I get with child as soon as possible after I was wed and, of course, it would be preferable that the child I bore be male—as if that is something any woman can control. Father even intimated that if my husband could not achieve the desired result quickly enough, he would find a fertile stand-in to service me. I felt my father viewed me much the same as one of his prized mares. My value to him lay only in the fact that I could be bred, and profit could be made from my offspring. That my husband-to-be was repugnant to me—he is old and fat and dirty, his teeth are rotten, and his breath and body stink—was of no concern whatsoever to my father."

"Did you tell your father your feelings about the marriage?" I asked. She shook her head.

"My father is not an approachable man. Not to his daughters, anyway. I told my mother, though. I asked her to intercede with Father on my behalf. She told me to stop behaving like a spoiled child and accept the duty I owed to the family.

"Father held a great celebration to announce my

betrothal. My future husband sat at my side and pawed at me throughout the feast. Later that night, when the household had all gone to bed, he made his way to my bedchamber and attempted to rape me. He could not wait until our wedding night. I clawed his face, scratching great bloody stripes across it until I escaped his grasp. Then, with a candlestick, I beat him about the face and head."

Her face looked animated and her dark eyes flashed as she described beating her betrothed. This was a side of her I had not seen before—Genevieve the warrior maiden. I thought it suited it her far better than being a priestess of a dead God.

She continued. *"By the time he was able to escape, crawling naked out into the hallway, with me following and hammering upon his bald and now bloody pate, the din had awakened the household, and his humiliation was witnessed by many.*

"The next morning, my betrothed angrily called off the wedding. Relations between him and my father have been strained ever since. My father was incensed by my conduct. 'Why did you not let him have his way?' he shouted at me. 'What difference would it have made? You were to be wed! You might that much sooner have become with child!'

"My father decided that if I would not have as husband the man he had chosen for me, then I would wed no man at all. Among our people, the holy

church expects the nobles to give of their wealth and lands for its support, in exchange for which the church protects their immortal souls, and also supports their rule while on this mortal earth. This year, instead of giving the church lands or silver, my noble father, Count Robert, delivered his daughter. I am to spend the rest of my life serving the church in the Abbey of St. Genevieve in Paris. It was considered a generous donation on his part. The abbess was well pleased to gain so high-born a member for her order."

The tone of her voice sounded bitter as she uttered these last words, and the light I had seen moments before vanished from her face. Her looks belied her earlier assertion that she was pleased to be promised as a bride to her God.

"What did your mother say?" I asked.

"She said I had acted like a fool," Genevieve answered. *"She said I was fortunate my father did not do worse."*

I recalled the words Genevieve had spoken earlier during our ride out from Ruda. She'd said that in her life she had had everything except her parents' love. I did not agree. Fine clothes and a palace for a home were not everything. It seemed to me that despite her noble birth, in many ways she had had no more freedom than did a slave. Her life had never been her own to live.

I could understand now why her brother had

intimated her return might not be welcomed. Her father would have to part with much silver to gain her release. Yet once she was freed, there seemed no way he could hope to recoup what she had cost him.

"*After your ransom has been paid, will you return to your family or to the church?*" I asked her.

"*There is no question. I will be returned to the abbey in Paris. My father has made it very clear that he will never again consider me to be his daughter, nor welcome me into his home.*"

"*Then why will he pay to ransom you?*" It made no sense to me.

"*He will pay to protect his honor,*" she said. "*I have heard you speak of honor, and I have come to understand that to you, to your people, honor is a different thing altogether than what men like my father mean when they use the term. My father's 'honor' is his pride. What he calls honor is based more upon his noble birth and his wealth and position, than on his actions. He values that other men must defer to him because of his rank. He will worry it might lessen him in the eyes of others if he abandoned a daughter— even one he now wishes he did not have—to the Northmen. And I am certain he could not bear the thought of anyone of his blood becoming a slave. His pride matters even more to him than his wealth. He will pay my ransom, though it will gall him to do so.*"

When we reached Wulf's house, Genevieve disappeared into the back room and did not reemerge for the rest of the afternoon. After returning the horses to the stables, I dressed myself in the feast finery one of Hastein's thralls had made for me back at his estate on the Limfjord. Had it truly been only weeks ago that we had been in Jutland, impatiently waiting to sail? It felt as though those days had occurred during a different lifetime.

Dusk was beginning to fall over the town, and Bertrada had just added more wood to the fire to brighten the dimness in the front of the house, when the door to the back room opened and Genevieve came out. She was wearing the dark red gown Hastein had given her, over one of the white linen shifts. The short black cape was draped around her shoulders. Her dark hair was twisted into a knot that pulled it up off of her neck.

She glanced up at me when she entered the room, then quickly looked down. I felt as though I should say something, but my mind emptied at the sight of her and my tongue felt clumsy in my mouth. Finally I managed to stammer, *"Perhaps I should get a torch to light our way."* It was all I could think of to say.

"Is it dark enough that we shall need one?" she asked.

"No," I said, mentally cursing my own stupidity.

Did I appear as witless as I felt? *"You are right. It will not be that dark until later when we return."*

Wulf was grinning broadly as he looked at us. *"Don't the two of you make a fine-looking pair,"* he said. Genevieve looked embarrassed, and I felt the same. It was a foolish thing for Wulf to say. We were not a pair, fine or otherwise. Genevieve was my prisoner. I was her captor. We were nothing more than that.

When we reached Hastein's quarters, I felt more confused than ever about why he had asked me to dine with him, and why I had to bring Genevieve. Besides Torvald, I was the only member of the *Gull*'s crew who was present. It was a small gathering: Svein and Stig, the captains of Hastein's two other ships, and—to my surprise—Ivar. This was a meeting of captains. I had nothing to say to them, nor did they have anything to say to me. At least the fare Cullain had cooked was very fine, and Hastein provided generous amounts of both ale and wine to accompany it.

Except for his initial greeting, Hastein ignored us. The meal was nearly finished when Genevieve whispered, *"Why am I here?"*

"I do not know," I told her. *"I do not know why either of us are here."* That very question had been worrying me more and more.

As if on cue, Hastein spoke. "Halfdan, I wish to speak to your prisoner. You will translate my questions for her." Ivar, who had drunk much wine during the evening, was now slouched back in his chair, one leg propped up on the table, staring at Genevieve through half-closed eyes. He leaned over and murmured something in Stig's ear, and both men laughed.

"Ask her where the towns her father rules are located," Hastein said.

Genevieve looked confused and somewhat suspicious when I explained to her what Hastein wished to know. *"I do not know how to answer his question,"* she said.

Hastein tried again. "Ask her if the towns her father rules are on the Seine River, or close to it."

"Oh, no," she said. *"They lie far to the south of the Seine. All except for Paris."*

"Ask her how large Paris is," Hastein continued. "Ask her how it compares to Ruda."

"Paris is far larger than Rouen," she answered. *"Though it is not as great as it once was, in the time of the Romans. There are many very old buildings in parts of the town that now are just ruins, where people no longer live."*

"How much larger than Ruda is it?" Hastein wanted to know.

She claimed that more than ten thousand people

lived there. I personally did not believe that could be true, but when I translated her answer Ivar sat up and began to take interest in the conversation.

"Ten thousand? Surely there are churches there. Ask her if there are," he demanded. "Probably many churches. And monasteries—ask her if there are monasteries, too."

"Oh, yes," Genevieve responded enthusiastically when I told her Ivar's question. *"There are many, many churches, and several monasteries, in and near Paris. The Abbeys of St. Germain and of St. Denis are the two largest. And of course there is the Abbey of St. Genevieve, the convent where I am a holy sister."* She frowned and looked at me. *"Why does he wish to know these things? Who is he?"*

Why does a hungry wolf wish to know where the sheep are pastured, I thought, but I did not say that to her.

"His name is Ivar. He is one of the commanders of our army," I told her. *"His father, Ragnar Logbrod, is the war-king who leads our warriors, but Ivar and my captain, Jarl Hastein, also command. We are at war with your people. They must know from which direction threats against us are likely to come."*

"Paris is no threat to you," she said. *"It is far upriver from here. And it is a peaceful town."*

"Ask her about the town's walls," Hastein told me.

"I told you, it is a peaceful town," she answered when I translated Hastein's question. *"There is a garrison of my father's men who are stationed there in a fortress on an island in the middle of the river. But the town itself does not have walls."*

Hastein and Ivar looked at each other, incredulous expressions on their faces, when I translated Genevieve's answer. Then Ivar began laughing.

"I did not like that man," Genevieve said as we made our way back to Wulf's house. I did not need to ask whom she meant. She'd looked frightened and angered by Ivar's harsh laughter at her description of Paris' defenses—or lack of them. After that, she had stubbornly refused to answer any more questions from him or Hastein. *"I do not trust them,"* she'd said. I thought it a wise judgment on her part.

I was wishing I had remembered to bring a torch when we'd left the count's palace. The night sky was shrouded with clouds, and the narrow streets of Ruda were dark.

My forgetfulness may have saved my life. Had my eyes been dazzled by the light from a torch, they likely would not have caught the slight movement deep within the shadows across the street from Wulf's house.

"Stay behind me," I instructed Genevieve as I

drew my sword. *"I believe there are men up ahead in the shadows."*

As I spoke, two men stepped into view in the street and drew their swords. At least they did not have shields or armor. No doubt that would have elicited difficult questions from the guards when they'd passed through the town's gate.

It is a tricky thing, fighting with swords but no shields. My brother, Harald, the finest swordsman I have ever known, said he considered it more akin to fighting with knives—though very long knives, to be sure. Few blows are actually struck, as the risk of being exposed to a counterstrike is too great if a blow is swung but misses. And it is dangerous to try and block blade with blade. If they should strike edge to edge, rather than using the flat of the blade to catch and block an opponent's cut, one or both swords might break. It is a dance mostly of advances, retreats, and feints.

The two men moved apart as they closed with me, intending to attack from different sides. I backed away, a step at a time, keeping my sword in front of me, ready to thrust or parry. Distance and balance—Harald had drilled them into me, over and over; I must maintain distance and balance. If you are off balance, you will be slow to react, he'd said. And you must maintain the proper distance from your opponent, staying out of reach of his blade until you are ready to strike with your own.

I could hear Genevieve, her breathing rapid and frightened, behind me. *"When I move,"* I told her, *"run for Wulf's door."*

I made a quick, feinting jab to my left with my blade. The attacker on that side leaped back, while the man on my right stepped forward. I turned and advanced toward him, three quick lunging steps, thrusting my sword at his chest. He stumbled back, swatting at my extended blade with the flat of his own as he did, but I had already withdrawn my weapon and was gone, circling to the right, putting him between me and his comrade. As much as possible, I needed to fight only one man at a time.

Genevieve had reached Wulf's door. It was latched. She pounded on it, shouting, *"Wulf, help me! Let me in!"*

The attacker on the left—the one now to the rear of his comrade—turned and looked back at her. "Leave her," the other one said. "It is him we want, and we must finish this quickly." I recognized his voice when he spoke. It was Stenkil.

The two men moved so both faced me again. Behind them, I saw the door to Wulf's house open, and Genevieve darted inside. At least she was safe. As the two advanced, I retreated and kept moving to the right, trying again to put one of my attackers behind the other. The street was narrow, though, and soon I would run out of room.

The warrior closest to me—Stenkil—leaped forward in two quick steps and raised his sword for a lunging cut, but I jumped back just as swiftly, staying out of range, and he held back his blow, rather than launching it.

The door to Wulf's house opened again and Wulf charged out, one of Bertrada's iron cook-pans in his hands. I thought perhaps he intended to use it as a club, but he ran up behind the farther of my two attackers and swung the pan at him, flinging a shower of glowing embers onto his back.

The man's tunic began to smoke in a dozen places where coals burned holes through the fabric and set the edges alight. He shouted out in alarm and pain, and swung around toward Wulf, raising his sword. As Wulf scurried away, the attacker in front of me glanced back over his shoulder to see what was happening behind him.

It was a fatal mistake. When he did, I lunged forward and raised my sword, feinting a cut at his head. Startled, he swung his own sword up in a desperate effort to block it. I swept the flat of my blade down under his and flung his weapon aside, then whipped my own in a quick chop that ended in the side of his neck. There was not much force to the blow, but my sword's edge was very sharp, and it cut a gash almost as deep as the width of the blade.

The other man was chasing Wulf back toward the open door, and gaining on him, when suddenly the numerous small fires smoldering on his tunic flared up into an angry blaze that covered his back and set his long hair alight. He staggered to a stop, trying to reach behind him with his free hand to swat at the spreading flames.

I pulled my sword free of Stenkil, the man I'd wounded, the blade slicing even deeper as I drew it back toward me. He dropped his own weapon with a clatter and clutched with both hands at the gaping wound in his neck, trying to stem the fountain of blood spurting from it. I darted around him to the burning man and rammed my sword into his back. He screamed and tried to turn, but I held him skewered on my blade and pushed again, pushed the point on through and held him there till he slumped forward onto his knees, finally dead, and slid off my blade onto the ground.

I wheeled back toward Stenkil, to find he was no longer a threat. He was staggering away down the narrow street, trying to escape, still clutching at his neck with both hands. I caught him at the corner and finished him with a single thrust.

6

COUNT ROBERT

Wulf was becoming more and more anxious as the day passed. "You cannot leave those dead men in my storehouse!" he complained. "Soon they will begin to stink. And if your people find them there, I may be blamed for their deaths."

He had not protested last night, when I'd suggested that we move the two men's bodies there. He had even helped me drag them in off the street. It was late morning now, though—nearly noon. I supposed he felt it was time—past time—for me to make other arrangements. It was a reasonable expectation on his part. The problem was that I did not know what to do. I did not want Ragnar to learn I had killed two more warriors from our army.

As often happens when a person delays making decisions that must be made, the choice of what to do was taken from me. I heard a clatter of horses' hooves in the street outside, and a moment later a fist hammered on the door.

"Halfdan," Torvald's voice cried. "Are you in there?"

I opened the door. In the street behind Torvald, Hastein and Ivar were mounted on horses. Torvald was holding the reins of two additional horses, saddled but riderless.

"Make haste," Torvald said. "Arm yourself. Full gear—brynie, helm, shield, and weapons. You are to come with us. Two riders—Franks—are outside the main gate, bearing a flag of truce. We ride to meet with them. Hastein wishes you to translate when we do. We have brought a mount for you."

Behind him, Hastein leaned over in the saddle and stared at the ground.

"Blood has been spilled here," he said. "Recently. And no small amount, either."

He straightened and looked at me. "Halfdan, do you know anything of this?"

Though I did not wish to volunteer what I had done, I would not lie about it—especially not to Hastein.

"Yes," I answered. "It happened last night. When Genevieve and I were returning here from your quarters. Two men attacked us."

Ivar looked me up and down. "It does not appear it was your blood that was spilled," he said.

"No," I agreed. "The blood you see is theirs. I killed them both." Torvald grinned, and Ivar looked impressed. Success at killing seemed to have that effect on him. Hastein, however, did not look pleased.

"They were Danes?" he asked. I nodded. He stared at me silently for a time, then let out a long sigh. "Were you going to tell me of this?" he demanded.

I shrugged my shoulders. In truth, I could not say. I had not made my mind up by the time he arrived at Wulf's door. "It is not you whom I did not wish to learn of these deaths," I answered.

"Ah, yes," Ivar said. "Father will be very displeased. He will take great exception to what you have done."

I hoped Ragnar would not wish to express his displeasure with a noose.

"Do you know who they were?" Hastein asked.

"One of them was Stenkil," I said. "The comrade of the man I killed earlier here in Wulf's house. I did not recognize the other."

Genevieve and Wulf appeared behind me in the doorway. *"Is your captain angry?"* she asked, looking at Hastein's stern expression. I nodded. *"That is not fair. You had no choice. Those men attacked us!"* she protested.

"What is she saying?" Ivar asked. When I told him, Wulf chimed in. "It is true," he said. "I saw it also. They would have killed Halfdan, had he not killed them first."

"It is fortunate for you," Hastein said, "that these two will speak for you. If you were merely defending yourself from attack—if you had no choice but to fight—there is nothing Ragnar can say."

"Nevertheless, I am certain he will say something," Ivar groaned. "He will not miss such an opportunity to complain about how badly our men lack discipline."

"There is more," I said. "Two days ago, Wulf saw Snorre and Stenkil together here in the street in front of his house."

Hastein sat silently atop his horse for a moment thinking about what I had just told him. Then he shook his head. "We will have to deal with this matter later," he said. "For now, we must learn what these Franks at our gate desire of us."

The Franks who had approached Ruda under a flag of truce had been sent by Count Robert, Genevieve's father. It seemed he was near and wished to parley.

"He wishes to negotiate the ransom for his daughter, the Lady Genevieve," one of the two riders advised. *"He has brought silver to pay it. He wishes to gain her release this day."*

"So he does not wish to wait for the meeting we proposed when we delivered the written messages?" Hastein murmured to Ivar under his breath. "What should we make of his impatience?"

"From what Genevieve has told me, I do not believe he is motivated by concern for *her*," I volunteered.

If Genevieve's ransom was to be negotiated now, I would need Hastein's assistance. "I do not know what price to ask her father to pay for her," I told him. "I do not know how much such a prisoner is worth. Will you negotiate for me?"

Hastein nodded. "I will," he said, then grinned. "I will enjoy it."

Since there were four of us, Hastein told me to tell the Franks that Count Robert could bring three of his warriors to the parley. "We can dispense with the other terms we had demanded earlier—that no one would wear armor or bear weapons. I do not believe he is here with treachery planned. He would not have come to Ruda's gates, and so swiftly, unless he truly wishes to free his daughter."

"The count does not wish to meet this close to the walls of Rouen," one of the Franks answered when

I told him Hastein's terms for a parley. He turned and pointed behind him, across the cleared fields that surrounded the town, toward the distant line of trees. *"He will meet you in the open ground behind us, halfway between the town wall and the forest. He does not trust you and does not wish to come so close to the rest of your army."* He gave a grim smile and added, *"And you, no doubt, do not wish to come too close to ours."*

"It is a reasonable request," Hastein answered when I told him what the Frank had said. Ivar agreed. "In his place, I would not trust us, either," he said.

"When shall we return?" I asked the Frank. *"When should we expect Count Robert to be here?"*

"Return?" he answered. *"You should not leave. The count will meet with you now, as soon as we tell him you are willing. He is watching us from the cover of the trees."*

When I saw him, I had no doubt that Count Robert was a warrior. His body was encased in iron: a long brynie of mail with sleeves that covered his arms to his wrists and a long skirt that hung to just below his knees, but was split front and back for comfort while riding. His shins were protected by unornamented iron greaves, and a plain helm of conical design adorned his head. All of his armor appeared well-made, but was simple and without decoration. And clearly, from the patina of minor dents and scratches that covered its surface, his armor had seen hard use.

When he neared the agreed meeting location, he held up one hand. The three riders with him— the two Franks we had spoken with earlier, plus another warrior who, like the count, was older— stopped. One of them was leading a packhorse laden with two sturdy leather saddlebags. Another held the reins of an extra horse that, though saddled, was riderless.

Count Robert walked his horse forward a few more paces and halted in front of us. He had a tanned, weathered face, framed by a close-cropped beard, and hard, expressionless eyes, the gray color of a winter sky.

"I am Robert," he announced, *"Count of Angers, Blois, Tours, Autun, Auxerre, Nevers, and Paris. I serve Charles, King of the Western Kingdom of the Franks, and I rule those towns for him, in his name. Who are you, and what lord do you serve?"*

"Tell him," Hastein said, "that my name is Hastein, and this is Ivar. Tell him we are Danes, and free men, and we serve no man."

The count's eyes flashed when I translated Hastein's answer. *"Are you someone who holds authority among your rabble? Am I speaking with* someone who can arrange for my daughter's release?" he snapped.

I did not need to consult with Hastein to be able to answer Count Robert's question. *"Lord Hastein"*—I chose to call him that, since this Frank would not understand "jarl"— *"is one of the leaders of our army,"* I told him. *"He is here to negotiate the Lady Genevieve's ransom with you, for he is also the captain who commands the warrior who captured her."*

For the first time, the count focused his gaze solely upon me. *"And that, I suppose, is you. My son told me of you."* I saw his eyes glance briefly down at the sword I wore.

"Ask him why he has come now," Hastein directed. "Ask him why he did not wait for the meeting that had been agreed upon. Ask him also if the other messages have been delivered to the high priests they were intended for, and if they intend to meet us when and where we had planned."

"The archbishops of Sens and Rheims have both received the message you delivered from the Bishop of Rouen," Count Robert answered, when I explained what Hastein had asked. *"They intend to ask for more time before they meet with you. They will be sending an envoy to you here at Rouen with that request. Men of the church can sometimes be slow to act. I did not wish the end of my daughter's captivity*

to be delayed by them. That is why I have come.

"*I am prepared to settle with you now for the amount of ransom I must pay to secure my daughter's release,*" he continued. "*I am prepared to pay you this day whatever amount we agree upon. But I must see my daughter and speak with her before we begin.*"

When I translated his request, Hastein shook his head. "He will see her when her ransom has been negotiated and weighed. Not until then. He will see her when we are ready to make the exchange."

"*How do I know she is alive? How do I know she is unharmed?*" the count protested. I thought it a reasonable concern. But Hastein would not budge.

"*Just days ago you received the written message from her, in her own hand, telling you she was unharmed,*" I told him, translating the answer Hastein gave. "*And you will see her before you must actually give up your silver to us. She will be able to tell you then that she is still unharmed.*"

Count Robert looked angry. I suspected he was not used to having others refuse him what he wished.

"*Very well,*" he said through gritted teeth. "*How much do you ask for the ransom of my daughter?*"

"Ten pounds of silver," Hastein said. I was so

astonished I just looked at him, and did not translate his words. It was a huge sum.

"Do not stare with your mouth open," Hastein told me. "If the amount we ask for appears to surprise even you, it will weaken our bargaining position. Now tell him what I said."

Count Robert's eyes bulged and his face turned red when I translated Hastein's terms into his tongue. *"Your figure is preposterous,"* he sputtered.

"I disagree," Hastein replied, smiling broadly at Count Robert's indignation. Hastein looked as though he was enjoying this greatly. "Tell him it is a fair and well-reasoned amount. Explain to the Count that four years ago, I led a raid up the Seine River that captured the monastery of St. Wandrille, downstream from Ruda. Priests of the Franks' church paid us six pounds of silver not to burn the monastery's buildings, and twenty-six additional pounds to free the sixty-eight prisoners we'd captured there. Six pounds of that latter amount were ransom for the abbot alone."

After I had translated, the count quickly offered, *"I will pay you six pounds of silver for my daughter's release."*

Six pounds of silver was more than I'd thought to gain. I thought we should accept. But Hastein, when he learned what the count had suggested, looked incredulous. Again he spoke, and I translated.

"You would pay the same ransom to free your daughter as was paid for one abbot or for one monastery?" Hastein exclaimed. "Frankia has many, many monasteries and many abbots—they are common here. But is there another Count of Angers, and Tours, and Paris, and all the many other towns you rule? There is not. You are not, in any way, a common man, and your noble daughter is an uncommon prisoner—one of special value. Does not the honor of your name and your position increase your daughter's worth? What would men say about you if it was learned you would rather clutch tightly to your purse-strings and let your own daughter be sold into slavery than agree to pay a greater ransom for a child of your own blood than was paid to protect the buildings of a monastery from being burned?"

"I will pay eight pounds," the count said, after I translated Hastein's speech. *"But no more."*

When I told him of Count Robert's offer, Hastein let out a loud sigh and shook his head sadly. "Explain to this Frank that the king of the Danes has but one queen," he said, "but he has many concubines. And he views the Franks as his greatest enemies, and treasures every victory over them, large or small. Tell him I am certain our king

116

will pay us at least eight pounds of silver for this girl, when he learns she is the daughter of so powerful a leader of his mortal foes—especially when he learns she is still a virgin whom he can deflower. Why should we ransom her to this Frank for eight pounds of silver, when we can easily sell her to our own king for the same amount, and by doing so gain his favor? Ask the count that."

I knew Hastein was bluffing. It was my decision what would happen to Genevieve if her father failed to ransom her. And I did not intend to sell her—to the king of the Danes or anyone else. I had come to know her too well—and had known the effects of slavery too intimately—to do that to her. I thought it was a fine argument that Hastein made, though, and I enjoyed seeing the effect it had on Genevieve's arrogant father. The count's face turned a most unhealthy shade of red, and his voice trembled with rage when he spoke.

"You shall have your ten pounds of silver," he snarled. *"And may God in heaven damn your heathen soul, if you even have one. Let us be done with this. I wish to spend no more time in the company of those who would use a father's concern for his defenseless daughter, and for her honor, as a weapon against him."*

I would have been more impressed with the count's speech had Genevieve not told me how little her father cared about her or her honor. It was, in truth, his own honor—or as she had explained, his pride—that he was protecting, and I felt no shame that we were making him pay a high price to do so.

The packhorse was led forward, and one of the count's men removed a scale from one of the saddlebags and began assembling it. Another began removing small, bulging leather sacks from the saddlebags.

"Is the spare horse for your daughter to ride?" I asked the count.

"It is," he answered.

"If I may take it, I will go into the town and fetch her," I told him.

When I entered Wulf's home, Genevieve, who was seated at the table holding baby Alise in her lap, looked up.

"You are back from meeting with the Frankish soldiers?" she asked.

"It is not just Frankish soldiers," I answered. *"It is your father, Count Robert. You must come with me now. Your ransom has been agreed upon. Your father brought silver to pay it, and you are to be freed this day."*

Genevieve just stared at me, speechless with surprise.

"I am happy for you, Lady Genevieve," Bertrada

said, reaching to take Alise from her.

"Aye," Wulf added, nodding his agreement. *"Though our home will not feel the same after you are gone."*

It was a gracious thing for Wulf to say. I remembered how reluctant he'd initially been for her to stay under his roof. What he said was true, though. Genevieve had become a welcome addition to the household, cheerfully assisting Bertrada with the cooking, the children, and the other chores Bertrada did. In fact, since Genevieve had come, the house was cleaner by far than it had been when I first saw it. And the gloom and tension that had seemed to permeate it in the days before Genevieve had arrived was no more.

She was wearing the red gown she had worn last night. *"I must change back into my habit,"* she said and went into the back room. Considering the temper her father had been in when I'd left him, it seemed a wise choice. He would be angry enough at her over the amount of silver she had cost him by her capture. If he interpreted the fine gown from Hastein as a sign she had in any way enjoyed her captivity, no doubt her welcome—if it could be called that—would be even grimmer.

We both were silent while we rode through the town and out the main gate. It was not a comfortable silence. I felt I should say something, but words would not come to mind.

"Will you be glad to return to the abbey?" I finally asked.

"It is not a bad life," she answered. *"It is quiet and peaceful. And I will not have to wonder or fear what the next day may bring. Life there is very . . ."* She paused and frowned, as if searching for the right word. *"Predictable,"* she finally said. *"Yes, that is it. Life in the abbey is very predictable. My life as a nun follows a set pattern, a strict routine."*

I would not wish my life to be so fixed. I would not want to know what path it would follow, day after day, year after year. I had known such a life as a slave.

"There is a religious holiday not many days hence. I suppose I shall be back in Paris, back at the abbey, by then. It is Easter, the feast when we celebrate the rising of our Lord, Jesus, the son of God, from the dead."

I thought it would be grim if the most you could look forward to, to break the monotony of your life, was a religious feast day. If such was the high point of Genevieve's life, though, I was glad for her sake that she would not miss it.

"In Paris, on Easter morning," she continued, *"there is a special mass in the Church of Saint Genevieve. The church was built on Mt. Genevieve by the first king of the Franks to become a Christian.*

*Special prayers and requests are offered at the Easter
mass by the people of Paris to Saint Genevieve, who is
buried in the church. We believe she gives extra con-
sideration to prayers made to her on that day, and
asks God to grant them."*

"Who is this Saint Genevieve?" I asked.

*"She is the protector of Paris. I am named for her.
Saint Genevieve lived long ago. She saved Paris from
the Hun army of Attila. Genevieve, who was a very
good and very holy woman, called upon God to spare
the town and when she did, God listened, and
Attila's army turned aside. Through the power of her
prayers, Saint Genevieve saved Paris when the power
of men, and of arms, could do nothing."*

I knew of this Hun she spoke of. He had been
a great and fierce warlord, and was remembered
even among the Danes, who knew him as King
Atil. I had heard tales about him during the long
winter nights in my father's longhouse.

*"This Attila lived many hundreds of years ago,
did he not?"* I asked.

"Yes," Genevieve answered. *"This happened
back during the time when the Romans still ruled
over these lands."*

*"And this Genevieve who saved Paris, she was
just a woman? She was not a Goddess?"*

"She was a very holy woman," Genevieve repeated.

"But she is dead, is she not?" I asked. *"Holy or*

121

not, she is dead, and has been dead for many, many years. Hundreds of years. Yet you pray to her?" I did not understand why the Christians would offer prayers to a dead person. What could such do to help the living?

"I do not expect you to understand, or to believe," Genevieve said. *"You are not a Christian. But I told you about Saint Genevieve because I wish you to know that on Easter morning, I will pray to her and ask her to protect you from your many enemies. Christian or not, I think you are a good man. I know that had I been captured by any of your people other than you . . . "* She shook her head silently, but did not express what she was thinking. She did not need to. We both knew what probably would have happened to her.

"I will always be grateful for how you have treated me," she said, beginning again. She turned and looked me full in the face, her dark eyes glistening as if they were wet with tears. *"I am certain I shall never forget you. You are truly a man who does not merely speak of honor, but who lives it."*

Her words surprised me. I would have thought she'd have been glad to forget me—to forget the time when she'd been a prisoner, to forget the killings she'd been forced to witness. I did not know what to say or how to respond, so I said nothing.

Later, as I watched her ride away in the company of her father and his warriors, I felt an unexpected pang of loss and, remembering her words, regretted I'd said nothing in return. I confess that in my heart, part of me wished that her father had not agreed to the high ransom we had demanded. Part of me wished that she was with me still.

7

ESCAPING A TRAP

"Ugh," Tore said. "They are starting to stink. We should have done this last night."

It was my fault we had not. Yesterday as we rode back into town bearing my new wealth, I'd been pleasantly surprised when Hastein had announced, "I have decided. We will not tell Ragnar about the two men you killed."

Ivar had said nothing, but looked at Hastein skeptically.

"The killings were clearly justified," Hastein continued. "They attacked you at night, by surprise, and without provocation. You had every right to defend yourself, and two witnesses have confirmed your story—though it is true that one of your witnesses, your prisoner, is now gone. Still, I heard her. Ivar did, too. We can confirm what she said if it should become necessary."

"I only heard her speak Frankish," Ivar pointed out. "I do not understand Frankish. I cannot say for certain what she really said—we know only what Halfdan told us she said."

"You are just being contrary," Hastein said dismissively. "I know you do not believe Halfdan lied to us. And you heard the other Frank, Wulf, confirm the story in our own tongue."

"If you feel the killings were justified, why should we not tell Ragnar?" I asked.

"Because he will be angry anyway," Ivar suggested. "Father does not like to have his orders disregarded, even for good cause. It is the frustrated king in him."

Hastein shook his head. "That is not the reason," he explained. "I wish to know who else was involved, if anyone. It seems obvious Snorre probably was, though it would be impossible to prove solely from the fact that Wulf saw Snorre and Stenkil talking together in the street in front of his house.

"We will make the two bodies disappear, then wait and watch what happens. Perhaps Snorre will make inquiries, trying to discover if you have been killed or injured, or if anyone knows where Stenkil or the other man are. That could help prove he knew in advance what Stenkil was planning to do. And I also wish to see how Stenkil's captain, Gunulf, will react to his disappearance. If Gunulf searches for Stenkil, and seems surprised that he has disappeared, he was probably not involved. But if he does not question the fact that one of his men has vanished, and if he does not try to find him—something a captain would normally do—it may show us Gunulf was aware Stenkil planned murder, but now that he has disappeared believes the safer course is to let sleeping dogs, or missing bodies, lie where they will.

"And finally, we do not know who the other man you killed was—whether he was a companion of Sigvid and Stenkil, from Gunulf's crew, or possibly one of Snorre's men. If the latter, that, too, could help us prove Snorre was behind the attack. So let us keep these deaths quiet and see what we can learn. It is always wise to discover whom to number among your enemies."

"You enjoy this, don't you?" Ivar said to Hastein, shaking his head. "This kind of devious plotting. I would far rather just confront my enemies and kill them."

I did not think what Hastein planned was devious plotting. I realized he was hunting. But he did not hunt beasts, nor use the skills of woods-lore—

the kind of hunting I was used to. He was hunting men—Snorre and, ultimately, Toke. He was seeking to put together, bit by careful bit, proof of their treachery—the kind of proof that would support bringing a legal case against them, at a Thing. It was a type of hunting I did not know. I had much to learn from Hastein.

Yesterday we'd stopped at Wulf's storehouse, and Hastein, Ivar, and Torvald had trooped in to examine the two bodies. "Put them in barrels; barrels with small holes drilled in them," Hastein had told Torvald. "Add some large stones and throw the barrels into the river. They will float downstream from Ruda, far enough away so no one in our army is likely to find them, and eventually sink."

Torvald had nudged Stenkil's body with his foot. "They are very stiff now," he'd said. "If we're going to try to pack these two into barrels this day, I'd better fetch an axe."

The thought of chopping the two dead men into pieces had seemed too gruesome to me. I'd persuaded Torvald to wait a day until the bodies began to loosen up again. When he'd arrived this morning, he'd brought Tore with him. Each of them was carrying a large, empty wooden barrel balanced on one shoulder.

Wulf watched nervously as we folded the two

noisome bodies double, then crammed each into a barrel. Though they'd begun to loosen, there was still enough of the death stiffness in them to make it hard work. The flies that had found the bodies swarmed around us, protesting the interruption of their meal and making it an even more unpleasant task.

"At least they have not begun to leak yet," Tore grunted as we lifted the filled barrels up onto a handcart Wulf had supplied to transport them to the river. "Their smell is bad enough, but leaking would be far worse."

"Get your gear, Halfdan, and we will take it on the cart, too," Torvald told me. "We are readying the *Gull* today. We leave Ruda at first light tomorrow."

I was surprised. I'd thought, from what Count Robert had told us, that the meeting upriver to negotiate the ransoms for the rest of the prisoners would have been canceled, or at least postponed.

"That is not where we are going," Torvald explained, when I asked. "Our entire fleet, save for nine ships whose crews will stay here in Ruda to hold the town, moves upriver tomorrow."

"Why?" I asked.

"We are going to fight," Tore said. He looked pleased.

"Ragnar thinks it suspicious that the Frankish

count was so eager to free his daughter," Torvald explained. "He suspects the Franks are even now moving their full army against Ruda. He thinks the count wanted to get her clear of the town before we learn of the Franks' advance."

Part of what Torvald said made sense. If the Franks were moving their army against us, Count Robert would not wish his daughter to be used as a hostage, hampering the freedom of his attack, even though their relationship was strained. However, I did not understand what our army was doing.

"If Ragnar believes the Frankish army is moving against Ruda, why are we taking our ships upriver?" I asked. We would be moving closer to the Frankish army, and danger. Surely it would be wiser to stay safe behind the walls of Ruda, or even retreat down the Seine toward the sea.

"Ragnar brought us to this land to fight the Franks and spill their blood, not to run from them," Tore answered.

I remembered the great fortified encampment that the Franks had been building as a temporary base for their army. I remembered the seemingly endless column of marching infantry and the numerous patrols of mounted warriors I'd seen. The Franks had many men—too many. Our army was too small, compared to the forces the Frankish king was gathering. We could not fight them and win.

"I have seen the Franks' army," I told Torvald and Tore. "It is vast. They far outnumber us."

"Aye," Torvald said. "They would greatly outnumber us if we just sat and waited for all of their forces on both sides of the river to join together here at Ruda and surround our army. When they come, they will bring thousands of infantry and siege machines and attack the town and our encampment on the island. With their siege engines, they could even threaten our ships out on the river. It is a style of fighting the Franks do very well. They can be very slow to react, but when they finally do bring their full forces to bear, they are very strong. But Ragnar is too canny to play the game according to the Franks' plan. The speed with which our ships allow us to move our army is one of our greatest strengths, and Ragnar knows well how to use it. When we fight, it will be a battle of his choosing."

The *Gull* was far more heavily laden upon leaving Ruda than she had been on the long voyage south to Frankia from Denmark. The sea chests of every warrior aboard—and no doubt, those of every warrior in the fleet—contained plunder taken from the churches, monasteries, and villages sacked by our raiding parties, as well as loot stripped from the homes and storehouses of Ruda when it had fallen. Silver candlesticks and the large silver goblets so frequently found in the Christians' churches, coins, jewelry, bolts of fine cloth, weapons, armor, and whatever else had struck our men's fancy now filled their sea chests. The deck of the *Gull* was cluttered with barrels filled with Frankish wine and ale, and casks of fine glassware and pottery packed in straw. There were also penned fowl, pigs, and even two sheep, all of which were destined for our cook fires. Under Torvald's direction, our crew pried up deck planks to gain access to the ballast stones in the bottom of the ship's hull, and threw enough overboard to compensate for the added weight we were now carrying.

The only plunder we did not carry with us was the army's prisoners—the ones still awaiting ransom, plus the women and children some of our warriors had taken to sell in the slave markets back in the north. Those remained under guard in Ruda, with the crews of the nine ships left to hold the town. Svein, one of the two experienced captains who followed Hastein, had been left in command of our forces there.

"Snorre and Gunulf, and their ships and crews, are among the nine staying to hold Ruda," Torvald told me. "Hastein made certain of that. You will not have to worry about Snorre's treachery while he is there, and Svein will keep an eye on both of them and report to Hastein what he observes."

My own sea chest was far heavier than when I'd begun this voyage. In addition to the ten pounds of silver I'd won as Genevieve's ransom, I had added to my possessions the fine helm, sword, mail brynie, and padded jerkin I'd taken from the body of Leonidas, Genevieve's cousin, as well as the long-bladed Frankish spear I'd taken from one of the cavalrymen I'd killed in the fight at the river.

To me, it seemed our attack on Frankia had already been a successful raid. Our warriors had won many fine goods and much silver from the Franks and, so far, our own losses had been relatively light. I wondered if Ragnar was wise to persist in his desire to make the Franks pay with blood, also.

If any other warriors among the *Gull*'s crew harbored doubts similar to mine, it was not obvious as we backed the ship away from the shore and headed upriver. The men around me laughed and joked as they rowed. Beside us on the river, the black shape of the *Raven*, Ragnar's ship, cut through the wisps of morning fog drifting over the water's surface. Behind us, the rest of our fleet followed, two or three ships abreast. For as far as I could see, their oars rose and fell, churning the river's surface and pulling us deeper and deeper into the heartland of Frankia.

We were not far upstream from Ruda when the first Frankish cavalry patrols began shadowing our progress from both banks of the river. The swiftness with which they appeared surprised me. It made me think Ragnar was probably right—the Franks must be closing in on the town. I wondered about the risk we were taking. What if the Frankish army ignored our fleet and attacked Ruda now, while only nine ships' crews remained to hold it? I did not know the size of each of the ships left there, or how many their crews numbered. At most, Svein could have no more than three to four hundred men under his command, and probably considerably fewer.

But when the Franks realized almost our entire fleet was on the move, the ranks of fast-moving mounted troops following our progress from either bank of the river quickly swelled far beyond mere scouting patrols. Ragnar's stratagem worked. Even before the sun reached its noon zenith, so many horsemen were traveling parallel to our course that broad plumes of dust rose high into the sky above either side of the river. Along each bank, an army of Frankish horsemen was moving, ready to attack if our warriors should land.

"The Franks have taken the bait," Hastein said,

a look of grim satisfaction on his face. I was glad he felt pleased. I did not. His words brought a worrisome image to my mind. We were the bait Ragnar was using to draw the Frankish army—or at least its mounted forces, the only ones fast enough to keep pace with our ships—away from Ruda. This seemed dangerous. When fishing, the bait often ends up getting eaten.

By now I was beginning to recognize sights along the river above Ruda, having passed this way and back twice before. For the first day, we traveled at a steady but easy pace, along the winding, switchback portion of the river that lay immediately upstream from the town. We camped the first night on several large islands in mid-stream, near where two smaller rivers converged with the Seine. The campfires of the Franks twinkled and flickered in the darkness on either shore. There looked to be hundreds of them. It was as though the land along both sides of the river had become the night sky, and the fires of the Franks were the stars.

We pushed harder on the second day, reaching and traversing the entire straight stretch of the river—the section where I had been brought to bay by the mounted Frankish patrols who'd hunted me after I had captured Genevieve. The islands where we camped on the second night lay in the first bend of the river just beyond the long straight run.

It was here, on the open flat land along the north bank of the river opposite the islands, where we'd been supposed to parley with the Franks to negotiate the ransoms for our prisoners. I remembered describing this location for Genevieve's brother, and telling him of the terms and conditions Hastein had set for the meeting.

I wondered if Genevieve's brother was out there now, in the darkness among the Frankish warriors camped on the north side of the river. I suspected he was. He'd said he hoped to someday have a chance to kill me. Was he now anticipating he would have an opportunity to fulfill that threat? It seemed likely that our armies would meet in battle. I wondered if he and I would face each other.

By early afternoon on the third day, we reached the two long islands in the Seine opposite the point where I had gone ashore and delivered the written messages to Genevieve's brother. Only eight days had passed since the *Gull* had last been here; eight days since I had last set foot upon this shore. Yet in that brief time, I had become a wealthy man, Genevieve had regained her freedom, and our army had sailed from Ruda, seeking battle with the Franks.

Torvald had said Ragnar would fight at a place and time of his own choosing. I remembered that

Hastein and Ragnar had studied the land carefully here, while Torvald had taken the *Gull* slowly along the channel between the islands and the north bank. I realized this must be the ground Ragnar had chosen. This was where we would fight.

The north bank rose up steeply from the river in heavily wooded slopes opposite most of the length of the first of the two islands, but a short distance downstream from where the first island was separated from the second by a narrow channel, the riverbank leveled out into an open plain that rose in a gentle incline toward the distant village.

Because of the steep and heavily wooded nature of the terrain abutting the river, for a time we had lost sight of the Franks following our progress along the north bank. No doubt they had swung wide from the river in order to pass around the rugged hills and ridges that overlooked its channel from that side. But when we neared the upstream end of the first island, I could see Frankish cavalry pouring from the tree line at the far end of the plain, and swarming like ants across the pastures and cleared fields surrounding the distant village.

A long black pennant was run up to the top of the mast on the *Raven*, and she swung sharply in to the shore of the downstream island. Torvald heaved on the *Gull*'s steering oar, and we followed. I could feel the keel grating along the bottom as we ground to a stop with the *Gull*'s bow nosed up against the edge of the shore. At Torvald's command, we pulled in our oars and stowed them in their racks.

Three other ships—Ivar's *Bear* and Stig's *Serpent* among them—tied up near us along the first island. The remainder of the fleet, led by Bjorn, passed us by. They continued upstream and made land along the north side of the second island, directly opposite the center of the plain, and within clear view of the village. The warriors from those ships quickly began setting up an encampment on the island, as our fleet had done each night of our journey since leaving Ruda. Some crews tented their sails above the hulls of their ships, making shelters onboard to sleep under for the night. Others pitched tents ashore. Men scattered across the island, gathering firewood for the night's cook fires.

Aboard the *Gull*, Hastein stepped up onto the small raised deck in the stern and addressed our crew.

"Do not bother setting up camp," he told us. "We will be moving the *Gull* once darkness falls. Use this time to rest or to ready your weapons and armor. But do not don them while it is still light and the Franks can see. We will cook and eat a meal before dusk. Be sure to eat your fill. Each man should carry water when we move out tonight, and pack a day's ration from the ship's store. It will be a long day tomorrow. Torvald, Tore, come with me."

Followed by Torvald and Tore, Hastein walked forward to the bow and leaped down onto the shore. Ivar, Stig, and several of their men were already waiting there. Together they walked down the island toward where the bow of Ragnar's ship was beached.

Odd pulled his cloak from his sea chest and rolled up in it on the deck. "Are you not going to try and rest?" he asked me. "We will get no sleep tonight, and the morrow will bring heavy work."

I felt too unsettled to even contemplate sleep.

"Why do we move tonight, while the rest of our army camps here?" I asked him. "Where are we going?"

Odd chuckled. "The camp being set up upstream is just for show. None of our warriors will sleep this night. We will use the cover of darkness to reach the ground Ragnar wishes to fight on."

"How do you know this?" I asked. What I really wished to know was why he knew, and I did not.

"Hastein told Tore of the plan, and Tore told

me," Odd explained. "Tore will command the archers from the *Gull* and a number of other ships tomorrow when we fight."

Tomorrow. What would it bring? What would the battle be like? There were thousands of warriors in our army, and surely at least as many in that of the Franks. The largest engagement I had fought in was the capture of Ruda's gate. Fewer than a hundred warriors, Dane and Frank together, had fought there.

Odd was watching my face. "You have never fought in a battle this large, have you?" he asked.

I shook my head. "No," I admitted.

"You will do fine," he said. "You fought well at Ruda. And you showed great resourcefulness and courage when you were holding off the Franks along the river before we found you there."

I appreciated Odd's words, but they gave me little comfort. When fighting against a single opponent, or even several, at least I could know what threats I must defend against. But fighting among so many warriors, and facing so many enemies, was not the same. Harald had told me, when trying to train me in the skills of a warrior during the brief time we'd had together: "A large battle is different," he'd explained. "Missile fire fills the air. Death can come from any direction, at any time. Men may not even see the warriors who slay them.

In a large battle, perhaps more than at any other time, surviving depends on luck. All you can do is fight as bravely and as well as you can, and meet with courage and honor whatever fate the Norns are weaving for you."

"Many will die tomorrow," Odd continued. "It is the way of a great battle. But death can find a man anywhere, at any time."

"How many battles—large battles, like this one—have you fought in?" I asked.

Odd removed the fur cap he was wearing, and rubbed his hand over the top of his bald head.

"Well," he said, "this will be a very great battle. It is likely to be one men tell tales of around the winter fires for many years to come. I have heard Torvald estimate our army numbers five thousand warriors, give or take a few hundred. I have never before fought as part of an army that large. But even in so great a force of warriors, the men we shall actually fight beside, and the enemies we shall directly oppose, will number no more than three or four ships' companies on either side. And I have fought in a number of battles of that size since I have served the jarl. I would guess ten at least. Jarl Hastein is a man not much given to peace. You will see that, if you continue following him."

Would I continue following Hastein? When I'd sought to join the crew of the *Gull*, it had been to gain experience as a warrior, and hopefully to win, in Hastein, an ally who might help me bring Toke to justice. Once Toke was finally dead—assuming I survived tomorrow to pursue the vengeance I had sworn to bring upon him—what then? When I had been a slave, I had dreamed of living the life of a warrior and a Viking. But that was before I had experienced it. I was no longer certain I would wish to spend my life fighting others, and stealing from them and killing.

Of course, I might have no choice to make. I might not survive tomorrow.

Odd must have interpreted my silence as worry about the coming battle. "You will do fine," he said again.

After Hastein, Tore, and Torvald returned from the war council with Ragnar, Tore called the archers aboard the *Gull* together in the stern. Though Tore, Odd, and I were the most skilled with bow and arrow, and the first to be called upon by Hastein, there were ten in all among the *Gull*'s crew who had brought bows on this voyage and possessed enough skill with them to warrant fighting as archers, if the need arose. Tore gathered all of them around him now.

"All of you should check your bows and your arrows, and make certain they are ready for use," he told us. "All of us will fight as archers in the coming battle, at least to begin with. But bring all of your weapons and armor with you when we cross the river—including your spears—for no one can know what the course of the battle will bring."

I was surprised Hastein would pull so many of our warriors from the main battle line. Since the fight at the gate in Ruda where we'd taken losses, our crew numbered only thirty-one, including Hastein, and two of our warriors were still recovering from wounds they'd received at Ruda and were not yet fit enough to fight. In this battle, a full third of our crew would fight as archers, instead of in the shield wall. What were Ragnar and Hastein planning?

"When do we cross the river?" I asked.

"We will be moving the *Gull* and these other four ships after darkness falls," Tore answered. "Two ships will be lashed side by side and anchored in the channel between the two islands. We will use their gangplanks, and those from other ships, to form a bridge across them for our warriors to move from the upstream island to this one. The other three ships, including the *Gull*, will be used to span the river from this island over to the north bank.

"The *Gull* will form the far end of the span. That means she will be the ship to be secured to

142

the river's north bank, and our warriors will be first ashore there. The ten of us will land first, as soon as the *Gull* touches the far bank. We must spread out quickly and search the shore for Frankish sentries. Surprise is essential to Ragnar's plan. If there are any Franks watching along the shore, we must find them and kill them before they can sound the alarm. Hastein and Ragnar do not believe there will be any sentries that far downstream in the woods, though. They think the Franks will expect that if our army does make an attack, we will strike at the flat, open shore directly across from our encampment, because if we attacked there, all of our ships could cross and land at once."

"Where are we going after we cross?" a warrior named Olof asked. I did not know him, other than by sight. He rowed at an oar toward the front of the ship. We had never had occasion to speak.

"There is a ridge that rises steeply above the plain the village sits on," Tore explained. "The ridge is clear almost to its crest along the side facing the village, but it is wooded on each end and its back slope. After we cross the river, our army will move through the woods up onto the back side of the ridge and wait there for morn. When day comes, we will move out onto the cleared slope below the ridge's crest and offer battle to the Franks from high ground."

I wondered what would happen if we did not achieve the surprise Ragnar and Hastein hoped for? What if the Franks *had* placed sentries in the woods across from this island? Even in the dark, they would see our ships moving long before we could maneuver them into position to span the river from the island to the bank. The sentries could sound the alarm and then fade back into the darkness in the woods before we even reached the shore.

Odd, too, had concerns. "Even if the Franks have no sentries along that part of the shoreline where we plan to cross," he said, "moving our entire army across the river in the dark without alerting the Franks will not be an easy task. Without question, the Franks will have sentries farther upstream, across from our encampment. Will not those sentries hear or see signs that we are moving? Where we plan to cross is not that far downstream."

"Ragnar has thought of that," Tore said. "When we are ready to begin the crossing, a small attack will be launched directly across the river from the encampment as a diversion. Five ships will cross the river there, and their crews will land on the edge of the plain. They will attempt to find and eliminate any Frankish sentries watching along that portion of the river. They'll form a defensive line as if preparing to hold the shore there for a larger assault to follow. The Franks will certainly respond by sending a force to push our warriors from the shore. When they do, our men will fall back to their ships. But the noise and confusion they cause will cover for us. And throughout the night, other men will move back and forth through the encampment, in and out of the light of the fires there, to create an illusion that many men are stirring on the upstream island, as if preparing to launch a larger assault from there in the morning. The Franks will be watching our feint at the encampment, and will not see our main force moving downstream in the darkness around their flank."

Unless there are sentries in the woods where we plan to cross, I thought.

I did not wish to question the plan in front of the other men. I did not know how great a role, if any, Tore had had in its making. After the rest of the men dispersed, though, I pulled him aside and spoke quietly to him.

"What is it?" he asked gruffly.

"Much depends on our army crossing the river undetected," I said. "I was wondering if we could do more to ensure there are no Frankish sentries watching from the woods across from this island."

"Ragnar does not think there will be Franks posted this far downstream from our main encampment," Tore answered. "And if there are, I have assured him and Hastein that we will be able to find and kill them quickly—before they can sound the alarm. Remember, there will be ten of us armed with bows."

I had long suspected Tore had little experience at hunting, or in the woods. This confirmed it.

"Let me look now," I told him.

"What? What are you saying?" he demanded. "You wish to cross the river in the daylight?"

"No," I explained. "I will lie hidden among the trees and undergrowth on this island, downstream from where our ships are anchored, and watch the far bank. I know the forest well. I know its ways. If men are hiding in the trees on the north bank, I may be able to see them."

Hastein approached us. "Are your men ready for tonight, Tore?" he asked.

Before Tore could answer, I spoke. "Tore was just suggesting to me that perhaps I should begin watching the woods now—the woods on the north bank where we shall cross," I lied. "To make certain there are no Frankish sentries hiding there. It is still several hours until dark. Few men can remain motionless that long. If sentries are there, I will see them."

Hastein looked at Tore approvingly. "It is a good plan," he said. "You are making good use of Halfdan's skills. I, for one, am not as confident as Ragnar that the Franks will post sentries only opposite our encampment on the island upstream."

Seeing Hastein's enthusiasm for the new plan, Tore wanted to go watch the woods with me. With difficulty, I dissuaded him. "Can you stalk as slowly and silently as a cat? Can you lie motionless in the dirt and undergrowth for hours?" I asked. "Even if insects crawl upon you and bite you? It is what must be done. If there are Frankish sentries, they will be hidden and watching. If you move, they will see you. Only if they see nothing moving, nothing at all, will they grow bored and confident and certain no one watches from our side of the river. Only then will they move about and give away their own positions."

There were three of them. Three Frankish warriors, concealed just back from the water's edge in the woods across from the downstream island. They were widely spaced—one opposite each end of the island, and one in the center—but between the three of them, they would be able to see anything that crossed the river from the island to the north bank, even in the dark.

I told Tore, and Tore told Hastein. Hastein immediately sent runners to fetch Ragnar, Ivar, and

Bjorn to the *Gull*.

"Your plan will not work, Father," Ivar said once he heard the news. "The Franks' sentries will sound the alarm long before we can position our ships to span the river. Your battle plan depends upon our army forming on the high ground of the ridge in a strong position before the Franks realize we have crossed the river. But if they send their soldiers into the woods, in response to their sentries' alarms, what we will have instead will be a confused, disorganized fight in the dark among the trees. We cannot win the decisive victory you desire that way."

"We have come too far to be undone like this," Ragnar answered. "We have led the Frankish cavalry away from their infantry. Their army is fragmented now. We cannot let this opportunity pass." He wheeled on Hastein. "How certain are you that Frankish sentries are in those woods?"

"I am certain," Hastein answered. "Halfdan saw them."

Given Ragnar's displeasure at having his plan foiled, I would rather Hastein had given Tore the credit. Ragnar glared in my direction. No doubt my appearance did not improve his impression of me. My face and hands were still smeared with the mud I had used to darken them, and my clothes were filthy from having slowly crawled on my belly almost the entire length of the island as I watched the far bank from hiding.

"You must face the facts, Father," Ivar said. "Your plan cannot succeed."

"Perhaps," I suggested, "there is a way."

The water was cold and the temperature of the air had dropped sharply after the sun had gone down. I was shivering and I could hear Einar's teeth chattering.

"How far downstream do you think we need to go?" he whispered. The cold was making him impatient. We had not even passed the end of the island yet.

We were floating with the current, hanging on to the raft we'd built in the channel between the two islands while dusk was falling. There was not much to it—just three logs lashed together, with cut brush tied on top and along the sides. Our clothes and weapons—just bows, one quiver of arrows each, and knives—were also tied on top of the logs and covered with cut branches. In the dark, from the far shore, the raft would look—I hoped—like a tree that had fallen into the river and was drifting downstream.

"Far enough so we can no longer see the end of this island," I answered, also in a whisper. "The third sentry I saw was in the woods almost opposite the island's end. We need to be far enough downstream from him that he cannot see us when we climb out of the river."

Only our heads showed above the surface of the water, and they were concealed by the brush we'd lashed to the logs. As the current slowly carried us past the end of the island, we began kicking our legs, gradually pushing the raft closer to the north bank.

"To your left," I whispered, once we'd rounded a bend and the island was no longer visible. "I see what looks to be a gap in the trees along the bank. Do you see it? Let us make for there."

The gap proved to be the mouth of a narrow stream. We pushed our raft into it, cut our clothes and weapons free, and climbed stiffly up into the stream's shallow channel, hidden by its banks and the trees that grew above them.

"Gods, that water was cold," Einar said as we shook ourselves as dry as we could and pulled on our clothes. "I was beginning to regret that you asked me to come with you."

I was glad he'd accepted. If two of us struck simultaneously at each of the sentries, we were far more likely to achieve silent kills. It was essential that each sentry die without making any sound to alert his comrades. I needed someone skilled with a bow to help me. But even more, I needed a woodsman like me—someone who could move through the forest silently, more like a beast than a man. There might be others possessing such skills within our army, but I knew only of Einar.

The first sentry was easy. He had fallen asleep, seated against the base of a tree, and we located him by the sound of his snoring. We did not even need our bows. We crept close, then I reached around the trunk of the tree and clamped my hands over his mouth and nose to prevent any outcry, while Einar killed him with his knife.

The second Frank had taken a position behind a large oak at the water's edge—a good hiding place from which to watch the river. It had taken me the longest to locate him during the afternoon, when I was watching the shoreline from the island. But now that the woods were cloaked in darkness, he moved about often, standing to stretch his legs or pacing up and down along the bank. Einar and I took up positions behind a bush no more than two spear-lengths behind him, and readied arrows on our bows. The next time he stood and stretched, reaching his arms up and rolling his head from side to side, we put two arrows into the center of his back. He flopped forward against the trunk of the oak, a single, strangled gasp escaping from his throat, and slid slowly down the tree to the ground.

The third sentry was the hardest. He had moved since the afternoon, and was now hidden in the midst of a large thicket with small trees and shrubs behind him as well as in front. Although we could dimly make out his shadowy form through the leaves and branches of the underbrush that surrounded him, we had no clear shot. Einar and I watched him for a time, but when he did not move from the thicket, Einar signaled to me and we backed away, deeper into the forest, so we could talk.

"The other two are already dead," Einar whispered. "This killing does not have to be as quiet."

What he said was true. But it still needed to be quick and certain. If we only wounded the Frank, he might still be able to sound an alarm before we could close with him and finish the job.

"We cannot delay too long," Einar continued. "The night passes. It will take time to move the ships into position and get our army across them."

"What do you suggest?" I asked.

"One of us must get in position to shoot. The other must move upstream of him, or down, and make noise—enough noise that he will move from that thicket he hides in and investigate."

His plan had the merit of being simple, and I could think of nothing better.

"Who will be the shooter?" I asked.

"You," Einar answered, and pointed downstream. "I will circle around that way. Be ready."

Einar moved off, quickly vanishing into the dark. I headed back in the direction of the river's edge, and took up a position that gave me a good view of the downstream side of the thicket—and hopefully the sentry, if Einar was successful in luring him from it.

Rap-tap. The sound startled me, even though I had been waiting for Einar to begin. *Rap-tap-rap-tap.* What was he doing?

Over and over, Einar repeated the pattern: *rap-tap, rap-tap-rap-tap.* It did not sound like any noise a beast would make. Yet it was not obviously a sound made by a man, either.

Rap-tap, rap-tap-rap-tap.

"Is someone there?" the Frank whispered.

Rap-tap, rap-tap-rap-tap.

"Carloman, is that you?"

Rap-tap, rap-tap-rap-tap. It sounded like it was getting closer.

The Frank stood up. I was watching him from behind the thick trunk of a tall ash tree, peering around its side, just above ground level, with one eye. I could see the Frank's head clearly now above the undergrowth, but my view of his body was still obstructed. With so much depending on a quick, quiet kill, I did not want to risk a shot

153

at his head in the dark.

Rap-tap, rap-tap-rap-tap.

I heard the quiet rasp of the Frank's sword being drawn from its scabbard, and he began edging forward, one cautious step at a time. I estimated that in three more steps he would be in the open.

Rap-tap, rap-tap-rap-tap.

"*Who goes there?*" I could hear the nervousness in the Frank's voice. I eased back behind the trunk of the tree until I was fully hidden by it, then stood up slowly. Listening to the rustle and crunch of the Frank's footsteps in the dry leaves and scattered acorn shells on the ground, I visualized where he was as I laid an arrow across my bow and pulled it to full draw.

Rap-tap, rap-tap-rap-tap.

I edged forward around the ash tree. The Frank was directly ahead of me, just clear of the thicket, peering into the darkness in the direction the sound was coming from. His right side was toward me. It was not a good angle for a killing shot.

"Psst," I whispered. The Frank spun toward me and I aimed my arrow at the center of his chest. I was close enough to see the whites of his eyes when they widened with shock and surprise, and to hear him suck in his breath in a frightened gasp.

I released my arrow and immediately lost sight of it in the dark. Just as it leaped off my bow, the Frank began scuttling back away from me, then staggered and fell out of sight into the cover of the thicket. I heard a *thunk*—I feared it was my arrow, sailing past him and smacking into the trunk of a tree. Almost immediately after, I heard a muffled thud followed by a brief rustle as the Frank hit the ground. Then there was only silence.

"Did you hit him? Is he dead?" Einar called in a loud whisper. I did not know. I didn't know if he was even wounded. I feared he was merely frightened and hiding. And now Einar had given his own position away.

"Shhh!" I answered, nocking another arrow on my bowstring. I moved to the other side of the ash tree and crouched low behind a bush, waiting. I was hoping that when he fell, the Frank had been too startled and distracted to be able to tell where I had gone. I was hoping he would be uncertain where I was now. Most of all, I was hoping he would be too fearful of losing his own life to risk calling out or blowing a horn to sound the alarm.

Eventually, I thought, he will try to move deeper into cover, in order to put more protection between himself and my bow. When he did, it would give his position away. I would have to risk a shot then, even through the brush. At this point, any shot was better than none.

But the Frank did not move. And as Einar had said, the night was passing. I could not wait forever. I would have to go to him. I would have to expose myself to view. Hopefully, he did not have a bow, too.

Pulling my bow to full draw, I stood and crept forward. When I reached the edge of the thicket, the Frank's body came into view and I understood what had happened.

One of the Frank's feet lay across a thick tree root. When he'd seen me and tried to retreat, his heel must have caught on it, tripping him. The arrow I'd aimed for his chest instead had struck him in the center of his forehead as he was falling. It was his skull the arrow had thudded into, not a tree. It was a miracle I had hit him at all, much less killed him. Had I released my arrow a split second later, had I aimed only a little to one side or the other, or jerked the bow the slightest bit when I released, my arrow would have missed him completely.

I heard Einar coming up behind me. "Is he dead?" he asked.

"Yes," I answered and turned to face him. "What was that sound you were making?"

Grinning, Einar held up his knife and tapped its handle against his bow: *rap-tap, rap-tap-rap-tap.*

He stepped forward to look at the dead Frank and gave a low, admiring whistle.

"A shot through the head," he said. "Perfectly centered. In the dark, and when your target was moving. I knew you were skilled with a bow, and confident of your ability with it. But this shot . . . " He looked at me and shook his head. "This is the stuff of legends."

8

THE FIELD
OF THE DEAD

From somewhere nearby, a bird chirped its first tentative greetings to the approaching morn. I opened my eyes. I had not been sleeping, only wishing I was.

I was sitting on the ground with my back propped against the trunk of a tree. My shield, helm, and weapons were beside me. The woods around me were filled with other warriors, mostly also seated or lying on the ground, a few standing. There was enough light—the strange, gray light of dawn, before the sun actually rises above the horizon—to see them clearly now. When we'd first arrived here, after stumbling through the forest, bumping into each other and trees, for what felt like hours, it had still been the deep, pitch-black dark of the last stretches of the night.

Torvald appeared from the slope behind me. His helm was strapped on his head, and his shield slung across his back. "Up, my lads. Up now," he said as he walked among us, occasionally prodding a sleeping man with the shaft of his spear. "The morn is upon us, and it is time."

He stopped beside Tore, who was sprawled against the trunk of a nearby tree with his head tilted back, mouth open, snoring loudly. Tore's unstrung bow and two quivers stuffed with arrows were propped beside him.

Torvald reached out, eased the bow away from Tore, and leaned it against the back side of the tree he was sleeping against. Then he jabbed the butt of his spear's shaft sharply into Tore's chest.

"Wake up, Tore," he said. "Would you sleep through the battle? And Gods, man, where is your bow? Did you leave it on the ship?"

Tore opened his eyes, looking dazed, and slapped at the shaft of Torvald's spear, but it was already gone. Torvald strode off, wearing a pleased grin, while Tore looked around him for his bow with a confused and increasingly anxious expression on his face.

I stood and stretched, made water against the side of a tree, then strapped my helm and sword on. Slinging my shield across my back, and the straps of my two quivers over one shoulder, I hoisted my bow and spear and joined the disorganized throng of warriors headed toward the top of the ridge just above us, where a steadily growing light was beginning to shine through the trees.

As I stepped from the last fringe of the forest into the open, just beyond the crest of the ridge, I paused and looked around at what was to be our field of battle. The face of the ridge had been cleared on this side so long ago that not even stumps remained. A long, grassy meadow—no doubt used as grazing land for the flocks of the nearby village—covered the sloping side of the ridge, flowing down and merging with the broad plain that extended from the river to the village.

The open, grassy hillside stretched perhaps two bowshots long. On its right, the sloping meadow ended at a large outcropping of rock. Just beyond, the end of the ridge fell off sharply down to the river. In the opposite direction, just past the left end of the open ground, the ridge turned and curved out onto the plain where it tapered down to nothing. That end of the ridge, beyond the far end of the hillside meadow, had never been cleared. The dense growth of trees on the long, sloping extension that reached out into the plain marked the boundary of what would be our left flank. Ragnar had chosen a strong position from which to offer battle to the Franks. They could attack us only directly from the front.

The Frankish village we'd seen from the river lay almost straight ahead, though it was still a considerable distance away. Numerous tents, smoldering cook fires, and tethered mounts of the army of Frankish cavalry that had followed us upriver along the north bank were scattered across the fields surrounding the village.

Hastein, Ragnar, Ivar, and Bjorn were all standing a short distance down from the tree line on the sloping side of the ridge, spaced evenly across its front. As warriors emerged from the woods above them, they called out, "What ship? Who is your captain?" Depending on the answer they received, they directed the men to the right flank, the left, or the center.

Two standards had been set up in the center of the hillside, their tall poles wedged into the ground and supported by piles of stones. The silk banners fluttered in the morning breeze, revealing the designs that adorned them: Ragnar's black Raven and Hastein's soaring Gull.

Someone slapped me on the shoulder as he walked past. "Fine work last night, Halfdan," he said. "I heard the tale of the shot you made in the dark." I recognized the warrior who spoke. His name was Hauk. He was one of the ten archers on the *Gull*'s crew, and rowed an oar toward the front of the ship. He had never spoken to me before this day.

Odd was walking behind him. He grinned at me and said, "Aye, your deeds are quite the story this morning. Your comrade Einar has been telling us of them." He jerked his head in the direction Hauk was walking. "Come with us," he said. "Our position will be on the slope above Jarl Hastein's standard."

Gradually our battle formation began to take shape. A shield-wall of warriors, standing shoulder to shoulder and three deep, stretched from one end of the grassy hillside to the other. Above the shield-wall, a short distance below the tree line running along the crest of the ridge, a second battle line composed entirely of archers was being formed. The archers had been divided into three blocks of warriors: the largest in the center, and two smaller behind and supporting the shield-wall on each flank.

Tore was walking along the archers' line in the center. He periodically stopped and spoke with one or another of the warriors he passed, checking their weapons, sometimes repositioning men in the formation.

When he reached me, he looked me up and down silently for a moment, his features expressionless. Then he said in a gruff voice, "Are you ready?"

I shrugged my shoulders. "I wish now I had taken the time to shoot each of my new arrows," I told him. "I should have checked them to see if there are any that do not shoot true."

"I do not think it will be a problem," Tore said, as he unslung his shield and quivers. "Much of the shooting we will do this day will be at close range. Move over a bit. I will be shooting from here, beside you and Odd."

"I have never seen this many men together at one time," I said, looking at the mass of warriors finding their places in the two long lines.

"It is an impressive sight," Tore agreed. "Our archers alone number close to a thousand. That is what Hastein says, at least. Five hundred of our men armed with bows are here in the center—and I command them," he added, as if to make certain I knew. "And over two hundred more are on each flank."

"It seems a lot of warriors to pull from the shield-wall," Odd said. "I wonder if we do not thin it too much. There look to be many Franks gathering across the way."

"Ragnar knows what he's doing," Tore replied.

The first units of Frankish cavalry were beginning to stream from their encampment, forming a line out on the plain facing ours. Behind them, the rest of their camp was a swarm of activity.

163

Ragnar and Hastein stepped out from the front line below us and after walking a few paces down the hill, they turned to face our army. Both had their shields slung across their backs and were carrying spears. Ragnar, who was also carrying a long-handled war-axe, began addressing us in a booming voice.

"Warriors! You who will fight here in the center of our battle line, around my banner and that of Jarl Hastein—hear me!"

At the sound of his voice, the men standing along the ridge stopped talking and turned to listen. When all were quiet, Ragnar continued. "We have journeyed here together, far from our homes and deep within the heart of our enemy's land. The Franks have been generous hosts. They have shared with us their goods, their silver, and their women." At this, many of the warriors laughed. Ragnar continued. "But we did not come this far merely to lighten the Franks' purses. We came because they are the only enemy of the Danes powerful enough to have ever threatened our homeland.

"We have traveled this far to carry war back to our enemies, the Franks. We have come to fight them here, in their own land. And I intend that we shall so badly bloody them that the Franks will never again dare threaten the lands of the Danes."

Up and down the line, men roared their

approval of Ragnar's words. Many beat their spears against their shields, making a sound like thunder. Ragnar held up his hands and the din gradually subsided.

"Let me tell you now of the error the Frankish king has made. He is so fearful of the threat we pose to his land and to his people, he has divided his mighty army. He is like an overly cautious and unskilled player of hnefatafl who tries to cover the entire board at once by scattering one piece here and another there."

Ragnar turned and pointed behind him at the rapidly swelling ranks of Frankish warriors forming out on the plain. "And he has placed some of the pieces of his army over there. This day, we are going to take those pieces, and destroy them."

Again the army roared its approval. I did not join in. What Ragnar described as only some pieces of the Frankish king's army nonetheless looked to me to be a very large and strong force.

Ragnar continued. "This will not be an easy fight. The Franks are doughty warriors, especially their horse soldiers, as any of you who have faced them before can attest. But we have already won the first advantage, by making this hillside the ground on which we shall meet. And I will tell you now how we shall fight this battle, and how we shall win it.

"The Frankish army that faces us is composed entirely of cavalry. They know but one way to fight: They will charge us. And because we have taken this strong position across the top of this ridge, with both of our flanks protected, they can attack us only from our front.

"The steepness of this hill will slow them when they come. Still, those of you who have not faced a charge by mounted warriors before, know this: It is a fearsome thing, to see a wall of horses and men bearing down upon you. But horses will not throw themselves upon the points of spears. You who are in the front rank of the shield-wall—and our most seasoned men should be there—must kneel and brace your spear butts firmly against the ground. Aim the points of your spears at the chests of the Franks' horses. That will keep them from charging through our line. Their charge will break when the horses reach our spears. You must hold fast, and trust that it will. And when it does, you warriors behind must thrust out with your spears, past the front rank, and strike at the faces of the horses and the riders upon them.

"My warriors, if you do not waver in your courage, I promise you our line will hold and the Franks' charge will break against our shield-wall like the ocean's waves break upon a rocky shore. And while the Franks are stopped against the points of our spears, our archers, standing on the hill behind and above you, will be pouring arrows into them, like the wind of All-Father Odin that carries death to those it touches.

"You, my warriors, are the anvil upon which we will break the Frankish army. The Franks will throw their forces against us this day, for they think this is their chance to destroy our army which has eluded them until now. But you who fight in the shield-wall will hold them, and you archers, standing behind, will strike them down, and bleed their army until it is weak. And then, while the Franks mill in front of our line, weakened and confused, the hammer will fall and crush them against you. A strong reserve of our warriors will be waiting, rested and eager to fight, in the woods beyond our left flank. They will fall upon the Franks from the rear. Together, hammer and anvil, we will enclose our enemies in a trap of sharpened steel, and we will destroy them in it.

"My warriors, do not fear death this day. The Gods themselves will be watching this great battle. They will look to see who fights bravely and scorns fear. Odin's shield maidens, the Valkyries, will carry our brave warriors who fall in this day's contest to the great feast-hall of the Gods, and their glory will be sung of there forever. It is a good day to die!"

I thought it a better day to live, but the army

once again roared its approval of Ragnar's words.

While Ragnar strode off toward the left flank, to address the warriors there, Hastein made his way through the ranks of the shield-wall and up to where Tore, Odd, and I were standing.

"Prepare a fire arrow," he told Tore. "Ivar will command the reserve force of our army. Once the battle is well underway, he will lead the reserve forward through the woods along the end of the ridge that juts out into the plain over there, beyond our left flank, to a position from which he can attack the Franks' rear. But he must stay well hidden and not attack until we give the signal—until all of the enemy's forces are committed. If he attacks too soon, it will be his men who find themselves encircled, not the Franks. When Ragnar tells you to—or when I do, if Ragnar has fallen—you must light the fire arrow and shoot it high above the field of battle, to signal Ivar to attack."

Hastein looked at Odd and me. "Did you hear?" he asked. "If Tore has fallen, one of you must shoot the fire arrow. The signal must be given in order to close the trap on the Frankish army."

"It is a fine plan Ragnar has made," Odd said to Hastein. "Our victory seems assured."

"Huh," Hastein answered. "Do you think so? Nothing is ever certain. Battle has a way of ignoring the plans of men."

A light breeze brushed gently across my cheek. The air felt crisp and cool, and I sucked in deep lungfuls of it, savoring each one. The sky overhead was a deep, cloudless blue, and although the day was fully arrived, the moon still hung above us, faintly visible. As I looked up toward its pale face, an eagle drifting with the air currents floated across it. I wondered if it was an omen. If so, what was its meaning?

"Are you looking for the Valkyries?" Odd asked.

"No," I answered. I would not wish to see them. Surely that would mean I was to die. "I am just looking. It is a beautiful day."

"Aye, it is a good day for fighting," Tore said. "We are fortunate it is cool. Wearing armor in the heat saps the strength, and I feel certain we will need all of our strength, and wish for more, this day."

By now columns of Frankish cavalry were pouring in a steady stream from their encampment, and the Frankish line was beginning to take shape. Many units had already formed into tight blocks of riders, who waited patiently on their motionless horses. A forest of upright spears topped with glittering steel points stood above the entire host. Within each block of riders, small flags fluttered from a few of the spears.

"Do you see the spears with flags?" Tore said.

"Those are officers. Captains, or leaders of smaller units. When they charge, try to kill the men with the flags."

A small group of riders broke away from the Frankish line and rode toward us. There were ten of them. They made their way slowly from one end of our line to the other, studying our ranks.

Torvald climbed up the slope toward us after they had passed. "Halfdan, did you see?" he asked. "Those Frankish officers, when they rode past? One of them was Count Robert, your captive's father. I am certain of it."

I had not noticed. But Torvald was probably correct. He had unusually keen eyesight. "I thought him an arrogant pig of a man," he continued. "I hope he comes within reach of my spear."

Tore, who had also been studying the group of Frankish riders, was now wearing a grim expression on his face.

Odd looked at him and frowned. "What is it?" he asked.

"Did you not notice?" Tore snapped. "Two of the riders, two of the Frankish commanders, were Bretons."

"Who are Bretons?" I asked.

"Their land lies to the south, along the coast of Frankia," he replied. "I recognized them by their armor and weapons. Breton horse-warriors are very hard to kill. Even their mounts are protected with mail. And they fight with javelins, and are very deadly with them. I was certain they were Bretons when I saw the quivers of javelins hanging from their saddles. This is a bad thing." Tore seemed unnerved.

I was surprised. Odd and Torvald looked surprised, too. "We have fought Bretons before," Odd told Tore. "And we have beaten them."

"Aye, we have," Tore said. "We fought them once, and did beat them then. But do you not recall? My brother was killed when we fought them before. And I saw him last night. In a dream."

"You saw your brother Torsten?" Odd asked.

Tore nodded. "I have not dreamed of him in years. I fear it is a sign. I do not think it is a good one."

From down in the shield-wall, someone cried out, "Look! They come!"

I looked up. Out across the field, the entire Frankish army—save for a single block of mounted warriors, no doubt their own reserve, that remained motionless behind their center—was moving forward at a slow walk. As they advanced, the rear ranks of each unit moved forward, filling the spaces in their formation, until all were arrayed in a single long line of horsemen. Gradually, their speed increased from a walk to a canter as they headed across the plain toward us.

"They waste no time in starting the battle," Tore muttered. "They must be eager for our blood." He reached inside the neck of his mail brynie, pulled out the silver Thor's hammer he wore on a leather thong, and touched it to his lips. "Strength and honor," he whispered, then tucked the charm away. Raising his hand and clenching it in a fist in front of his face, he said again, this time in a louder voice, "Strength and honor."

Odd raised his own hand in a clenched fist, also making the sign of the hammer, and touched it to Tore's. "Aye, strength and honor, my comrade," he said. "This day we will face together whatever fates the Norns have set for us, with strength and with honor."

All along the line of archers, warriors quickly strung their bows, pulled arrows from their quivers, and readied them on their strings. Tore stepped out in front of us.

"Archers!" he cried. "We will shoot our first volley on my signal, and shoot it as one. Hold fire until you hear me cry 'loose.' After the first arrow, shoot as swiftly as you are able, and mark your targets well."

I felt awed by the Franks' discipline and their control of their mounts. They were coming at a full gallop now. The thunder of thousands of hooves shook the ground where we stood, yet their line remained even as they swept toward us.

On our left and right flanks, the Frankish soldiers charging at our line were beginning to lower their long spears, pointing them at the shield-wall. The riders approaching our center looked to be carrying shorter spears in their hands. They held them down by their sides as they rode. I raised my bow and began searching for a target.

"I knew it. It is the Bretons. They are attacking our center," I heard Tore murmur to himself. "Ready!" he shouted aloud.

All along the line, archers pulled their bows to full draw. I looked out at the rapidly approaching line of riders, and picked the man who would be my target. I tried to focus my sight, the killing look, on his chest, just above his shield, and drive all else from my mind. I could not control my thoughts, though. I could not stop hearing the thunder of the hooves, nor counting the moments till the Franks' line would crash into ours.

"Loose!" Tore shouted. Hundreds of arrows arced out from the hillside, and fell into the charging horde. I watched my arrow soar out toward the line of Franks, but lost it among the cloud of shafts. I could not see where it hit, but the man I'd shot at did not fall.

As the swarm of arrows descended upon the

charging Franks, horses stumbled here and there and riders fell. Many shields had arrows embedded in their surface, some so thickly they looked like the backs of hedgehogs. But in the center, among the Bretons, few riders went down. Now that they were closer, I could see that their horses' chests and necks were protected by thick, quilted skirts, covered with mail. On some horses, arrows had struck the armor and become caught in the links of mail, and now flopped back and forth ineffectually.

I nocked another arrow on my string and raised my bow again, drawing as I did. The Bretons were keeping themselves well covered, crouching behind their shields as they rode.

Tore was holding his bow at full draw, too, but did not release. "Show yourselves, damn you," he said. "I can find no target." He loosed his arrow at the same time I launched mine, and we both clawed another from our quivers.

By now the Bretons had reached the base of the ridge and began climbing it. They were so close I could see the flying clods of earth their horses' hooves kicked up. Below me, the warriors in the shield-wall readied themselves for the impact. Those kneeling in the front rank huddled behind their shields, the second and third rows pressed close behind, their spears extended.

But there was no impact. The Bretons did not

try to crash through our shield-wall. Suddenly a rider in the fore of their charging line raised his arm and brandished a short spear above his head. At his signal, the line of charging Bretons straightened up in their saddles as one, cocked their arms back, and hurled the javelins they were carrying. I launched my arrow at a rider's face as he did, but saw it skim harmlessly past his head.

Though smaller than a normal spear, the Bretons' missiles were far heavier than an arrow, and the force with which they were thrown—made even greater by the speed of the charging horses—caused them to strike with tremendous impact. I saw a warrior below me in the shield-wall try to block a javelin that was flying at him. Its sharp steel head splintered through the planks of his shield, knocking it back against his helm and face. Then the spear's point, now colored red with gore, suddenly jutted from the back of his head. Many warriors, more than I could count in the instant I looked, were knocked backward by the Bretons' missiles. I saw a warrior near Hastein stagger back and fall, clutching at a javelin through his neck. Another warrior standing beside Ragnar's standard was flung back by a missile that pinned his shield to his chest.

As soon as they launched their javelins, the Bretons cut their horses hard to the right in unison. They were superb riders. All along the center of the line, our archers were loosing at them, but the Bretons had turned so their large shields were facing us, and those and their horses' armor kept most from suffering serious harm. As they rode along our line, many whipped another missile down at the ranks of our Danish warriors they were passing.

I raised my bow, but did not draw yet. I was determined to make this shot count.

Again the Bretons wheeled their horses in unison, turning as one back toward their own lines. As they did, they swung their shields around to cover their backs.

A Breton making his turn in front of me found his way obstructed by a riderless horse that failed to turn with their formation. He sawed at his reins with both hands, urging his horse around it, and his shield, hanging now by its long strap around his neck and shoulder, flopped sideways. I drew and released, aiming for the point between his shoulder blades, but by the time my arrow reached him, he had kicked his horse forward and was twisting in the saddle. The arrow—shot hard enough at this distance to pierce his mail—hit him in his right shoulder. He jerked upright at the impact, then slumped forward against his horse's neck, but managed to stay in the saddle and escape.

As the Bretons headed back to their own lines, horns sounded and all along our battle line the rest of the Franks began withdrawing. On each of our flanks, where regular Frankish cavalry had attacked, rather than Bretons, Ragnar's plan appeared to have met with some success. In the disorganized melees that had resulted when the Franks' charge had been stopped against the spears of the shield-wall, and our archers had poured their fire into them, many of the Franks' mounts had gone down. I could see many riders on the ground—some motionless, others climbing to their feet or trying to stagger back toward their own lines. As I watched, groups of Danish warriors sprinted out from our shield-wall, cutting down the Frankish wounded.

It was a different story in the center. A few of the Bretons' horses had fallen to our arrows. A few of the Bretons themselves had been hit, too, and knocked from their mounts. But we had lost far more men than our attackers. All along the center of the shield-wall, men were down. Some were writhing in pain at the javelins piercing their bodies, others lay motionless with the stillness of death. As the thunder of the Franks' hoofbeats receded, it was replaced by the moans and cries of wounded men and horses.

Our heaviest losses had occurred around the

two standards—the Bretons had concentrated their fire there. The shield of almost every man around the standards had been pierced—some by more than one missile. To my relief, I saw that Torvald and Hastein still stood, though both were pulling on the shafts of javelins embedded in their shields. Ragnar, too, had escaped harm.

In their zeal to strike at our leaders and the warriors who guarded their standards, the Bretons had not aimed any of their fire at the second line along the ridge. None of the archers had fallen.

"Did you bring any down?" Odd asked me. "Did you kill any?"

I shook my head. "I shot four arrows," I said. "But only my last struck its target. And though wounded, even that rider still managed to regain the Frankish line."

"I did no better," he said. "I, too, got four arrows off, but none brought down man or horse. Their armor is too heavy. How did you fare, Tore?"

But Tore did not answer. He was striding down the slope to meet Hastein, who was climbing toward us.

"It is no good," Tore exclaimed to him. "Ragnar's plan. It is no good against the Bretons."

"Then we must change the plan," Hastein told him. He continued walking, Tore following beside him until he stood just below Odd and me.

Hastein's shield, though pierced with two holes where the heads of javelins had struck it, did not look to be badly damaged. I noticed it was not a shield I'd seen him carry before. Although painted in the colors and pattern he favored, it was considerably thicker than a normal shield and covered on both front and back with leather.

"You three are my best archers," he said in a quiet voice so others would not overhear. "How can we deal with these Bretons? We cannot continue to take losses like we did in this attack and not bleed them in return."

"At Ruda, we broke the Franks' charge by bringing down their horses," I suggested. We had done so at Tore's direction, then, and it had worked well. I was surprised he did not suggest it again here.

"At Ruda, the horses were not armored," Tore said bitterly. "These are Bretons."

"We must shoot at their horses' heads," I told him. "It is the only unprotected target. All of us must launch our first arrows together in a volley as before, but wait to shoot until they are very close. Wait until just before they are ready to launch their own missiles to make certain we can hit our marks. Their horses' heads are unarmored. Hit the head, and the horse will fall. And if enough fall, it may even throw off the fire by the other riders around them."

"The head of a galloping horse is a difficult target," Odd protested, shaking his head dubiously.

"That is why we must wait until they are very close," I explained.

Tore shook his head. "I do not like it. I do not like this at all. But Halfdan is right. It is the best target we have." I wondered fleetingly what he did not like—the difficulty of the target, or that I had thought of it?

"Do it then," Hastein told him, and returned back down the hill to his standard.

"At least the Bretons did not shoot their spears at us," Odd said.

"Do not expect that to last," Tore replied.

Out on the plain, the Franks had reformed their line and were beginning to walk their horses in our direction again. "They are coming," I said.

Tore hurried out in front of the archers' line. "Archers!" he shouted. "Listen to me. We must change our tactics. These are Bretons we face, not regular Frankish cavalry. Do not waste your arrows on shots that their armor will deflect.

"Again you must hold your fire until my signal. We will let them draw closer this time before we loose. You must mark as your target the unprotected face of a horse in the front rank of the charge." A low grumbling passed up and down the line. Odd was right. The front of a horse's head was a small target, particularly when it was moving as fast as the Bretons were riding. "We must break the Bretons' charge," Tore continued. "Our comrades' lives depend upon it. And spread yourselves out— stagger the line. Every other man move up the hill a few steps. Bunched together as we are now, we will make too easy a target for the Bretons' javelins."

When Tore rejoined the line, Odd moved up the hill, and stood behind us. I searched through my quiver and found an arrow I had made long ago in the shed of Gudrod the Carpenter. It was one I knew shot true.

As the Bretons neared, I picked my target. The rider held his shield high across the front of his body and peered intently over its top as he rode. He protected himself well, but I did not care. His horse, a fine black stallion, had a white star-shaped patch between its eyes. That would be my target.

"Ready!" Tore cried. I pulled my bow to full draw and looked past the sharply pointed iron head on the end of my arrow out to the white blaze that was my target. It was constantly moving—the horse's head was jouncing up and down as it ran. I would have to lead it. But how to judge how much? How swiftly was the horse approaching? I focused my eyes on the white patch of hair and tried to free my mind of conscious thought, giving myself over to the arrow and my bow. The Bretons raced on. They were almost to the base of the ridge.

"Loose!" Tore shouted.

My arrow leaped forward off my bow, then seemed to float toward the oncoming horse. It flew so straight I could not see its shaft—only the three feathers of its fletching.

Suddenly the arrow was there, dark against the white patch. Blood gushed around the shaft embedded in the horse's skull. As its galloping hooves struck the ground, the horse's front legs seemed to fold under it, no longer possessing the strength to support its weight. Its massive body plowed into the ground, the impact flinging its rider forward over its neck. He hit hard, landing on one shoulder and the side of his head, and did not move after he stopped rolling.

Up and down the oncoming wave of Bretons, horses and their riders were down or falling. Fully a third of the charging line fell. But of those riders who escaped harm, many now realized where the danger lay. Although some of the Bretons still hurled their javelins at our warriors in the shield-wall, as in their first attack, most launched their missiles up the hill at the line of archers who had just struck down their comrades. Exposed, with no shields to protect us, we paid a heavy price for the Breton blood we'd spilled, and fell like wheat before the scythe.

Hauk, he who had spoken to me earlier that morning, who had been shooting from a position in our line just three men down from me, fell with a javelin piercing his chest. The warrior beside him took a javelin in his thigh. And many others fell, too—our mail brynies alone were no match for the heavy, hard-thrown missiles.

I saw a Breton with a thick black beard cock his arm back to launch his javelin. His eyes were locked on mine, and I knew he was aiming at me. His mouth was open, but in the din of battle, I could hear no sound coming from it. I raised my bow, drawing as I did, and snapped off a shot at the gaping hole of his mouth. Just as I loosed, he whipped his arm forward. The deadly spear arced up toward me. I watched it coming, but could not move.

As the Breton's missile flashed past me, slightly to one side, I saw my arrow strike him in the eye. He flopped backward off his horse. At the same instant, I heard a scream of pain from just beside me. I turned toward the cry and saw Odd seated on the ground, his legs splayed out in front of him, clutching with both hands at a wooden shaft protruding from his belly. The bloody, barbed head of the javelin was sticking out of his back. Odd's legs were jerking in spasms and as I watched, his chest heaved and blood spurted from his mouth.

"Odd!" Tore cried and knelt beside him.

Below us, the Bretons had wheeled their mounts to the right, as with their first charge, just before reaching our line. This time, though, the hillside was littered with the bodies of fallen horses and men. The tightness and order of the Bretons' formation disintegrated while they struggled to guide their mounts over or around the fallen. As they did, our archers that remained standing poured fire down on them. More Bretons fell, and those men's bodies and mounts further blocked the way for those who sought to escape.

A rider below me was whipping his horse furiously with the haft of a javelin, trying to force it between two riderless horses that blocked his way. He held his shield high, covering his side and head. I shot an arrow into his thigh, through the skirt of his long mail brynie. He screamed and lowered his shield, reaching for the wound. Another arrow from farther along our line—I could not see who shot it—struck him in the side of his face and killed him.

Another Breton, seeking an unobstructed path, spurred his horse so close to our line he was almost in range of the spears that reached out for him as he galloped across the front of our shield-wall. I turned, tracking him with my bow, and as he passed in front of me, I stuck an arrow into the side of his horse's head. It staggered for a few more strides then sagged to the ground. As the Breton tried to leap free, two warriors lunged out from the shield-wall and stabbed their spears into him.

Abandoning all efforts to maintain any sort of unified formation, the remaining Bretons spurred their horses desperately back toward their own lines. Fewer than half of the Bretons who had made the second charge returned to the Frankish side of the field.

Hastein again climbed the hillside up to our line. He had a grim expression as he surveyed the number of dead and wounded archers lying along the side of the ridge.

"Where is Tore?" he asked me.

"I am here," Tore said, from the hillside behind me. He was still kneeling beside Odd, who now was stretched out unmoving on the ground. I walked up to them with Hastein.

Odd was dead, his throat cut. Tore was holding a bloody knife in his hand. He looked up at us, and I saw tears streaming down his cheeks.

"He could not have survived," he said. "He was my comrade. He has been my shipmate for years. I could not let him suffer so."

"I need you," Hastein told him. "You must leave him now."

Tore wiped his knife on the grass and sheathed it, then picked up his bow and stood. "I am ready, my Jarl," he said.

"You have done well. You and your men have broken the might of the Bretons," Hastein told him. He looked again at the numerous dead and wounded archers who lay upon the hillside. "But at a very high price."

"No man can escape his fate," Tore said woodenly.

"How goes the rest of the battle?" I asked.

"On our flanks, the enemy has not come close to breaking the shield-wall, and their losses have been far higher than our own. Ragnar's plan was a good one. But in the center . . ." Hastein sighed and looked around again at the numerous warriors lying dead or wounded on the hillside. "It is the way of battle. We could not have anticipated the Bretons being here, this far north of their own lands."

Hastein looked out across the field of battle, in the direction of the Frankish lines. He squinted, then called Torvald up from the shield-wall.

"I need your eyes," he told him. "They are sharper than mine"

As Torvald reached us, I saw that he was staring

at Tore, at the tears on his cheeks. For once he did not taunt him.

"The Franks look to be realigning their forces," Hastein said. "Can you tell what they are doing?"

Torvald stared hard at the Frankish line. "They have moved their reserve up into the main line," he finally said. "The remaining Bretons are formed in a single rank in front of them, in the very center."

I did not understand how Torvald could do it. To me, the distant Frankish line looked nothing more than a confused, swirling mass of tiny figures.

"If they are committing their reserve, this will likely be their final attack," Hastein said. "They will give their all, but if they do not break us, I think they will withdraw from the field. We must stand against their attack and hold them, while Ivar closes the trap."

"What do you wish me to do?" Tore asked him.

"We must destroy the remaining Bretons when they charge. They will be trying to weaken our line in the center, around the standards, and create gaps in the shield-wall just before the Franks' main charge hits it. It is what I would do. Their only chance for victory now is to kill our leaders and hope that doing so breaks the army's will to fight. It is up to you, to the archers, to stop them. I need one more volley of arrows from your men. As with this last attack, aim it at their horses' heads when they draw near, to break their charge and disrupt their fire. But hold your fire until the last possible moment, just before the Bretons launch their own missiles, and make every shot count.

"This time, bring your men down closer and shoot from just behind the shield-wall," Hastein continued. "Tell them that as soon as they loose their arrows—before the Bretons can return fire—they should take cover behind us. Let our shields give you shelter this time."

I could feel the earth shaking under my feet as the Frankish army galloped toward us one final time. The Bretons no longer had enough warriors for their line to stretch across our entire center. They had closed in, concentrating their attack around our standards, as Hastein had predicted. As they charged, their line was as straight and even across its front as it had been in their first attack. After their last charge, the remaining Bretons must surely have known they rode to almost certain death. I stared out at them, wondering how these men found such courage. Then I nocked an arrow on my bowstring, selected a target, and prepared to kill him.

Tore did not give the cry, "Loose!" until the Bretons were climbing up the slope toward us and raising their javelins to throw. Though many archers in our army would never shoot again, still the missile fire that struck the Bretons was withering. All along their line, horses fell, throwing their riders to the ground.

I shot, watched long enough to see that my arrow was flying true, then scurried down behind the back row of the shield-wall. Moments later, I heard thuds, the splintering of shields, and screams of pain as the javelins launched by those Bretons who had survived smashed into the ranks of warriors around the standards of Ragnar and Hastein.

This time the Bretons did not wheel aside. They drew their swords and spurred their mounts forward, urging them against our shield-wall, hacking and battering furiously at the spears that stabbed out at them and slashed at their horses' faces.

Moments later, the warriors of the Frankish reserve—a tight mass of riders five ranks deep, fresh troops unhindered by any archery fire from our lines—thundered up the slope of the ridge behind the Bretons and smashed against the shield-wall, too.

The Bretons' fire, concentrated at the center of our line, had felled enough men in the front two ranks below the standards to create gaps in the shield-wall. Though other warriors pressed forward to take the places of their fallen comrades, trying to close the holes in the line, the Franks spurred their horses forward, pushing into the openings, stabbing down left and right with their spears at the warriors who tried to block their way.

Many men on both sides fell. But our line was stretched thin. As warriors fell, there were fewer and fewer to step forward and take their place. And the Franks, five ranks deep of fresh warriors, kept pressing in, their spears stabbing down, their battle-crazed horses kicking and slashing with their hooves.

Most of our archers were still milling ineffectually behind the shield-wall. I looked around wildly for Tore, and saw him a few feet down the line from me. As I watched, he flung his bow and quiver to the ground behind him, picked up the shield of a fallen Dane, and pushed his way into one of the rapidly widening gaps in the shield-wall as he drew his sword.

Hastein, Torvald, and the warriors fighting closest to them had been pushed back almost to the standard pole. Our line there was only moments from being irretrievably broken. Four Franks had forced their horses forward into the widening gap in our line in front of Hastein's standard, and others were pressing close behind them.

I ran back up the hill to a position just behind

Hastein's standard, and pulled an arrow from my quiver. The Franks atop their horses towered above our men. They held their shields tight against their bodies to protect against the thrusts of spear and sword that reached up at them, while they stabbed down at the faces and chests of our warriors with their long, broad-bladed spears. They gave no thought to the lone warrior standing farther up the hillside behind the standard.

They were so close, I could have hit them with my helm if I'd thrown it. In quick succession, I shot arrows—one, two, three—into the faces of the leading Frankish riders pressing forward into the crumbling shield-wall. Seeing them fall, Torvald lunged forward past one of the suddenly riderless horses and stabbed his long sword into the belly of the fourth rider who'd pushed into the gap, reaching under the edge of the Frank's shield and forcing his blade through the links of his mail brynie.

"Archers!" I cried. "To me!" I loosed another arrow, and another Frank who'd pushed his way into the gap fell backward, an arrow in his eye.

Hastein turned and looked behind him. Spotting me, he pointed with his sword. "Halfdan!" he cried. "Look to Ragnar!"

I turned to where Hastein was pointing. The Franks had forced a wide hole in the shield-wall in front of Ragnar's standard. Only Ragnar and one of his housecarls still stood in front of it, trying to keep the Raven banner from falling. As I watched, a rider hurled his spear into the housecarl's breast, then spurred his horse forward. Its shoulder crashed against Ragnar, knocking him to the ground. The Frank drew his sword and hacked at the banner pole, while Ragnar rolled aside to avoid the stomping hooves of the horse above him.

I swung my bow up and shot. My arrow hit the Frankish rider in the side of his head, just in front of his ear. Blood spurted from his mouth and nose as he fell sideways from his horse.

Ragnar staggered to his feet and swung his long axe with both hands, nearly decapitating the dead man's horse. As it fell, another rider urged his mount forward through the crush of bodies and raised his spear to stab at Ragnar's back, but Ragnar spun to face him and swung his great axe again, striking the Frank in his leg just above the knee, severing it.

Other archers had joined me on the hillside now. We poured our fire into the Franks at point-blank range. Hastein shouted to me again. "Where is Tore?" he cried. "We must give the signal!"

But Tore was lost somewhere among the swirling mass of warriors hacking and stabbing at each other in front of the standards. I ran back down the slope to where Tore's quivers lay on the ground, and dumped their contents onto the grass, searching for the fire arrow. When I found it, I pulled my flint and steel from the pouch at my belt and struck them together, over and over, showering sparks over the bundle of dried grass and tinder Tore had lashed to the arrow's tip with strips of frayed linen. Finally some of the loose threads caught and held the sparks. The bundle began to smoke. I blew on the smoldering embers until they burst into flame, then lay the arrow across my bow and shot it arcing over the field of battle, showering sparks behind it like a falling star.

A moment later, even over the screams of beasts and men, and the clashing of steel, I heard it—the distant peal of Ivar's horn.

9

GRIM FRUIT

The battle began in brave and desperate deeds, but it ended in slaughter. Ivar and his men poured from the wooded ridge extending along our left flank, and fell upon the rear of the disorganized swarm of Frankish horsemen that were pressing forward to attack our shield-wall. The warriors along the back of the Franks' line, recoiling from Ivar's assault, spurred forward into the rows of riders in front of them, pushing them forward against the bristling hedge of the shield-wall's spears. In the end, the Franks were packed so tightly together by the press of their own men and mounts, they could barely move at all. They bravely tried to fight, but we swarmed around them, stabbing and hacking with our spears, swords, and axes in an uncontrolled orgy of killing. We let their blood wash away the fear of death we all had felt, and our anger and sorrow for the many comrades we had lost.

Many songs and stories have been composed about the great victory we won that day. But there is much that is never told in the tales that skalds spin. The screams of the wounded and dying, and the blood—the thick, red blood that was splattered over everyone and everything, soaking the ground until it squished underfoot—such things are not remembered in song. Nor are the weeping of wives and children when they learn they will never see their husbands and fathers again. War may be glorious in tale and song, but it is grim in fact.

Some few of the Franks' army escaped by breaking through the encirclement on the river side, and fleeing desperately from the field. Their leader, Count Robert, must have been among them, for his body was not found. Others, several hundreds of them, threw down their weapons and were taken prisoner. But most of the Franks—thousands of them—died that day.

We made the Frankish prisoners do the grim task of fetching the dead from the field of battle—our dead only. We left the Frankish dead where they fell, though many of our warriors wandered among the bodies, stripping the slain Franks of their weapons, armor, and valuables. After the battle, not a man among our army, no matter how poor, was not equipped with brynie and helm. And the markets of Hedeby and Ribe would be flush for many months after our return to the north with captured Frankish armor and weapons offered for sale or trade.

For days after the battle, the sky overhead was black with circling carrion birds, and foxes and wolves skulked in the fringes of the trees, waiting for night to fall so they could sate their taste for flesh.

We also forced the Frankish prisoners to fell trees in the forest, haul the cut wood out onto the plain, and construct a huge pyre. Ragnar announced that in three days' time, we would hold a funeral feast and burn our dead.

The mood in our army was grim. Every ship's company had taken heavy losses. Among the *Gull*'s crew, three of our ten archers had died—Odd, Hauk, and another warrior who'd bled to death from a javelin that had skewered his thigh. And two others were wounded, one badly. Four of our crew who'd fought in the ranks of the shield-wall had also been slain, and almost all the rest had wounds of some nature. Although one man had lost a hand, another an eye, and a third would probably walk with a limp for the rest of his days, all of our injured would likely recover if they did not develop fever. But our crew, which had numbered thirty-nine when we'd sailed from the Limfjord, had now been reduced to twenty-four warriors, and five of those would not be well enough to fight again this season. We did not even have enough men left to man all thirty of the *Gull*'s oars.

Around the cook fires of the army, men complained bitterly about the losses we had suffered, and questioned Ragnar's wisdom in challenging the Franks when it had not been necessary.

Tore, in particular, was vocal in his anger. "What did we gain from this battle?" he grumbled to anyone who would listen. "What did any of us gain? Are we wealthier men as a result of this victory? Does anyone truly believe our own homes are safer because of the Franks we killed here? Their numbers are vast. There will always be more of them. But who will replace our comrades? Who will replace our warriors who died?"

I, too, thought the battle had been ill-considered, given the heavy losses we'd suffered, though I did not voice my feelings as Tore did. It was true we had utterly crushed the force of Frankish cavalry that had faced us. But they had been only a part of the entire army the Franks' King Charles had mustered. And his was only one of three Frankish kingdoms. Like Tore, I did not believe we had crippled the might of the Franks. I did not see how this victory had truly made our own land any safer.

Ragnar was aware of the army's discontent. "Even if from no one else, he has heard it from Ivar," Torvald told me. "They almost came to blows. Ivar is a son who does not hesitate to criticize his father, and he speaks his mind bluntly. Ivar weighs the success of a campaign more by silver won than blood spilled, and by his measure the plunder we have won so far from the Franks does not nearly compensate for the men we've lost. And now our army is too weak, in his judgment, to achieve any further successes on this campaign."

"What of Hastein?" I asked. "What does he think about the battle?"

"The jarl is keeping his own counsel so far," Torvald answered. "Though he is very concerned about how many men we have lost from the *Gull*'s crew. And Stig, too, lost more than a few warriors from the *Serpent* in this battle. Between the two ships, Hastein has lost many experienced warriors who followed him."

At least Svein and the crew of the *Sea Wolf* had been safe back in Ruda. Perhaps Hastein would draw men from their crew to help us man the *Gull* when the time came for the long voyage home.

"Would Hastein have risked this battle had he

known the cost we would pay?" Tore demanded. "I do not believe so. The jarl is wiser than that. I think he was misled by Ragnar."

Torvald shrugged his shoulders. "I do not know the jarl's mind, nor do you, Tore. But do not be too quick to criticize Ragnar. His plan did accomplish what he sought to do: We crushed the army of Franks who faced us. Years from now, men will remember only the victory. They will forget the cost."

"I will not forget," Tore said. "I will never forget Odd. He was my comrade for many years, on many voyages. We fought side by side in many battles. I will not forget him and I will never believe this victory was worth his death."

Torvald shook his head as Tore stomped off angrily. "He should watch his tongue," he said. "Though many may be unhappy about this battle, Ragnar is still our war-king, and he is a powerful and dangerous man." He looked down at me. "Hastein wishes to speak with you," he said. "You are to come with me to his tent."

When we reached Hastein's tent, I was surprised to see Ivar and Bjorn were there, sprawled in front on the great bearskin Hastein used to entertain guests. All three were drinking wine. From Bjorn's appearance, I suspected he had been for some time.

"Ah, it is the hero of the battle," Ivar said, mockingly raising his cup to me as I approached. I frowned, not understanding what he meant.

"Oh, do you not know?" he said. "Your name is on many men's lips. It is said that but for you, Father would have been killed in the battle. And possibly Hastein, too. I thank you for saving Hastein, but do not expect me to show gratitude about Ragnar."

"Shut your mouth, Ivar." Bjorn spoke in a thickly slurred voice. "He is still our father."

Hastein stood and beckoned me to follow him into the tent. Inside, he filled a cup with wine and handed it to me. "Do not mind Ivar," he said. "He is just angry. But not at you." I wondered what had angered Ivar so. He had never struck me as one who cared overmuch about the lives of common warriors.

"Have you not heard the stories men are telling about you?" Hastein asked. I shook my head. "I suspect Ragnar himself may have started some of them. But they are not undeserved. But for your rallying of the archers, and your signaling Ivar, we might well have lost the battle. And there might not have been a successful river crossing, or a battle at all, had you not found and killed the Frankish sentries."

Perhaps it would have been better, I thought,

if the river crossing had failed. Many deaths would have been avoided.

"Why do you say Ragnar may have started the tales?" I asked.

"Warriors like a hero," Hastein said. "They are stirred by tales of brave and daring deeds. The army is in a dangerous mood now. Ragnar knows they are, and wishes to distract them. Tales of your deeds may be one way he is trying to. The Gods are another."

"The Gods?" I asked.

"Ragnar is now saying that this victory was a gift to our people from the Gods—from Odin, in particular. He is calling the battle a victory of our Gods over the White Christ. He plans a great sacrifice at the funeral feast to thank them. I think he feels our men are less likely to question his decision to fight the Franks if they believe the victory over them was a gift from All-Father Odin. It is, of course, unwise to be ungrateful to the Gods.

"But I did not call you here to discuss these matters. I am thinking of making you captain of my archers."

I was dumbfounded. I did not know what to say. "But Tore . . ." I stammered.

"Tore failed me dangerously during the battle," Hastein answered. "He forgot the responsibility I had entrusted to him. Had you not found and shot the fire arrow, the battle's outcome might have been very different."

To command the archers who fought under so great a leader was an honor I had never even dreamed of. It was a long way for a former slave to have come.

"You have not given me an answer," Hastein said. "What would you say, if I asked you to command my archers?"

I realized Hastein was not saying he wished me to command—he was asking me what I *would* do *if* he offered it to me. Was this some kind of test? Or was he still undecided in his own mind?

Tore had saved my life that day in Ruda when Toke's man, Snorre, had tried to stick a knife in me. Though perhaps not a friend, he was a comrade. I could not do this to him. And becoming the captain of Hastein's archers would bring me no closer to fulfilling my vow and avenging Harald's death. I had a different path to follow.

"I do not think it would be fair to Tore," I told Hastein. As I spoke the words, I doubted if Tore would have had any concern at all about being fair to me were our roles reversed. No matter. "Tore saw the Franks beginning to break through our shield-wall," I continued. "He joined the line to try to help drive them back. Once he was caught up in the fighting . . ."

I did not finish. I had been planning to say Tore had just forgotten about the fire arrow once he was caught up in the fighting. But that, I supposed, was Hastein's point. And although I believed Tore's actions were at least in part a reaction to the grief and anger that had filled his heart at Odd's death, I feared Hastein would not think that any excuse at all.

"I am honored," I told Hastein. "But I do not feel I have the experience to lead other warriors, especially ones as seasoned as the *Gull*'s crew. There are still too many things I do not know and have not done. Tore is more fit to lead the archers than me."

Hastein stared at me silently for some time, as though he was trying to read my thoughts and know what was truly in my heart. "I am not certain I agree with you," he finally said. "But for now, we will leave things as they are. Tell no one what we have spoken of."

As I was walking away, I could hear Ivar complaining again to Hastein and Bjorn about the battle.

"Great victory? Hah!" he said. "Ten thousand people. Dozens of churches and monasteries. And with no wall protecting it all. Capturing that would have been a great victory. This was more of a disaster."

✦ ✦ ✦

The day of the funeral feast, the sky was dark with clouds and threatened rain. For Ragnar's sake, I hoped the storm would pass. If the funeral pyre would not burn because of rain falling from the heavens, it would be hard to convince our army that the Gods themselves had given us the victory. If they had, surely Thor, the thunder God, would not prevent us from honoring our dead.

The funeral pyre had been built far out on the plain, away from the ridge and the field of battle. It was a long platform, as tall as a man, built of layers of large, crisscrossed logs. The hollow interior of the pyre was filled with dead brush and the branches that had been cut from the felled trees. Its top—the platform on which our dead had been laid—was built of smaller logs, laid side by side across the framework to create a level surface.

It was a very long pyre. There were many dead to burn. One hundred and eleven longships had rowed upriver from Ruda. Every crew had lost warriors in the battle.

We arrayed ourselves around the long platform in our ships' companies, and listened as Ragnar— standing atop it, so all could see and hear him— told us how favored we all were to have been a part of so glorious a victory, and how our valiant dead were already feasting in Valhalla with the Gods.

I could not keep my thoughts on Ragnar's words. I kept looking over my shoulder at what lay behind us. A solitary oak tree, huge and ancient, towered over the plain not far from the pyre. Frankish prisoners, dozens and dozens of them, sat or squatted together on the ground near it, surrounded by armed warriors from the crew of Ragnar's ship, the *Raven*.

Oak trees were sacred to Odin, the God of war and death. Sacrifices to the one-eyed God were often hung upon oak trees, although I had never seen other than beasts sacrificed that way. I remembered now with horror that Hastein had said Ragnar planned a great sacrifice to the Gods, to give thanks for the victory they had given us. I could not tear my eyes away from the Frankish prisoners huddled miserably near the giant oak. I wondered if they knew or suspected what awaited them.

The pyre was lit, and the roaring flames began to consume the bodies of our dead. A huge plume of dark smoke rose into the sky. What followed next was a scene I wish I could erase from my memory.

Each ship's crew chose a victim from among the terrified Frankish prisoners-—a sacrifice to be offered to Odin in honor of the ship's crewmembers slain in the battle. One by one, the Franks were marched beneath the ancient tree and hoisted by nooses that Ragnar, acting as godi for the sacrifice, tied around each of their necks. Up into its branches each prisoner was pulled, kicking and struggling in a desperate dance of death.

When the time came to hang the *Gull*'s wretched sacrifice, Tore eagerly stepped forward and helped haul upon the rope. He asked me to join him, to honor the memory of Odd, but I declined. I could not. I had killed Franks in battle, but this was different. The man standing before us was weeping and begging us for his life. He would surely not have surrendered had he thought this might be his fate. There was no honor in this. It sickened me.

I turned away and began walking toward the river. I had to leave. I could not listen any longer to the cries of the terrified Franks, nor see the desperate panic in their eyes as they awaited their turn to die.

I was standing at the edge of the river across from the downstream island, staring at the current flowing by. How many days would it take for the water passing by me now to make its way to the sea?

I had wandered there after leaving the sacrifice, hoping that being in the forest might bring my troubled heart some peace. It did not. I realized that my feet had led me to a spot not far from where I had killed the third Frankish sentry. Was there nowhere I could escape from death?

I felt exhausted. Weariness weighed on my body and my heart. Every night since the battle, my sleep had been fitful and restless, and my dreams had been haunted by ghostly faces of men I had killed. Some of the faces I did not even recognize. But all of the faces told me, speaking in strange, whispering voices, "You killed me."

Last night, the dream had been different. Last night, a woman had appeared. She was very, very old. Her face was wrinkled and her cheeks sunken. Her hair, which flowed long and unbound over her shoulders and down her back, was as white as snow. Yet despite her aged visage, she stood erect and tall, and there was a strange, almost glowing beauty about her features.

A small pair of blackened iron scissors—my mother had had a similar pair—hung by a cord from her belt. The old woman unhooked them, and held them out in her palm for me to see.

"You did not kill them," she said. "I cut the threads of their lives. You were just an instrument." But the faces of the men ignored her and kept whispering, "You killed me, you killed me."

The sound of someone approaching startled me from my thoughts. I stepped behind a tree, hoping to remain unseen. I had no wish for company.

A voice called out, "Halfdan, are you here?" It was Einar. I stepped forward and let him see me.

"I was looking for you after the sacrifice," he told me, as he drew near. "Torvald said he saw you coming this way." He studied my face for a moment, then said, "You look troubled."

"Do you ever dream of men you have killed?" I asked him. "Do they ever visit you in your sleep?"

He shook his head. "I have not killed that many men. And the ones I have killed deserved to die. Their deaths do not trouble me."

I wondered why he thought the sentries we had killed deserved to die. They were merely doing their duty, trying to protect their own comrades and people. And what of the Frankish warriors who had been hung this day? They had laid down their weapons and surrendered, believing we would spare their lives if they did. Why did they deserve to die?

"I do not know what I am doing here," I told Einar. "I swore to try and avenge my brother's death. Why am I here, killing men whose names I do not know, whose faces I do not recognize, who had nothing to do with Harald's murder? I loved Harald, but how can anyone's death, even his, be worth all the blood I have spilled?"

Einar stared at me in silence for a time, peering into my eyes as if trying to read the thoughts behind them. "You have changed greatly since the first time we met," he finally said.

Had I? Even then, he had called me a "rare killer." Somehow, even at our first meeting, he must have seen into my heart; he must have seen in me what I was to become.

"None of us can choose our own fate," he continued. "We are but men. Rarely can we even understand what role our lives play in the great pattern that the Norns are weaving. We can but face the twisted paths our lives follow with as much courage and honor as we are capable of.

"You do not seek to avenge just one death. Others died with Harald. My own kinsman, Ulf, fought and died beside him, and you have also sworn to avenge the deaths of the innocents, the women and children whose safety Toke falsely promised. You have pledged, on your own honor, to avenge the infamous deeds of one who has no honor. You have pledged to rid this world of a Nithing—one who is neither beast nor man. That is no small thing."

I shook my head. "How does that justify all I have done? Only a stone's throw from here, in that thicket over there, I killed a man with whom I had no quarrel. How did that killing honor my oath?"

"You are just a man, Halfdan," Einar replied. "Why do you expect to understand the ways and plans of the Norns? Everything happens for a reason. Although to you, at this moment, your path seems to have strayed far from your purpose, you must trust fate. Your time here in Frankia, and all that you have done—including killing that Frank, and the two others, in these woods—were steps carrying you forward along the road to your vengeance."

The funeral feast was held that night on the center of the island in the Seine where our encampment had been set up. I was glad when darkness fell and the great oak tree out on the plain was no longer visible. Until the night hid them, the grim fruit that hung from its branches could still be seen, swaying slightly in the breeze.

A bonfire had been built atop the low hill forming the high point of the island, and a number of tables of various shapes and sizes had been set up around the hilltop for the chieftains to dine on. I supposed the tables, benches, and chairs had been taken from the nearby Frankish village, whose inhabitants had fled when they saw their army defeated. The rest of the army, grouped together by ships' companies, were seated on the ground at smaller fires scattered around the base of the hill.

The crew of the *Gull* were gathered seated or

lying around two cook fires we'd built. Numerous Frankish horses had been captured in the battle, and a number of them had been slaughtered earlier in the day to provide fresh meat for the feast. Casks of very fine Frankish ale, looted from a monastery downstream from Ruda that our army had sacked, had also been provided to every crew.

"Ragnar paid for this," Torvald told me, patting his hand appreciatively on the cask propped beside our fire. "He bought them all from the warriors who took the monastery where they were brewed. He has provided the feast ale for our entire army." I wondered if Ragnar thought the army's good will could be regained so easily.

I had eaten my fill, and drunk enough to dull my mind sufficiently so it was no longer possessed with images of men kicking and jerking as they choked to death. I did not feel in a celebratory mood, though.

Ragnar stood up beside the bonfire in front of the high chieftain's table and addressed the army. When he began speaking again about how greatly the Gods had shown favor toward us, I stopped listening.

Suddenly I realized Ragnar was calling out my name.

"Halfdan!" he cried. "Where are you? Stand and come forward."

I was startled and did not move, wondering if perhaps it was some other Halfdan whom he summoned.

Torvald, who by now was well into his cups, picked up a stick and threw it at me. "Get up," he said, grinning broadly. "Go on, or are you too drunk to stand?"

Slowly I rose to my feet. Seeing me rise, Ragnar called out, "Come forward. Stand here beside me, before the army."

When I reached the hill and took my place beside him, Ragnar placed one hand on my shoulder as if we were comrades. Then, in a loud voice, he continued the tale he had apparently been recounting.

"Many of you may not realize how perilous was our position at the center of the shield-wall. Three times the fierce Bretons attacked us there, and so many of our warriors fell before their fire that our line grew thin. In their final attack, the Franks threw their entire reserve against our center, striking at our banners and seeking to slay Jarl Hastein and me. The Frankish army's commanders knew that rare is the army that will not break if its leaders are slain.

"For a time, in the center, the Franks had as close a chance to grasp victory as did we. The Frankish cavalry hacked more than one breach in our shield-wall. Many fine warriors, many fine comrades to us all, were slain trying to hold our line. But though fierce we fought, and many Franks fell, still more and more of the enemy pressed toward our standards.

"Torgeir, my standard bearer, fell with a Frankish spear through his heart. I myself was thrown to the ground by the charge of a mighty Frankish champion. He tried to trample me beneath the flailing hooves of his warhorse, and with his sword he hacked at my standard, trying to bring the Raven banner down."

Ragnar paused for a moment and stood silently, looking back at the upturned faces watching him raptly. He was, I had to admit, a skilled tale-teller.

"There is a prophecy," he continued, in a voice so quiet that men in the back of the assembly had to lean forward and strain to hear, "that a witch-woman once made about me. She said that I will not die until the raven falls. I have a raven that I raised from a chick. It has shared my home and followed me on my travels for many years. I have always believed it was this bird whom the witch-woman spoke of. But when I saw the Frankish champion's long blade chopping at my Raven banner, the witch-woman's words echoed in my mind and I could feel the shears of the Norns brushing against the threads of my life. I could hear the approaching hoofbeats of the Valkyries."

Ragnar turned and took something from the table where he'd been seated and held it high over-head for all to see. It was an arrow. One of *my* arrows. I recognized it from the color and pattern of the thread securing the fletching to the shaft.

"But for this slender shaft," he told the listen-ing warriors, "your war-king would have been burned this day with the rest of our dead on the funeral pyre. This arrow, shot strong and true, struck down the Frank who sought to slay Ragnar and fell the Raven banner. And the same strong bow shot the fiery arrow high above the field of battle to signal mighty Ivar that the time had come for his fierce warriors to fall upon the Frankish rear and crush their army against our shield-wall."

"Halfdan," he cried, turning back to me. "This is your arrow, is it not?"

"It is," I replied.

"Halfdan Strongbow, take back your arrow, for we have enemies yet to fight. And accept this token of my gratitude, and of the honor you are due."

Ragnar slipped a torque from his arm. It was made of three thick wires of gold, twisted together like a rope, and capped on either end with intricately cast golden dragon heads. It was far more valuable than any single item I had ever seen, much less owned.

Ragnar hung the torque on the arrow and extended both to me. When I took them from him, and slipped the torque on my own arm, he shouted, "Hail, Strongbow!"

All around the hill, the warriors of the Danish army roared their approval, echoing, "Strongbow! Strongbow!" While the army shouted and cheered enthusiastically around us, Ragnar spoke to me in a quiet voice. For once, his eyes did not look cold or angry as they gazed upon me, though they held no warmth, either.

"I am in your debt, young Halfdan," he said. "In more ways than you may realize. It is no small thing. Some day you may find my gratitude more valuable even than this torque."

I felt dazed. In the back of my mind, I recalled Hastein telling me of Ragnar's need to distract the army from its anger. I knew this had been as much for his benefit as for mine. Yet I had been honored by our war-king before the entire army.

Ragnar was continuing his tale of the battle. Behind me, I heard a voice calling "Halfdan!" It was Hastein, who was seated at the high chief-tain's table with Ivar and Bjorn. He was holding an ornate drinking horn, decorated with silver at the tip and around the mouth. "Come around here," he said. "I wish the army to see that this night you sit at my right hand."

Hastein made a place for me beside him on the bench. When I took my seat, he held the horn out and Cullain, who was hovering behind him, filled it with ale from a cask at the end of the table.

"To a life filled with honor and glory. You have made a good start this day," Hastein said. "You have won a name for yourself, from a great war-king." He drank a long draught from the horn, then handed it to me.

"To honor and glory," I echoed and drank from the horn. I held it out for Hastein to take back, but he shook his head.

"This horn is fit for a hero," Hastein told me. "It is yours—a gift from me."

Ivar raised his own cup. "Hail, hero," he said, a sardonic smile on his lips and slightly glazed look in his eyes, and drank.

Hastein continued, "It was a fortunate day for me when the Norns caused the threads of our lives to cross. I am well aware that Ragnar is not the only one whose life you probably saved. I, too, am in your debt."

"To the many debts you are owed," Ivar said, his voice beginning to sound slurred. He drank again.

Bjorn, who had been silent until now, looked at Ivar disgustedly. "Must you mock everyone and everything, brother?" he said. "It is not Halfdan's fault our army is no longer strong enough to attack Paris."

"Ah, yes," Ivar said. "That, in truth, is the pity of all this. Capturing Paris would have been my idea of a great victory."

Ivar's words called to mind what Einar had said to me earlier that afternoon. "Everything happens for a reason," he'd told me. And I also recalled the last conversation I had had with Genevieve.

"Perhaps," I told him, "there is a way."

10

PARIS

An owl hooted nearby, and was answered by another in the distance. The woods were otherwise silent, except for the muffled sound of hooves on the thick mat of fallen leaves that covered the forest floor, and the panting of horses ridden hard all night.

There were five hundred of us, mounted on Frankish cavalry steeds captured in the battle. Another hundred of our warriors, led by Ragnar himself, were cutting across country on the far bank of the river. We'd ridden east all night, as fast as we could push the horses. It was essential that we reach Paris by dawn.

Over three days' time, we'd ferried horses

across the Seine to the south bank of the river. Frankish scouts had initially watched from a safe distance—ever since the battle and the sacrifice of the prisoners, they had been reluctant to draw near. But during the afternoon of the first day, Ragnar and Hastein had sent out strong patrols of mounted warriors to drive the scouts away and establish a screen of mounted pickets. After that, we'd finished the crossing and readied our army for its strike upriver free from watching eyes.

Ships bearing the rest of our army would follow as swiftly as they could. Bjorn, whom Ragnar had left in command of the fleet, understood the need for speed. But every ship was undermanned due to losses in battle and the large number of warriors detailed to this overland attack. It would be at least a day after our initial assault before the fleet could join us in Paris. It would be up to us—our small, mounted, attack force—to take and hold the town. If our plan failed—if we lost the element of surprise or if our attack was repelled by Paris's defenders—we would be deep within the land of our enemies and badly outnumbered.

I rode beside Hastein and Ivar at the head of the column. Hastein and the fifty warriors he would lead during the attack were disguised in captured Frankish armor and shields, most of which had been taken from Franks slain in the battle. Because I'd previously taken my armor from a Frank I'd killed, I already looked the part I needed to play.

Hastein hoped to be able to penetrate at least some distance into the town before its citizens realized they were under attack. All of us fighting under Hastein's command had tied strips of red cloth around our sword arms, so our comrades could recognize us during the assault and not mistake us for Franks. Ivar and the rest of our warriors were not disguised—they would not commence their own attack until after Hastein was in position.

I wondered if Genevieve would be in the church, the one she'd told me of, when we attacked. It seemed likely. She'd said the church was located at the abbey where she and the other nuns lived. If they were servants of their God, surely they would be in his temple during the feast day's ceremony of worship.

She had called the feast Easter. It was the day when the Christians celebrated their God, the White Christ, rising from the dead. Fortunately Ragnar had not sacrificed all of the Frankish prisoners we'd captured in the battle. When I'd questioned them, they had been able to tell us on which day the Easter feast would be held.

The night was still black, though dawn was not

far distant, when we passed just to the south of yet another long, looping bend in the river. We'd ridden past several such turns during the night, and at the sight of each my anxiety had increased. Each serpentine twist and turn of the river would add to the time it would take our ships to reach us. The closer we drew to Paris, the more I worried this plan was too risky. If it failed, I feared I would be blamed. I was beginning to wish I had said nothing to Ivar and Hastein about what Genevieve had told me of the Easter feast.

Just before the course of the river swung away from us again heading sharply north in another bend, we struck a road leading east and followed it. A short distance farther on, the forest ended. Ahead of us, beyond a wide swath of open fields and pastures, loomed a large hill. Even in the dim light cast by the stars and moon, we could see the angular outlines of buildings covering its sides and top.

Hastein held up his hand and our column halted. "Dawn will soon be upon us," he said to Ivar and me. "We must conceal our men and horses farther back, among the trees of the forest. Halfdan, you know what to do."

I knew, but I did not like it. I had to ride alone into the Frankish town, and scout the locations we would attack. A solitary rider dressed like a Frankish warrior and speaking the Frankish tongue would raise no alarm. Or so Hastein believed. But if he was wrong . . .

As I drew closer, I could see that the river curved in a great, sweeping loop around the base of the hill and the town that had been built upon its sides. Out in the river's center, opposite the hill, a large island was connected to the shore by a bridge. It was the fortress Genevieve had described. A stone wall encircled the island. Above it peeked the tops of several tall buildings located within.

Not far downstream from the island, on flat, open land near the river, a large building I judged to be a Christian temple towered above a sprawl of smaller buildings, orchards, and tilled fields, all enclosed by low stone walls. I suspected the complex was a monastery. Though I had never seen one before at such close range, Torvald had described them, and had pointed one out to me on our journey up the Seine River on the way to Ruda. Because of the riches they contained and their lack of defenses, they were his favorite target to attack when raiding. I remembered Genevieve had said there were several in Paris. This looked to be a large one. Ivar would be pleased.

From what Genevieve had told us, I'd known that the town would not be surrounded by walls. I was still anticipating, though, that sentries would at least be guarding the roads leading into it. I'd been worrying what I would say when they stopped me. How would I brazen my way past them? What would they think about the unfamiliar accent with which I spoke their tongue?

But there were no guards. How could these Franks be so complacent? Did they feel they were safe from attack because the vast encampment of their main army lay little more than a day's ride to the west? Did they believe that their army could reach Paris before ours if our ships should head upriver? Or were the folk of Paris entrusting its defense to Saint Genevieve and their God, as they had centuries ago when the Huns had threatened?

The road began to climb. As I entered the outskirts of the town, I was surprised to see many of the buildings I passed looked abandoned and in poor repair. Others, though, were clearly inhabited.

Even the ruined buildings were imposing. Paris was not at all like Hedeby. Besides being much larger, most of the homes and structures here were not built of timber or of wattle and daub, nor the roofs of thatch. It was a town built of stone—even the streets were surfaced with it.

Ahead, beside a doorway leading into the courtyard of a large house, a dog tethered by a chain began barking and growling as I neared. My horse's ears twitched nervously at the uproar it made. My first impulse was to shoot an arrow and silence the beast, for the din it was making would surely awaken everyone inside the surrounding buildings. But I forced myself to ignore the savage-looking hound's snarling threats and its lunges toward me that were jerked short by the chain. I rode on, affecting an unconcerned air. Somewhere a door creaked open and I could feel eyes peering at me as I passed. Then the watcher slammed the door shut with a curse, though whether it was directed at me or the dog, I could not tell.

Within the town, most of the streets appeared to be laid out in a regular grid. The road I was on, which had approached the hill at an angle, was an exception, but it ended a short distance inside the town's boundaries, at an intersection with a broad, straight thoroughfare that climbed steeply up the side of the hill. I followed this new road, the clip-clopping of my horse's hooves on the stone paving echoing loudly in the empty street.

As I approached the top of the hill, the road passed a long, towering structure—a massive building larger than any I had ever seen before. It dwarfed even the count's palace in Ruda. At first I hoped it might be the Church of St. Genevieve, the building I was searching for. But when I drew nearer, I could see that much of its upper levels were in ruins. Down along the street, recessed into the outer wall, were a series of shallow stalls, many containing wooden benches or tables for displaying wares. I realized that this was probably the town's marketplace. What must it have been like in its glory, when the Romans still ruled this land? What sorts of wares had been sold here then? I marveled again that so great a people, so vast an empire, could fall.

At either end of the enormous market square, broad, straight roads ran parallel to each other down the hill toward the river. As I crossed the second of these I saw that it led directly to the bridge, and the island fortress.

In the time it had taken me to reach the town and ride up the hill to its center, the darkness of night had faded away into gray dawn. Somewhere nearby, a single bell rang, its peals echoing off the stone walls, signaling the approach of the morn. Cocks crowed, as if in answer. The town was beginning to awaken. I feared I was running short of time. I did not know how soon the Franks would come to the Church of St. Genevieve to offer their Easter feast prayers.

There proved to be four of the Christians' temples among the many buildings atop the hill, and I saw what looked to be others down along its slopes. I thought the Franks' zeal for building so many temples excessive, especially considering they worshiped only one God. They'd have been wiser to have expended their wealth, labor, and stone on a wall to defend their town, for their God would not protect them this day.

Fortunately, only one of the temples I found was connected to a monastery-like complex. I felt certain it must be the church and abbey of St. Genevieve. I wondered if Genevieve was sleeping in one of the buildings that lay before me. Once her father ransomed her, I had thought I'd never see her again. I had forced myself to put her out of my mind. Had the Norns now chosen to weave the threads of our lives together again?

"There is a road that approaches the town from the south," I told Hastein and Ivar when I returned to where they were waiting with their men. "It will not take us long to reach it from here if we cut across country. It is the same road I left the town on."

"Why circle around to the south?" Ivar asked. "Why not just ride straight to the town from here?"

"From this direction, once we clear the edge of the forest, the land between it and the town is all flat, open ground," I explained. "Now that it is daylight, we would be seen long before we could reach the town. We would lose the element of surprise much sooner. But to the south, the land rises. Our approach from that direction will be through wooded hills. And along the southern road, once we draw close to the town, there is a vast burial ground. It is a very strange place, and looks to be very old. The Franks—or perhaps it was the Romans—have built stone houses there for their dead, and there are also many stone monuments honoring them. There are enough of the death houses, and they are large enough, to provide cover for you and your men to hide among, right at the very edge of the town, until it is time for you to attack."

"And the rest of us?" Hastein asked.

"I found the temple Genevieve described," I told him. "It is in the center of the town, atop the hill, as she said. Those of us who are disguised as Franks will need to continue on into the town as soon as we reach it and get closer to the temple. Once the Franks realize they are under attack, those worshiping there will probably try to flee to the safety of the island fortress. We must be close enough to stop them."

"How will my men and I know where to go?" Ivar demanded.

"The road you will be on—the road that approaches the town from the south through the burial ground—runs straight through the town, up over the top of the hill, and down to the river. It is the road that leads directly to the bridge that crosses to the island."

Just as we reached the burial ground south of the town, dozens of bells began ringing. I feared we had been discovered, and our plan was doomed.

"Have they seen us?" I exclaimed. "Are they sounding the alarm?"

Hastein shook his head. "No," he said. "I do not believe so. I have heard this before. Many of the Christians' temples have bells. Though sometimes they do use their bells to sound an alarm, I think they are ringing them now to summon the folk of Paris to worship. I think we have arrived just in time."

The front of the Church of St. Genevieve looked out over a broad open courtyard, paved with square-cut blocks of pale stone. Hastein and I approached cautiously on foot along a side street and peered around a corner into it. The rest of Hastein's men—fifty warriors disguised as Franks—waited on horseback out of sight around a bend in the road.

As we watched, the bells began pealing again. Hastein had been correct. Some of the ringing sound was coming from a square, stone tower attached to the church in front of us. Other bells from other temples across the town joined in, filling the air with a deafening clanging. I would not like to live in this town. I did not understand how the Franks who did could stand the noise.

The square before us was crowded with folk hurrying toward the open doors of the church, answering the second summons to worship being voiced by the temple's bells. Most were on foot, but a large party had apparently arrived only moments before on horseback. They were now dismounting near the stone steps that ran across the front of the building.

"Look," Hastein said. "That man there, with his arm in a sling—the one helping the woman in the red gown dismount from her horse. Do you see him?"

I nodded. I did see him, and I recognized him. "It is Count Robert," I said. I wondered if his arm had been injured in the battle. I wondered if the woman by his side was Genevieve's mother.

"The count is not wearing armor," Hastein said. "Few of the men here are. They are dressed in their feast-day finery. It will make our work easier."

Some of the men, the count included, were wearing swords. But as Hastein had observed, most were not dressed for a fight. Only a small guard of five warriors were wearing armor and carrying shields.

The count and his party waited until everyone

else in the square had entered the church. Three Christian priests wearing ornate robes stood just outside of the church's open doors, greeting all who entered. One of the priests, the most richly dressed of the three, was wearing a very tall and awkward-looking hat and holding a staff with an elaborate, curved top that shone in the morning sun as if it was made of gold.

"That one is a bishop," Hastein whispered to me. "A high priest of the White Christ. He must be the Bishop of Paris. The prisoners we take here will be rich prizes indeed."

As the bells finally stopped ringing, the count and his party climbed the steps of the church. The five armored warriors remained with the group's horses. Count Robert and the bishop bowed stiffly to each other. Then the count, accompanied by the woman in the red gown, walked into the church at a slow, measured pace, followed by the rest of their party. When all had entered, the bishop and his priests followed.

"Come," Hastein said. "Let us get back to the horses."

When we rounded the bend in the road, we found Tore with a bloody sword in his hand, standing over the bodies of three dead Franks—two men and a woman.

"What happened here?" Hastein demanded.

"They came from down the street," Tore answered. "At first I thought they were going to just pass us by. But then one of the men began babbling something at me. I did not know what he was saying. I feared he would become suspicious when I did not answer, so I thought it best to make sure he could not raise an alarm."

I walked closer to where the dead Franks lay sprawled on the pavement. Neither of the men was armed, and by their dress, all three looked to be common folk. The woman had been cut down from behind. She must have been trying to flee when Tore had killed her. I wondered if she had cried out in fear, or had tried to call for help, when Tore had attacked the men folk. The bells would have covered the sound of her screams if she had.

They had doubtless been on their way to worship at the Church of St. Genevieve. Their piety had cost them their lives. What, I wondered, had they been planning to ask their God for this feast-day morn? To protect them and their town from the Northmen?

"Do not just stand there," Tore said to me. "Help me drag them into this alley so they will be out of sight."

I did not move. I just glared at him.

"What?" Tore demanded, scowling back at me.

"Leave them!" Hastein barked, as he swung up

onto his horse. "To your mounts. We must go."

We rode in a double column out into the square, directly toward the guards. They watched our approach curiously, but without alarm. Their shields and spears were slung on their saddles, and they were squatting in a circle, throwing dice.

"*Have you come from the army encampment?*" one of them called out, standing up as we drew near. Perhaps he recognized we were not from the town's garrison. "*Who is your captain? What scara are you with?*"

Hastein drew back his arm and hurled his spear into the Frank's chest. As he fell back, other Danes spurred their horses forward, riding over the startled Franks, stabbing down at them with their spears. It was over in moments.

"Tore," Hastein said, "take twenty men and circle the church. Post warriors on all sides, at every door. Let no one escape. The rest of you men, dismount and form a line here." After he'd finished giving orders, Hastein raised a horn to his lips and blew a single long note. It was the signal for Ivar, telling him we were in position. A moment later, Ivar's horn answered, acknowledging that he had heard.

The church door opened and a man peered out. The horn and the noise of the brief struggle must have drawn him. At the sight of the dead bodies, he slammed the door closed again. A short time later, the bells in the church tower began ringing furiously.

It took time to persuade the Franks in the church to surrender. Count Robert, who led the negotiations on behalf of those inside, quite reasonably suspected that to do so might merely substitute one danger for another. *"How do I know you will not just slay us if we surrender?"* he demanded. *"As you did my warriors who surrendered to you after the battle downriver? Our scouts told us what you did. If I am to die, I would rather die fighting. At least I may kill some of you before I am slain."*

"In his place, I suspect I would feel much the same," Hastein told me, when I translated the count's words. "Ragnar's sacrifice will likely cause problems in our dealings with the Franks for years to come."

At first, the count was unmoved by Hastein's promise that if those in the church surrendered, he would personally swear an oath upon his honor guaranteeing their safety. But in the end, Hastein's powers of persuasion won the day. It seemed to be his threat to set the church afire and burn all who were in it alive that finally swayed the count. He walked out of the church, laid his sword upon the ground, and surrendered.

Soon messengers arrived, and told us Ragnar

and his men had, with little difficulty and few losses, captured the tower on the north side of the river that guarded access to the bridge leading from that bank to the fortified island. The stone tower guarding the bridge leading to the island from the Seine's south bank fell even more easily to Ivar's assault. Only two Frankish guards had been manning it. They had left the tower's gate open, awaiting the return of Count Robert and his party from their morning worship. The gates on the island sides of both bridges were closed, however, and Frankish warriors from the fort's garrison, manning the ramparts of the walls above, hurled spears and shot arrows at our warriors when they'd ventured out along the bridges to try and inspect them.

By the time I arrived there with Hastein, Ragnar and Ivar had already felled trees to use as rams. They were hauling the trimmed trunks onto the ends of the two bridges in preparation for a coordinated attack against the island fort's gates.

We had brought Count Robert and the Bishop of Paris with us. Ivar greeted us as we rode up. "Tell the count to order the garrison to surrender," Ivar said. "He commands the Frankish garrison in Paris, does he not? They are his men. Tell him to tell the warriors inside the fort that if they do not surrender, we will kill the count and the bishop here in front of them, while they watch."

"So much for the oath and honor of Northmen," the count sneered when I translated Ivar's instructions to him. *"So we will not be harmed if we surrender? I should have known better than to trust you. I will not do so again, and I will not help you trick the warriors in the fort into surrendering."*

Hastein sighed. "Tell him we will not really kill him," he said. "I have given him my word he will be safe. I will not break it. But the warriors in the garrison do not know that."

"I will not lie to my men," the count snapped, when I explained.

"We are wasting time with this," Ivar said. He turned to one of his men. "Find me a rope," he ordered. "Long enough to reach down to the bridge from up on top of the battlements of this tower."

"What are you going to do?" I asked him.

"One of the two guards who manned this tower resisted us and was killed, but we took the other alive. No one has made any promises to him."

I turned to Hastein. "If the garrison on the island surrenders, will you guarantee their safety, as you did those in the church?" I asked him.

"I will," he answered.

"Let me try to persuade them," I said.

I walked out onto the bridge. I was carrying my shield and kept it in front of me, but even so stayed far enough back from the island fort's walls to be well beyond range from any but the hardest thrown spear.

"I wish to speak to the commander of the garrison," I shouted. I could see the helmed heads of several Frankish warriors who were watching me from the wall above the gate.

"Who are you?" a voice answered. *"I am the captain in command."*

"My name is Halfdan," I called out. *"I am a Dane. I speak for the commanders of our army."*

"Speak, then," the voice said.

"We have captured the town," I told him. *"We have taken many prisoners. Your leader, Count Robert, and the Bishop of Paris are among them. You can see them there."* I turned and pointed back toward the tower on the south bank. When I did, Hastein and three other warriors marched the count and the bishop out into view upon the bridge.

"It is their wish that you surrender and avoid further bloodshed," I lied. Behind me, I heard the Count exclaim indignantly.

"Do not . . ." he shouted, then cried out in pain. I turned and saw that Hastein had clubbed him down with the hilt of his sword.

"I do not believe you, Northman," the Frankish captain said. *"Count Robert clearly does not wish us to surrender."*

"We will kill you all if we are forced to storm this fort," I argued.

He laughed. *"We will take our chances."*

This was not going well. Behind me at the tower, Ivar's man was lowering a rope from the battlements down to the bridge. A noose had been tied in its end.

"I told you we have captured many prisoners," I said to the Frank. *"We will hang them, one by one, from that tower wall, until you surrender. You will have to listen to them plead for their lives. You will have to watch them die. We will hang the Bishop of Paris and Count Robert himself, if we must."* The latter was not true, of course. Hastein had given his word. But though Count Robert might refuse to lie to his men, I felt no compunction about it— particularly if my lies might save lives.

"I do not believe you, Northman!" the Frank shouted, but his voice did not sound as certain as before.

Ivar wrestled a Frankish warrior whose hands were bound behind his back out onto the bridge below the tower rampart, and slipped the noose over his head.

"Quickly!" I cried to the Frankish captain. *"It is*

in your power to save this man's life—to save many lives. This man is one of your comrades. Do not make him die needlessly. You and your men will not be harmed if you lay down your weapons and surrender. We swear it. If you do not surrender, he and other prisoners will be killed, and eventually you will be, too."

Two more of our warriors had by now joined Ivar's man atop the tower ramparts. At Ivar's signal, they began hauling on the rope. The helpless Frank was hoisted slowly up off the bridge, his feet flailing wildly. The bishop, still standing between two of Hastein's warriors, dropped to his knees and began to pray.

Please, I thought, looking up at the Frankish captain watching from the island. Let no more of your people die needlessly this day. Spare this man, for it is certain Ivar will not.

"Let him down!" the captain shouted. *"I will surrender the fortress."*

11

HOLDING
THE PRIZE

The town and fort had fallen, but our army still needed to consolidate and protect our victory. Though they might not be warriors, the citizens of Paris greatly outnumbered us. And even if they remained peaceful, and did not pose a direct threat to our small force, many had fled the town when they'd realized it was under attack. Some would surely reach the Frankish army before long and alert it to our presence in Paris.

Ragnar assigned two hundred of our men to take control of and man the island fort, and confine the soldiers of the town's garrison there under guard. Count Robert and the bishop were also to be confined in the fort. As the only member of our force who spoke the Franks' tongue fluently, I remained there to assist Ragnar during the garrison's surrender.

While I was aiding Ragnar, Hastein returned to the Church of St. Genevieve. The priests, plus a number of nobles captured among the worshipers there, were marched under guard to the fort so they could be exchanged for ransom, used as hostages in the event we were attacked, or both. Hastein and his men released the remainder of the Franks who'd been inside the church when we'd surrounded it. We could not confine and guard them all.

Mounted raiding parties raced through the town and surrounding countryside, sacking every church and monastery they found, gathering their valuables before the Christian priests could hide them. The abbots and monks of the monasteries and the priests of the churches who had not already fled by the time our raiders reached them were also seized, and held with the other prisoners of value in the island fortress.

By the time all from the fort's garrison were disarmed and secured, Hastein had returned to the island with the additional prisoners from the Church of St. Genevieve. Neither Genevieve nor any other nuns or priestesses were among them.

"Has a raiding party been sent to the Abbey of St. Genevieve?" I asked him.

"No," he said. "Not yet. We did loot the church, though. The wealth the priests had amassed there was astonishing. The Christians' God may not be as strong as our Gods are, but he is certainly wealthy—or his priests are, at least."

"I would like to help search the abbey for plunder," I said. "When you send warriors there, I would like to go with them."

Hastein had been pacing along the rampart atop the fort's wall as we talked, studying the island's defenses. He stopped and turned to look at me. A slow smile spread across his face.

"You would like to search the Abbey of St. Genevieve for plunder?" he asked. "Ah. Do you plan to take her prisoner again?"

I could feel my face turning red. "No," I said. In truth, I was not entirely sure why I wished to go to the abbey. I told myself it was because I wished to make certain Genevieve was not harmed when the abbey was looted. It could be a dangerous time.

"Take ten warriors and go there now," Hastein said. "You will be in charge."

It was my first command. I felt nervous, and wondered if the warriors assigned to me would follow my orders.

"This is a community of women, of priestesses," I told the men as we approached the abbey gate. Several of the warriors came from ships other than the *Gull*, and I did not know them. They grinned and nodded to each other appreciatively. "These are holy women to the Franks," I continued. "You will not harm them. It would anger the people of the town unnecessarily."

One of the men who'd laughed a moment ago now scowled and spoke up angrily. "Are you saying we cannot pleasure ourselves with the women of this town?"

There were thousands of women in this town. There was nothing I could do about most of them. It can be a bad thing to be a woman in a town that falls to an enemy army. But I would not let Genevieve be harmed.

"I speak only of these women, these priestesses," I answered. "They are not to be molested by you, or by anyone in our army."

"You are not my captain," the man retorted. "I do not even know who you are. Why do you think you can tell me which women I can or cannot have?" He was heavily built, and though I had never seen him fight, he looked old enough to be an experienced warrior.

I could not let his insolence go unchallenged. Holding my hand up to signal we should stop, I turned my horse and guided it back to where the man who'd spoken now sat staring sullenly at me from atop his own mount.

"You do not know me? My name is Halfdan," I told him. "Though to Ragnar Logbrod, and the rest of the leaders of our army, I am known as Strongbow. You are free to disregard what I have just told you about the women who live in this abbey. But if you choose to do so, I promise you will not live to enjoy any of them. And you should know that you would not be the first warrior in this army I have slain because he disobeyed my orders."

The warrior who had challenged me glared, and I could see the muscles in his neck tighten. His right hand twitched, as if it wished to reach for the hilt of his sword.

My shield was slung across my back. I was holding my bow, unstrung, in my right hand and the horse's reins in my left. If he went for his sword, I would be at a disadvantage. If he reaches for it, I thought, I will stab the tip of my bow into his eye. With my knees, I nudged my horse even closer to him, lessening the distance between us. I wondered if any of the others would join in the fight, or if they would just watch to see who died.

But he did not want to fight. Perhaps he could see the death—his own—that was in my eyes. He shrugged his shoulders and looked away. "As you wish," he said. "The priestesses will not be harmed."

The gate to the abbey was closed when we arrived. I dismounted and hammered on it with my fist. A small door set within the larger gate swung open. Standing just inside was a short woman in a gray gown, with a white mantle and hood like the one Genevieve had been wearing when I'd first seen her. She had a frightened look on her face. Two other women, dressed similarly, were standing behind her.

"I am looking for the person in charge of this abbey," I told them.

The short woman let out a long sigh, closed her eyes for a moment, and said, *"Praise God!"* I wondered if this was how Frankish priestesses typically greeted a stranger. I saw no reason she should be glad to see me.

"I am Abbess Adelaide," she told me, opening her eyes. *"I am in charge of the abbey. Have you come to help us escape from the Northmen? I have been praying to the Blessed Mother of Jesus to rescue us. Surely she has sent you here."*

I thought it unlikely, although my mother had once told me the Christians' God worked in mysterious ways. I realized the abbess believed we were Franks. I and all of the warriors with me were still wearing captured Frankish armor, and I had spoken to her in Latin—though my use of that tongue sounded very different to my ears from the

244

way the Franks spoke it. Perhaps she thought I was a Breton, or from some other distant province of the Franks' lands.

"Were you and the prie . . . the nuns of the abbey in the church when it was captured?" I asked her.

"We were not," she said. "We were on our way to the church, but were late. It was Sister Helen's fault. I was quite annoyed at her and feared the Bishop would be angry at us all. But now I see that it was God's will. He—or perhaps it was Saint Genevieve herself—was protecting us."

"All of you are here in the abbey now?"

She nodded her head. "I was leading our sisters, and had just reached the gate to the church, when I saw armed warriors encircling it. I knew something was very wrong. We turned around and returned here, and have learned since that it was the Northmen," she answered. "So far they have not come here, but I fear sooner or later they will. I do not believe we will be truly safe unless we escape from Paris. The Northmen are pirates and savages. They are not likely to respect the fact that we are the brides and servants of Christ."

"You were right to worry that the Northmen will come here. It has happened sooner rather than later," I told her. "My men and I are Danes."

Her eyes grew big, and she tried to slam the narrow door shut in my face. I caught it and pushed it open, sending her staggering backward. Stepping inside, I lifted the bar securing the main gate.

"Do not be afraid," I told her. *"If you do not resist, you will be safe. I have told my men they are not to harm any of you. But I want you to send these two women here with you to gather all of the nuns together in one room. Do it right now. You will be safer if you are all together, while my men are searching the abbey."*

"Searching?" she said. *"What are you searching for?"*

Anything of value, I thought. Anything at all. I had seen some of the treasure looted previously from Frankish churches and monasteries. Hastein was right. The wealth accumulated in the name of the Christians' God was astonishing: plates and goblets of silver and gold, silver candlesticks with great thick candles of fine white wax, rich gowns worn by the priests, and intricately embroidered cloths used to cover the altars to their God. Many also contained generous supplies of the finest wine and ale, and bountiful amounts of the best meats and other provisions. Servants of the White Christ lacked for nothing. We would take it all.

"Just do as I say," I told her. *"Do it now."*

The abbess turned to the two nuns with her. *"Quickly,"* she said, her voice trembling. *"Gather the sisters together. Bring them to the chapel."*

✦ ✦ ✦

I spotted her as soon as I entered the chapel. Genevieve and the rest of the nuns were huddled against the far wall watching the door nervously.

The abbess was walking just in front of me. She had led me there. One of the nuns called out to her when we entered the room.

"Is it true, Reverend Mother? Are the Northmen here, in the abbey?"

I thought it a foolish question. Did she not see me standing behind the abbess? Then I remembered the armor I was wearing. To these women, no doubt I appeared to be a Frank.

"It is true," the abbess said.

The women began chattering to each other in frightened voices. *"Silence!"* the abbess said. *"We must all pray together now for God's mercy. And we must thank him for answering the prayers we have already offered. This man is the officer commanding the Northmen who are here. He has promised me we will not be harmed."*

All eyes in the room now looked at me. When Genevieve's eyes met mine, her hand flew up to her mouth and her face turned as white as the mantle she was wearing. She staggered back and would have fallen had the woman beside her not caught her.

I do not know what I had thought—or perhaps

hoped—her reaction might be. But I certainly had not expected this. Did the sight of me so horrify her?

I stared at Genevieve, watching the other nuns help her to a nearby seat, my mind numb and blank. Suddenly I became aware Abbess Adelaide was speaking to me.

"*Poor Sister Genevieve,*" she was saying. "*She was captured by your people. It was a harrowing experience for her. She saw her own cousin killed. Her father paid a ransom, and she was but recently freed and returned to us. It must terrify her to see you, after what she has been through.*"

"*I did not know,*" I lied. "*I do not wish to cause her or any of your nuns distress. I merely wished to be certain you all were safe here, while my men search the abbey. I will rejoin them now.*"

Ragnar was more cautious than the Franks had been. A screen of mounted sentries watched all of the approaches to Paris. Mid-morning of the day after we captured the town, we received a warning that a large force of mounted Frankish troops was approaching from the west. By now, most of our warriors except those acting as pickets had returned to the safety of the fort, bringing their plunder with them. If the Franks attacked in force, we could hopefully hold out against them on the island until our fleet arrived.

While Ivar remained in the fort, preparing our warriors to defend it if necessary, Hastein and Ragnar headed out to meet the approaching Franks. I rode with them to serve as their interpreter. We were accompanied by a guard of one hundred warriors—a force strong enough to allow us to conduct a fighting retreat back to the island if the Franks did not honor the flag of truce we carried, yet small enough to show we did not seek battle.

The Frankish army had approached Paris along the same road from the west our own force had traveled only yesterday—the one from which we'd first seen the town. By the time our party rode out of Paris and onto the edge of the flat, cleared land that lay between the town and the forest, the Franks had already begun pouring from the mouth of the road onto the plain ahead of us. There were thousands of them. As each unit of cavalry exited the forest, they turned, some heading north toward the river, others to the south, gradually forming a great line of mounted troops that curved in an arc around the base of the hill.

"They intend to throw a circle around the town," Hastein said.

"It does not matter," Ragnar answered. "When we leave, it will be by the river." I hoped he was right. I hoped Bjorn would arrive with the fleet before the Franks attacked.

A small party of Franks, five mounted warriors, separated from the milling mass of their army and rode toward us, bearing a flag of truce. Ragnar, Hastein, and I, displaying our own white flag, rode forward to meet them, accompanied by two of our warriors. We halted a few paces apart.

"My name is Lothar," one of the Frankish warriors announced to us. *"I bear a message from King Charles for the leader of your army."*

"Tell him he is speaking to our army's leader," Ragnar told me. "Tell him my name is Ragnar, and I am our war-king."

When I translated Ragnar's words, the Frank answered, looking at Ragnar as he spoke: *"Then tell your war-king this: King Charles marches on Paris with his entire army. The forces you see here, the cavalry that is even now encircling the town and blocking your escape, are just its vanguard. Many thousands more of infantry follow behind. Yet even this advance guard of mounted troops you see before you numbers far more than the army you fought before."*

We have, I thought, finally awakened the sleeping giant. And now it is rushing toward us, angry and eager for our blood.

"As you yourselves have already discovered, Paris is an easy town to attack, but it is difficult to defend.

If you are foolish enough to stand and fight against us, you cannot hope to win. Be assured, we will show you no mercy. None of you will leave our lands alive.

"But you do not have to die, although you deserve to. King Charles has authorized me to extend this offer to your army." From the expression on the Frank's face as he related the Frankish king's terms, it looked as though the words themselves tasted bitter in his mouth. I had no doubt his personal wish was that we would refuse the offer and choose to fight.

"Release all prisoners you have captured," he told us. *"Do no more damage to this town, or to Rouen. Agree to these terms and agree now that you will leave Paris and our lands without delay. Do these things, and King Charles will give you safe passage down the Seine to the sea. He will also allow you to keep the plunder you have already captured.*

"It is a generous offer," the Frank concluded. *"Far more generous than you deserve. Accept it, or risk losing all. If you do not agree to King Charles's offer this day, it will be withdrawn and we will attack."*

I agreed with the Frank. I thought it a generous offer. We had already won much wealth. If we accepted the Frankish king's terms, we could keep it all, lose no more of our men, and return safely to our homes.

Ragnar disagreed. Reluctantly, I told the Frank his response.

"Ragnar, our war-king, gives this answer to your King Charles. We hold many, many hostages, including Count Robert and his family, and the Bishop of Paris, plus many of your nobles and priests. If you attack us, we will kill them all. He says you must know he speaks true when he threatens to do this. You know the fate more than one hundred of your warriors suffered at our hands after we defeated your army before in battle.

"If you attack, we will also set fire to this town and burn it to the ground. We will destroy all its great buildings, all of its great churches. Then, when the town is ruined and the hostages are dead, we will take our plunder and we will sail down the river to the sea. We do not need your safe passage to leave your land. We will do so whenever we please."

"You follow a fool, Northman. A fool or a madman," the Frank said to me when I finished. I feared he spoke the truth. *"I will take your war-king's message to King Charles. For myself, I am glad you chose to fight. We in our army have many deaths to avenge. And while you wait to receive our wrath, think on this: You have no ships here. How do you plan to escape us?"*

Ragnar's face was red and his beard was quivering. His entire body was shaking, he was so angry.

"I am war-king!" he thundered. "I have made the decision for our army. If the Franks attack, we will kill the prisoners and we will burn the town. We cannot appear to be weak and lacking will."

"I gave my word," Hastein answered. "I will not break it. If the Franks attack, we must show our strength and will by fighting them, not by slaughtering unarmed captives. I will allow no one—you included—to dishonor my name. The prisoners we hold surrendered because of my personal oath to them that they would not be harmed. I will not be an oath-breaker. I will not allow you to make me one."

"They are Franks. They are our enemies!" Ragnar shouted. "This is war."

"Hastein is right, Father," Ivar said. "This is about our honor. We would not deserve to be called men if we abandoned it, war or not. Burn the town, if you wish. But we cannot kill these prisoners. Breaking our oath to them would be Niddingsvaark."

The argument had been going on all afternoon, ever since we'd returned to the island fort from the parley with the Franks. Hastein had asked me to remain with him, in case the Franks sought to negotiate further.

I thought we were wasting valuable time. It would not be easy to burn a town built of stone. The buildings, especially the larger ones, would need to be filled with combustibles. Our men should be out in the town taking care of that now. Once the Franks attacked, it would be too late. We would have to pull all of our warriors back to the island. But while our leaders argued, our army sat idle.

"I wonder why the Franks have not attacked us yet," Ivar said.

I, too, was surprised the Franks had not attacked. They had nothing to gain by waiting, and much to lose. Sooner or later, Bjorn and our ships would arrive. The Franks must certainly have seen our fleet moving upriver to join us. Once Bjorn reached Paris, our numbers would be greatly increased, and we would also have the means to escape, if we chose to.

"It is because they fear the fierceness of our threat," Ragnar snapped. "They do not realize we lack the will to fulfill it."

"I do not agree," Hastein said. "I do not think they mean to attack at all, if their king can find a way to avoid it. I do not believe he has the stomach for it. I think the Franks' King Charles is a cautious man. He will seek a less dangerous way to resolve this."

"Dangerous?" Ivar asked. "What danger threatens the Franks' king? He has arrayed thousands of warriors against our six hundred. We are the ones in danger."

"King Charles faces many dangers," Hastein explained. "We must look at this as he will view it. A king cannot rule if his people no longer trust him and will no longer follow him. King Charles knows this. But he has been making serious errors ever since we attacked his land. He divided his army, mistakenly believing that the best way to protect his people. He expected us to avoid battle and retreat before his approaching forces. But instead he lost thousands of his warriors when we attacked. Many of his people—the kin of those who were slain, as well as members of the army who lost so many comrades in arms—will now be angry that his ill-considered decision cost so many their lives.

"King Charles also erred by failing to protect Paris. He badly misjudged how quickly and boldly we could strike. If his error were to result in the destruction of the town and the death of the hostages, including the Bishop of Paris and Count Robert, who knows what his followers might do? Do not forget there are three Frankish kings now, and they often fight among themselves. If Charles becomes too weak because his followers no longer trust his leadership, one of his brothers may try to take his realm."

"So what do you think he will do?" Ivar asked.

"I believe he will look to silver to do the work of steel," Hastein replied.

✦ ✦ ✦

Paris was quiet that night. Most of its folk, not wishing to be caught in the midst of a battle, had fled to the encircling lines of the Frankish army. We did not have the means to stop them—nor, for that matter, the desire to. If we were forced to try to burn the town, it would be easier to destroy it if its inhabitants were not present to fight the fires.

A heavy screen of pickets, nearly two hundred of our warriors, watched the Frankish army all night from hiding places among the buildings along the outer fringes of the town, guarding against the possibility of an assault launched under cover of darkness. But the Franks did not attack. Looking out at their hundreds of cook fires burning on the open fields surrounding the town, I wondered whether the Frankish army's leaders were arguing like ours over what course they should follow when morning came.

The morning sun had halfway completed its journey from dawn toward noon when a handful of riders headed out from the Frankish lines, bearing a white flag and seeking another parley. Once again I rode out to meet them with Ragnar and Hastein.

The Frankish officer Lothar, who had delivered the Franks' terms yesterday, was one of the party that met us. Today, however, a different man was clearly in charge. He wore a dark red cloak trimmed with white fur over his mail armor, and his sword belt and horse's harness were richly ornamented with silver. He wore no helm; instead, atop his head was a heavy crown of solid gold, studded with colored stones and jewels.

As our party reined our horses to a halt in front of them, the crowned Frank spoke to Lothar.

"Which one is Ragnar, their war-king?"

"There," Lothar replied, pointing at Ragnar. *"And this one,"* he added, gesturing at me, *"speaks for him. He speaks our tongue."*

The Frankish leader looked at me curiously. He had a long face, framed by a carefully trimmed beard—it had been shaved until its width along the line of his jaw was no wider than the strap of a helm. His hair was light brown and sparse on top, and he wore it shorter on the sides than did most of the warriors who were with him.

"My name is Charles," he said to me. *"I am king of these lands and of the western Franks. What is your name?"*

"I am Halfdan, known among my people as Strongbow," I answered. When I said the latter, King Charles's eyes flicked momentarily to the bow lashed to the side of my saddle, then his focus returned to my face. There was something about

his manner—an arrogance, a haughtiness—that made me take an instant dislike to him.

"I wish you to give my greetings to the leader of your army," he said, nodding his head toward Ragnar. *"His name is Ragnar, is it not? My captain said his title is war-king. What is he king of? Is he of royal blood?"*

I wondered if this Frank would find it more agreeable to deal with a king. Would his pride be too offended to be defeated by a mere pirate?

"Ragnar is the war-king who leads us," I explained. *"He was chosen by our leaders to command our army—to lead us in war. He was chosen for his skill, not because of his family or birth, though he is related by blood to Horik, King of the Danes."*

"Is this the Franks' king?" Ragnar demanded. "What does he say?"

"This is King Charles," I told him. "He asks me to give you his greetings."

"Tell Ragnar I speak to him, king to king," King Charles said. *"Tell him I respect and honor his skill at war. Tell him I wish there to be peace between our peoples. Tell him I need him to leave my lands."*

"It is customary," Hastein said, when I translated the Frankish king's words, "when one king submits to another, for tribute to be paid. Ask King Charles if he is willing to pay tribute to Ragnar and our army if we consent to leave." I glanced at

Ragnar, and he nodded his agreement.

"Who is this man who speaks?" King Charles asked when I translated what Hastein had said.

"His name is Hastein. He is one of the leaders of our army. He is a jarl—*he rules over many lands and people in the name of King Horik."*

"So this is Hastings," Charles said, looking at Hastein appraisingly. *"I know of him. He has troubled my lands before."*

The king of the Franks looked back at me. *"Tribute? Yes, that has a better sound. It is more honorable to pay tribute to a powerful enemy, than to pay ransom to pirates, murderers, and thieves."*

"What is he saying?" Ragnar demanded.

"I think Hastein was correct," I said. "I think he will pay to see us leave his land."

12

A SEASON OF PEACE

In the end, the process was not so different from haggling over the price of a horse—although the details were far more complicated. It was understood by all, of course, that King Charles was buying the departure of our army from his kingdom. But he needed additional concessions from us in order for his people to accept the bargain he struck.

Ragnar and Hastein agreed that we would release all of our prisoners. No Frank we'd captured, not even the lowest born, would be carried away and sold into slavery. They also pledged not to destroy Paris and Ruda or any of the many monasteries and churches our army had overrun.

In return, our warriors would keep all of the

plunder they had already seized, and we would be paid tribute—a vast amount of tribute—in recognition of our victory. In truth, it could not be called ransom, for the sum was too great. The Franks would pay us seven thousand pounds of silver to buy peace.

King Charles explained that it would require time—several weeks at a minimum, and possibly until midsummer—to raise the funds needed to pay such a sum. The king's coffers alone, we were told, could not pay so great an amount. The churches of the land that we had not already stripped of their wealth would be pressed to contribute, on the grounds that they would be securing the safety of their own. And the nobles and common folk would be taxed.

Until the tribute was paid, we would continue to hold, as hostages against King Charles fulfilling his end of the agreement, our most valuable prisoners: Count Robert, the bishops of Paris and Ruda, and three abbots we'd captured—two from Paris and one from a monastery below Ruda. The other prisoners, including those held at Ruda, would be released forthwith. While we waited, our army would remain quartered in the island fortress at Paris. So we would not have to raid the countryside to find provisions for our men, the Franks agreed to supply us with cattle, ale and wine, and other foodstuffs to keep our warriors well fed—and hopefully content and peaceful—pending their eventual departure.

Hastein and Ragnar agreed that while our army waited to receive payment of the tribute, if any Dane injured a citizen of Paris, or took any of their possessions, they would be tried and fined by the leaders of our army. The fines would be paid to the injured Franks. If a Dane killed a Frank without justification, he would be hanged. The latter was harsh—in our own land, deaths were often settled by payment of wergild, not life for life. But no one wanted random violence to jeopardize the peace settlement, nor the payment of the tribute.

"Besides," Ivar said when he learned what Ragnar and Hastein had promised to enforce, "Father will be delighted to have the opportunity to impose more discipline upon our warriors."

Bjorn and the fleet arrived on the evening of the day the negotiations of the peace settlement were concluded. They'd thought they would face battle, or perhaps a hurried evacuation of our forces from the town, for large numbers of Frankish cavalry had shadowed their progress the entire journey upriver. Instead they found us celebrating our easy victory and the wealth we all would be receiving from the Franks in exchange for peace.

I was involved in every aspect of the negotiations of the peace accord, due to the need for an interpreter to facilitate the communication between our leaders and King Charles and his advisors. I found it heady indeed to be a part of so momentous an event. It was enlightening to watch such great men resolve the fates of armies and towns, and of so many people. Only a year ago I had been a slave. Now I was in the company of kings.

Once the negotiations were concluded, however, my services were no longer needed. I found myself with no responsibilities and time on my hands. I did not know what to do with it.

"I am going to make more arrows," Tore told me when I asked him how he planned to pass the weeks until the tribute was paid. "I lost many of mine in the battle. I have only enough left to partially fill a single quiver."

"I plan to eat and drink as much as I wish to," Torvald answered when I asked him the same question. "The Franks have cheeses the like of which I have never tasted, and their butters . . . There must be something about the grass here in Frankia that their livestock feed on. And their bread, and the wine . . ."

"We should come up with a plan and kill Snorre," Einar proposed when I spoke with him.

263

"A message has been sent downriver to summon the rest of our ships from Ruda. In a matter of days, Snorre will be here in Paris. We are prohibited by the peace treaty from harming Franks, but Snorre is not a Frank."

I found Einar's suggestion the most appealing. Now that the war with the Franks was over, it was time to take steps to fulfill my oath. I intended to raise the matter with Hastein, but an unexpected diversion presented itself only two days after the peace accord was reached that distracted me from my purpose.

I was in the immense palace inside the island fort where Count Robert and his family had lived before the town fell. The town's garrison had been quartered there, too. Now our army occupied it. Two of its rooms had been claimed as quarters by Hastein and the crew of the *Gull*—a small room for Hastein himself and a larger one for the rest of us. I was in our new quarters, helping Torvald and Cullain set up the ship's cooking gear in a deep, stone hearth built into the wall on one side of the room. I found the hearth an amazing thing. A channel to carry the smoke away had been built right into the stone wall above where the fire was laid. I thought it a much better arrangement than merely letting the smoke rise through the room toward a hole in the ceiling. The air inside the room remained much clearer.

A warrior whom I did not know entered our quarters with another man trailing behind him. "I am looking for a warrior named Halfdan," he called out. "I believe he follows Jarl Hastein."

"I am Halfdan," I told him.

"This Frank came to the town-side gate looking for you," he said, indicating the man behind him. "At least we think he is. We could not understand what he was saying, other than your name and the jarl's."

The Frank's face brightened when he saw me. As he hurried toward me, the guard who'd brought him turned and left. It seemed obvious the Frank recognized me, but the recognition was not mutual. Though he looked vaguely familiar, I could not place him.

"Who are you?" I asked.

"I am Gunthard," he answered. When the look of puzzlement did not leave my face, he added, *"I serve Count Robert. I was with the Lady Genevieve when you captured her."*

I remembered him now. He was the Frank I had wounded in the shoulder. The one I had left in the ancient hilltop fort with the servant woman Clothilde. He'd seemed a decent enough man, and brave. I was glad to see he had survived.

"How is your shoulder?" I asked him.

He shrugged and winced slightly when he did. *"It is healing,"* he answered.

"Why are you here?" I asked.

Gunthard glanced from side to side, then leaned forward and whispered to me in a conspiratorial tone. It was totally unnecessary. Even if he'd shouted, no one else in the room could have understood what he said.

"I have come from the Lady Genevieve," he told me.

"I see," I said, but I did not. *"Why are you here?"* I asked again.

"The Lady Genevieve sent me to give you a message. She wishes to meet with you."

Now I was truly confused.

"Why?" I said. *"When?"*

"Now," Gunthard answered. *"She is waiting in the Church of St. Severin. It is just across the river, in the town just beyond the bridge tower."*

This made no sense to me at all. I had seen the expression on Genevieve's face when she'd recognized me in the abbey. She had not looked as though she wished to see me again. Not then, nor ever.

It had to be a trick. Someone must wish to lure me off the island and into the town. But who would use this Frank, and the name of Genevieve, to bait such a trap?

I searched my memory, reviewing the ever-growing list of enemies I had made, but only one person seemed to fit these particulars. Genevieve's brother had sworn he would kill me. He'd seemed impulsive and hotheaded enough to try. I wondered if he was in Paris now. He'd been angry at me before because I'd stolen his sister and killed his cousin, Leonidas. No doubt the humiliating capture of his father had stoked his anger and offended his haughty pride even more. I could think of no one else who might be setting such a trap. Though I seemed to have made enemies aplenty among our own army, none of them would know of Gunthard, or be able to convince him to act on their behalf.

The wisest course would be to not go. But my curiosity—plus, no doubt, the feelings of boredom and impatience that were already replacing the excitement of the campaign—won out over wisdom.

"Wait a moment," I told Gunthard. I walked over to my sea chest and donned my padded jerkin and mail brynie, then took my sword belt, sword, and small axe from the chest and armed myself. After a moment's hesitation, I added my quiver, bow, and shield.

Torvald had been watching me curiously ever since Gunthard had arrived. "What are you doing?" he asked me now.

"I am going into the town," I said.

"Are you expecting trouble?"

I was, but did not wish to appear the overly nervous type. "Not necessarily. No man should venture from his home without his weapons," I answered, affecting an unconcerned tone, "because one never knows when he may need a good spear." It was a saying I'd heard Hastein use before. I liked the sound of it.

"Hmm. Or apparently a bow, either," Torvald said. "Your spear seems to be the only weapon you are not carrying. I think I will come with you. I am growing bored here." He walked over to his sea chest and retrieved his own sword from it, but left his armor and shield behind.

"Who is this man?" Torvald asked as we followed Gunthard through the palace. I noticed the Frank seemed familiar with it, certain of where he was going—much more so than I was. I supposed he had lived here before our army had evicted the count's household.

"He serves Count Robert," I answered.

Torvald looked surprised. "Where is he taking us?"

"To one of the Franks' temples just across the river. He says someone is waiting there. Someone who wishes to see me."

"A Frank?" Torvald asked.

I nodded. "He says Genevieve, the count's daughter, is there."

Torvald was silent for a time, as though pondering what I had told him. "I do not think I understand," he finally said. "Why are you so heavily armed? She was a small woman, and did not strike me as being particularly fierce of disposition."

"She will not be there. I believe this is a trap. In fact, I am certain of it," I told him. "And I thank you for coming with me." I was truly glad to have his support, for I did not know how many enemies awaited me. "If we are forced to kill any Franks this day, Hastein and Ragnar are more likely to believe we had to if it is you who tells them."

But when we reached the church, only a single person was visible inside. Torvald walked the entire length of the church, from rear doors to altar, just to be certain no one else was hiding. Then he told me with a smirk, "I believe I will return to the fort now. I do not think you need my help here after all."

Genevieve had been watching Torvald with a puzzled expression ever since he and I had arrived. Neither of us had yet spoken to the other. I was too dumbfounded at seeing her to know what to say.

Finally she broke the silence as Torvald left. *"What was your friend, the giant, looking for?"* she asked. *"And why are you armed? What did you expect to find here?"*

"Enemies," I answered and felt foolish as soon as I said it.

Genevieve glanced over at Gunthard with a puzzled frown. He, too, looked confused. *"What did Gunthard tell you?"* she asked.

"He said you were in this church and wished to see me." She glanced again in the direction Torvald had gone, but said nothing. After a moment I added, *"I did not believe him. I did not think you would be here."*

"Why?" she asked.

"I saw the way you looked when you recognized me in the abbey."

Genevieve glanced away when I told her that. After a moment she turned her gaze toward me again. *"Why did you come there that day?"* she asked me. *"Why did you come to the abbey?"*

"I knew our warriors would loot it. They were going to every church and monastery in Paris. I feared for your safety."

"That is why?" she asked. I could not read the expression on her face—it told me nothing. I shrugged my shoulders in answer. That was why I'd gone. At least in part. But I had also just wished to see her again. I certainly did not intend to admit that to her, though.

My answer apparently did not satisfy her. *"Why did you care?"* she pressed me. *"Why did you care for my safety? Your promise to me had been fulfilled. While I was your prisoner, you honored your word and never harmed me. But my father had already ransomed me. I had already been returned to my people. You owed me nothing."* After a moment she added, *"We are enemies."*

Yes, we were enemies. That was the heart of the matter, was it not? To her, I was just a Northman and a pirate. I was a murderer—a ruthless, cruel killer. She had called me all those things before. Why had I been surprised when she was horrified to see me again?

"Is that why you asked me to meet you here?" I said. I could not keep my voice from sounding brusque. *"You were curious to know why I came to the abbey? I only wished to make certain you were safe. That is all. Now, if you will excuse me, I must return to the fort."*

I turned to leave. *"Wait,"* she said. *"I did not mean to appear ungrateful. I thank you, not just for myself, but for all the sisters in the abbey. Had it not been for you, who knows what might have happened to us. Even the abbess said you were not what she expected a Northman to be."*

That was faint praise. *"You are welcome,"* I said and started to leave again.

"In the abbey, when I saw you," Genevieve said.

I turned back toward her. Her face was very pale, but when our eyes met she blushed, and turned aside, so her mantle hid her features. *"I had thought you were dead,"* she murmured.

I tried to make sense of her words, but could not. *"I do not understand,"* I told her.

"The battle," she explained. *"My father was wounded, and barely escaped with his life. My brother Drogo was killed, or so we believe. It is certain he was not among our soldiers who escaped. We heard that many, many died on both sides. I do not know why, but I believed you were among them. I believed you were dead. And then I saw you."*

I still did not understand.

"I thought you were dead," she said again, her voice catching. *"And then you were there, standing before me."*

"Why did you care?" I asked, shaking my head in surprise.

"Why did you come to the abbey?" she countered, looking into my eyes. *"Why did you care what happened to me?"*

Neither of us answered the other's question. Not that day, at least. There are some things too fragile, too delicate, to be put into words. They are like thin ice. To venture directly onto it would risk destroying it.

In the weeks that followed, Genevieve found reason to venture out of the abbey nearly every day. She paid frequent visits to her mother and father—to comfort them, she said. They had been forced to live in greatly reduced circumstances within the island fort, due to our army's takeover of the palace and her father's continued status as a hostage. From what I knew of their relationship, I wondered if Genevieve's visits came as a surprise to her parents. Perhaps they thought that becoming a servant of the White Christ had evoked in her a new sense of appreciation for them.

Even though the terms of the treaty forbade any Dane from molesting the peace of the inhabitants of Paris, it was still not a place where an attractive young woman—even a nun—could wander safely alone. On her daily walks from the abbey to the fort, Genevieve was always escorted by Gunthard. It came to be our practice that I would usually accompany Genevieve when she returned to the abbey while Gunthard trailed a discrete distance behind.

I found our walks to be a pleasant diversion during the weeks of enforced idleness while our army waited for the tribute to be paid. They gave me an opportunity, for the first time in my life, to have a comrade—no, more than that, a friend, for that was what Genevieve came to be—my own age.

And although we came from vastly different backgrounds, I came to realize that Genevieve and I had more in common than just our age. Neither of our lives had ever truly been our own to live.

I had been a slave for most of my life. And now I was bound by my oath to devote myself to avenging the deaths of Harald and the others. I had sworn not to rest until Toke and his men had paid for their treachery with their lives.

And Genevieve? Her father had considered her as merely a valuable commodity to be bartered for his own gain. When she had tried to resist and live her own life, she had been given to the Christian priests and priestesses, as if she was a piece of property. She now faced a long and lonely life as a servant of the White Christ.

But during these days while the Danish army was quartered in Paris, during this brief season of peace, she and I stole a few hours of each day for ourselves.

Rarely did we plot a direct course back to the abbey. Instead, we wandered together about the town. It was an opportunity for me to learn about Paris, a fascinating place unlike any I had ever seen. For me, it provided a window into the distant past, into the histories of entire peoples and ancient times when mighty empires had risen and fallen. And Genevieve was an enthusiastic guide, who

274

knew much about the town's history and was eager to share it with me.

She told me of the Parisii, the ancient tribe who had lived on the island in the river before the Romans came. She explained how the Romans had built a city here after they'd conquered Gaul, and had patterned it after distant Rome itself, filling the town with great monuments and buildings such as the forum—the name she called the great market-place that I'd passed that first morning I'd entered Paris—huge public bathhouses, and an arena.

"What is an arena?" I asked.

She took me there. A huge, stone-lined circular pit with sloping sides had been built beyond the fringes of the town on the lower eastern slope of the hill—Genevieve called it Mount St. Genevieve, though it was hardly a mountain. The jagged remnants of thick walls loomed around the stone-lined crater, hinting that once a great structure had towered above the ground. Stepped, evenly spaced rows of stone benches lined the sides of the pit's interior.

"The spectators sat on those benches," Genevieve explained. *"And before the arena fell into ruin, there were many additional rows of seats above ground level. Thousands at a time could watch the performances here."* She shuddered. *"The Romans could be very wicked. They made men fight each other—or*

fierce beasts—to the death, for their entertainment."

It must have been enormous before it had fallen into ruin. Genevieve was right—it did seem an evil thing to build so vast a structure for no purpose other than to watch men kill each other. Killing was not meant to be entertainment.

"What happened to this place?" I asked, looking at the crumbling walls.

"For hundreds of years, this was a land of peace under the Romans' rule. Towns such as Paris did not have walls, because they did not need them. Then tribes of barbarians attacked the borders of the empire, and Rome's armies could not keep them out. Paris was sacked more than once by bands of barbarians raiding into Gaul. In desperation, the citizens of the town used stone from this arena, and from the forum in the center of town, to build the walled fortress on the island, where they could take refuge in times of danger."

"But they never attempted to build a wall around the town itself?" I asked.

She shook her head. *"Once the Franks conquered Gaul, peace came to the land again. It has been hundreds of years since an enemy threatened Paris."*

Or looted it, I thought. That is why the plunder we took was so rich.

"Did the Franks drive away the barbarians, the ones who'd sacked Paris? Did they fight and defeat

them?" I asked her. It seemed a thing worth knowing. If the Franks had once before managed to conquer foreign raiders who'd threatened their land, they might do so again.

"*No,*" Genevieve said. "*It was the Franks who had raided Gaul and sacked Paris. They themselves were the barbarians. But in the time of Clovis, one of the greatest kings of the Frankish people, they finally conquered Gaul and settled here. It was King Clovis who led the Franks to convert to Christianity. He built the Church of St. Genevieve here in Paris, and he is buried there. Since the time of Clovis, the peoples of Gaul—Romans, Gauls, and Franks—have been one and have lived together in peace.*"

I thought it an amazing story. I wondered if Ragnar knew it. It made his dream of finding a kingdom to rule through war and conquest seem almost plausible.

It was a carefree time, the happiest I had ever known—happier even than the brief period when Harald, Sigrid, and I had lived together as family. For most of my life, the only feeling of belonging I had ever experienced was of belonging to Hrorik, my father, as his property. After I was freed—and before Harald was killed—I had for the first time been part of a real family. I'd had a brother and sister who had cared about me, and had taken care of me and showed me more kindness than I had ever known.

Yet I always knew Harald's and Sigrid's feelings toward me had been based in large part on what I was, rather than who I was. After all, I had lived in the same household with them for my entire life, but they had not cared about Halfdan the thrall. It was not until I became a legitimate member of their family, until I was acknowledged as Hrorik's son and their brother, that their feelings toward me changed.

With Genevieve, it was different. The feelings she'd initially felt toward me, the fear and mistrust, had changed despite the fact that *what* I was—a Northman, a pirate, an enemy—had not. Her feelings toward me were based on who I was: on the man who was Halfdan. I asked her about it one day.

"Do you not think it strange," I said, *"that we have become friends?"*

"What do you mean?" she asked.

"It is not just that we are different peoples—that you are a Frank, and I a Dane. I stole you from your own people, and held you for ransom." And, I thought, I killed your cousin when he tried to stop me. I did not say that, though. I did not wish to call that memory back to her mind.

She was quiet for a few moments, reflecting on

what I had said. Then she answered, *"What you say is true. But there is another side to it. No one has ever shown as much true care for me, for my well-being and safety, as you have. My father and mother, whom I once believed loved and cared for me, would have wed me to a hateful man whom I despised, in the hope that Father might one day gain his lands. Surely a father and mother should care more for their own child than that. Yet you, who should be my enemy, who owe me nothing, have repeatedly honored and protected me. I find it strange that you have, but I am grateful for it."*

The look in Genevieve's eyes, the warmth of her manner when she told me those words, made me imagine she found it more than merely strange. She made me feel that she enjoyed and valued my company. I, in turn, was grateful for her time and attention. She did not have to make her daily excursions from the abbey to visit her family. They surely did not expect it. I knew she did it so she could spend time with me. It was, at the same time, both a very pleasing feeling and an uncomfortable one. I was not used to finding so much enjoyment in the company of a woman.

My mixed feelings were exposed one day when she took me to see another of the great Roman buildings of the town. This one, like most of the ancient stone structures, was very tall, with high, arching windows and vaulted ceilings. *"During Roman times, this entire building was a great bathhouse,"* she told me. I was impressed. I'd thought the low, single-room bathhouse my father had built onto the side of his longhouse a fine and comfortable place to bathe. This building looked as though half the population of Hedeby could have washed in it at the same time.

"Later, King Clovis used this as his royal palace," she continued. It was certainly big and fine enough to be a palace. I had noticed that many of the Franks—particularly the common folk—did not seem all that familiar with the practice of bathing. It did not surprise me that a Frankish king would think so grand a building wasted as a mere bathhouse.

The thought of bathing carried my mind back to the river below Ruda. As I looked at Genevieve now, in my mind I was recalling how she had looked in the water; her beauty revealed by her thin, soaked shift; her long hair billowing in the water around us. She caught me staring at her.

"What are you thinking?" she demanded. *"Why do you look at me like that?"*

Embarrassed, I blushed. *"I was, it was . . . nothing,"* I stammered. *"I was just thinking. My mind, my thoughts, were elsewhere."*

"*I do not believe you,*" she said. "*The redness of your face reveals that you are not being truthful. I thought we had become friends. Is something troubling you?*"

I summoned my courage. "*When you told me this was a bathhouse,*" I began, "*my mind traveled back to the day when I took you to bathe in the river below Ruda.*"

Now it was her turn to blush. "*You should not think of such things,*" she said. "*It is wrong.*"

"*I cannot help it,*" I admitted. "*And I do not feel it is wrong.*" She blushed again, and looked away. Now it was she who appeared troubled.

"*It is getting late,*" Genevieve told me, and began walking quickly up the hill. "*I must return to the abbey now.*"

281

13

THE GIFT

I was waiting at the town-side gate of the fort for Genevieve. She'd come once again to the island to visit her parents. Einar had seen me standing near the gate, and had come over to talk. I was feeling distracted and wished he would go away.

"Have you seen Snorre yet?" he asked. I shook my head. I had not even thought about him recently. My mind had been consumed with thoughts of Genevieve.

"The ships from Ruda arrived yesterday. He and his men are quartered here on the island now, in the palace. You should be careful."

I appreciated Einar's warning, but I did not wish to think about Snorre just now. I was trying to plan what I would say to Genevieve when I saw her.

"It is surely fate that has brought Snorre to Frankia," Einar continued. "It is a sign that the Norns wish to help you fulfill your oath of vengeance."

My oath. I realized with shock and great shame that in the past few weeks I had completely forgotten about it. I had forgotten that I had sworn to avenge the deaths of my brother, Harald; of his men; and of all who had died in Toke's attack on the Limfjord estate. Back when I'd sworn the oath, I had even prayed to Odin, asking for his help. My prayer came back to me now: "Let my heart not feel peace until my oath is fulfilled."

I had been wrong, very wrong, to allow the pleasure of Genevieve's company to drive my duty from my mind.

I did not want Einar to realize that I had been neglecting my oath. I did not wish him to lose respect for me. I mumbled some excuses and promised that although I did not have time now, we would speak more later. We agreed to meet in my quarters at the end of the afternoon.

When she finally appeared, Genevieve seemed somber.

"What is the matter?" I asked her. *"You look as though something is troubling you."*

"My father told me today that King Charles has completed gathering the silver he needs to pay the tribute to your army. The king's men will be bringing it to Paris within a matter of days." She looked at me and forced a smile. *"I suppose I feel sad,"* she added. *"Soon my friend will sail away forever."*

I was surprised to learn of the news her father had given her. I'd spoken with Torvald earlier that morning and he'd said nothing of this. I felt certain that if Hastein had known of it, Torvald would have also—and he'd have told me. Although we had confined Count Robert to the fort on the island, apparently he still somehow had access to Frankish spies and to the news they carried from their king.

Genevieve and I crossed the bridge and began climbing the long, straight road that led up to the hill's summit. Normally we would have been talking eagerly to each other, planning what sights we would visit as Genevieve made her circuitous return to the abbey. But this day, we were both lost in the silence of our own thoughts.

Finally Genevieve turned to me. *"I am sorry, Halfdan,"* she said. *"But I wish to return to the abbey now. My heart is troubling me. There are things I wish to think about alone, and to pray over."*

I did not protest. Today everything seemed changed. I found that being with her brought me more pain than pleasure.

"I will be myself again tomorrow," she promised. I did not know if I could be. I had remembered my oath. I had remembered that I was a killer. It was my fate. I should never have forgotten it.

I was deep in thought, and paying little attention to my surroundings, as I made my way back to the island fort. But when I walked out onto the bridge leading from the town to the fortress gate, my attention was jerked back to the present. Snorre and another warrior stepped into view from the shadowed opening of the gate ahead. They began walking down the bridge toward me.

Snorre and his man were both wearing mail brynies, and swords hung at their belts. Though I, too, was wearing my sword and my dagger was also stuck in my belt, I wore no armor. I stopped, then took a step back, and another. There are times when flight is the better choice.

I realized that the man beside Snorre was looking at something beyond me with an evil grin on his face. I glanced over my shoulder and saw two more warriors, armed and armored as Snorre was, approaching along the bridge from the shore side. They must have been hiding in the gate tower when I'd passed through it. I had nowhere to go. It was either fight or leap into the river. As Snorre and his men drew closer, I stepped toward the edge of the bridge and glanced down at the water flowing beneath it.

"I know you are quite a runner," Snorre said, leering. "You were the only one swift enough to escape the night we killed your brother. But how well can you swim?"

I could not believe Snorre would be so bold as to attack me here on the bridge in plain sight. I looked beyond him at the gate. Where were the guards?

"There is no one there to help you," Snorre said. "My men are guarding the gate this afternoon. I volunteered them for the duty. I thought it the least we could do, since we were not able to help with the battle or the capture of Paris."

They were close now and had spread out, boxing me in. I could not afford to wait longer to see what Snorre would do. His intentions seemed obvious. With my back to the bridge's edge and the water below, I drew my sword and dagger from their scabbards and extended the sword in front of me, prepared to thrust or parry, with my dagger ready in my left hand.

"He drew on us," Snorre said to his men. "You all saw it. You are witnesses now. I merely sought to speak with this boy, but he has drawn his sword and threatens me with it. I have a right to defend myself. We all do."

Snorre and his men grabbed their sword hilts, but before their blades could clear their scabbards, an arrow flashed between Snorre's legs and thudded into the planks of the bridge just in front of him. Had it been shot a hand's span higher, it would have unmanned him.

"Do not draw your blade, One-Eye," a voice called out. "You nor any of your men, or I swear to you my next arrow will kill you."

It was Einar. He was standing above the gate on the rampart of the fort's wall. As I watched, he fitted another arrow to the bow he was holding.

Snorre spun around to look up at the rampart, his hand still on his sword hilt, but neither he nor any of his men finished drawing their weapons. It was a very short shot from the rampart down to the bridge, one any skilled archer could make with ease.

"You!" Snorre exclaimed, when he saw Einar. "I have always thought it suspicious that Toke's men were slain when they hunted this boy, but you returned to your village unharmed. Now I know the truth of it—the hound was in league with the fox. You will pay for your treachery then, and your interference this day. I will see your blood on my sword."

"Do not count your enemies slain until you have killed them, One-Eye," Einar said. "And you, of all people, should not accuse others of treachery. You serve a man who murdered his own brother. Halfdan, come this way. Give them a wide berth, so I have a clear shot at this snarling dog."

I edged around Snorre and the warrior beside him, keeping my weapons up and at the ready. As I passed him, Snorre jeered, "Once again, you run away, boy. You cannot do so forever. Be a man, for once in your life. Let us take two horses, just you and me, and ride out into the countryside. Away from the town, away from your comrades and mine, and we will settle the differences between us as men do."

"What is between us will be settled," I told him. "You can be certain of it." But I intended to do it my own way.

Einar told me he had been watching Snorre ever since his ship had arrived from Ruda. "Remember, it is not you alone who has a blood-debt to pay. Toke and this one-eyed dog are responsible for the death of Ulf, my sister's son. By following Snorre, I thought to learn of his habits and identify his comrades. When plotting a man's death, it is always better to know more about him than less. But when I saw him and his men take over the guarding of the gate, I suspected he was up to no good and fetched my bow. It is a good thing I did."

I agreed. Together we went to see Hastein. We found him in his quarters, playing a game of hnefatafl with Ivar.

"I need to speak with you," I told him.

Hastein looked irritated at the interruption. From the positions of the pieces on the board, he appeared to be losing.

"I am busy, in case you cannot tell," he snapped.

"It is a matter of some importance," I said.

He glared up at me. "Speak, then. Speak or be gone."

I would have preferred not to raise the matter in front of Ivar. When I'd seen that he was there, I should have waited. I should have left and come back later. But I hadn't, and now Hastein was impatiently waiting for me to declare what was so important. I had to continue.

"It is Snorre," I said. "I can wait no longer. It is time. I need to kill him."

"I am beginning to like this man of yours," Ivar said. "Things are never boring for long when he is around."

The following day, shortly after noon, Gunthard appeared at the entrance of the room where the *Gull*'s crew was quartered in the palace. I was standing near the hearth, watching Cullain begin his preparations for the evening's meal and talking with Torvald and Tore about the news Hastein and Ragnar had just learned. A messenger had arrived from King Charles. Wagons loaded with the tribute were en route to Paris.

"*I have a message for you from Lady Genevieve,*" Gunthard said, handing me a folded piece of parchment. When I opened it, I found a brief note written in Genevieve's hand.

"*My dearest friend,*" it said. "*There is one more thing I wish to share with you here in Paris, before you must leave. And there is a boon, a gift, I wish to ask of you. I cannot come to the fort. Please follow Gunthard. He will bring you to me.*"

I was tempted not to go. I needed to speak with Hastein again. Yesterday evening, we had begun forming a plan to deal with Snorre. It was far from finished, though. But this might be the last chance I would have to see Genevieve.

I folded the parchment, stuck it in the pouch on my belt, and retrieved my sword from my sea chest.

"You have been summoned by this Frank again?" Torvald asked.

I nodded. "If Hastein wishes to see me, tell him I will be back before dusk."

"Do I need to come with you, to protect you?" Torvald asked. I glanced sharply at him. He was

290

grinning. "Like the last time?" he added.

"Is Halfdan in danger?" Tore asked.

"Very much so," Torvald told him. "He goes to meet the Frankish girl who was his prisoner." I blushed as they both erupted in laughter. It was useless trying to explain to them. They would not understand. Genevieve was just a friend. She could never be more. It was not my fate.

Gunthard led me to a part of town I had not previously explored with Genevieve. I wondered what she planned. There were none of the town's large buildings here, only houses. Some of the bigger ones appeared as though they might date back to Roman times, but others looked to be of more recent and more ramshackle construction.

We stopped at the doorway of one of the latter, a narrow house crowded between two others. *"Why have we come here?"* I asked Gunthard.

"Lady Genevieve is waiting for you inside," he answered.

I did not understand. *"What is this place?"* I said.

"It is the house I grew up in," he told me. *"It was my parents' home, but they have been dead for many years. It belongs to my brother and his wife now. They are not in Paris, though. They are in Dreux, with her family. They were afraid to return until your army leaves the town."*

He knocked once on the door and it immediately swung open. Genevieve was standing inside. *"I will leave you now,"* he said.

Genevieve looked pale and had an anxious expression on her face. Her hands were clasped in front of her. She was wringing them nervously. *"Please come inside,"* she said. *"Do not stand in the street."*

"Why . . ." I began as I stepped through the doorway, intending to ask her the reason we were here, but she put her fingertips against my mouth to silence me.

"Please," she said. *"Let me speak. I have thought much about what I wish to say to you, but if you interrupt me, I fear the words will fly from my mind and I will forget them.*

"You have told me of your belief in fate. My own fate—to live a life of faith and devotion to my God— was pressed upon me. Yet I have sworn to accept it. I have pledged myself to serve God for the rest of my days. I will not—I cannot—dishonor such an oath once I have given it. I know that you, who are the most honorable of men, can understand that. I will give my life to my God.

"But once you asked me if I had ever wished to have a living husband, rather than be a bride of Christ. I told you there was a time when I had dreamed of such. I did not tell you all, though. That

292

dream I once held, which I know is now lost to me forever, has become so much more painful since I have known you. I cannot keep myself from wondering how different, how sweet, my life might have been, could I have spent it with someone like you."

I could not believe the words my ears were hearing. I could not believe what Genevieve was now revealing lay within her heart.

"I cannot bear," Genevieve said, her voice catching, *"to spend the rest of my life wondering what might have been. I will spend the rest of my days serving my God, because I have sworn to. But I must have something to help me through the thousands of lonely nights that lie ahead. I must have more than just a lost dream. I must have one sweet memory to cling to."*

Her lip was quivering and her eyes looked wet, although she shed no tears. She pulled her mantle up over her head, dropped it on the floor, and shook her long hair loose.

"What I am about to do is a terrible sin," she whispered and stepped toward me. *"But I do not care. Help me, Halfdan. Help me make this day a memory to treasure, one that will comfort me through the long years that lie ahead."*

14

THE ROAD

I had eaten sparingly and drunk only water. I would have to be light on my feet and have my wits about me this night.

It was our army's final day in Paris. The Franks' tribute had been weighed, counted, and divided among our men. All of the ships were loaded and ready to sail. Tomorrow we would head downriver toward the sea and begin our long journey home. Tonight, a final great feast was being given by Ragnar for all of our warriors before the army disbanded.

"Father will wish to make certain every man fully appreciates the glory and treasure their mighty war-king has won for them," Ivar explained.

A suitable location was needed—one where all could gather together and Ragnar could address the entire army and be heard. I'd suggested, through Hastein, the old Roman arena. Ragnar was pleased with the site. He thought it would serve his needs well. It suited my plans—mine and Hastein's—also. After all, the arena had been built for the purpose of watching men fight to the death.

A broad, raised platform ran across one side of the arena. Genevieve had called it a stage. She had told me that during Roman times, stories were sometimes acted out there for the townspeople. It was a thing I had difficulty understanding. Tales were for telling. It was the sound of the tale-teller's voice, his words, and the skill of the skald at crafting images that each listener could picture in his own mind that gave stories their power. It would seem undignified and weak to have men stand in front of you posing and pretending, instead.

The platform proved convenient, though, for Ragnar's feast. Long tables had been set up across it, and all of the chieftains of the army, every ship's captain, was seated there. Torches blazed around them so they could be visible to all. Snorre was among them, toward the left end of the stage. Stig and Svein, the two captains who followed Hastein, were seated nearby.

The rest of the army clustered around fires

scattered across the arena's floor. We of the *Gull*'s crew and the warriors from Hastein's other two ships had a place just in front of the center of the platform. Torvald had claimed it early, at Hastein's direction.

Ragnar's final address to the men had been droning on for some time now. Before him, other, lesser chieftains had also spoken. I'd stopped listening long ago. I was remembering my last hours with Genevieve. As I thought of her and of what we had shared, I held in my hand a small cross of gold, mounted on a slender chain of the same metal. She'd given it to me when we had parted.

"I wish you to have this token," she'd said, taking it from around her neck and pressing it into my hand. *"I will hope that occasionally, in the years to come, it will cause you to remember me."*

I would not need anything to help me remember Genevieve. I would never forget her.

I had given her a gift, too, though it looked poor and shabby by comparison to hers. To replace the cross she'd given me, I gave her the small, worn, simple cross of silver I wore around my own neck on a leather thong. Before handing it to her, I used the point of my dagger to carve the symbol ᛉ in the back of the cross. As I did, I remembered the last time I had used my knife to make this rune. I had cut it on the face of a man I had killed, as a sign.

"This symbol," I told her, *"is the first letter of my name in the writing of my people. When you see it, remember me. Remember this day especially, but also all of the days we have shared."* A memory was what she'd said she wanted from me. A memory was all that I could give her.

She took the cross and asked, *"How do you come to wear this? It is a symbol of my God, of his son, Jesus Christ."*

"My mother gave this cross to me, on the day she died," I told her. *"It is from Ireland, where she was born. She told me that wearing it might cause her God—your God—to watch over and protect me. I give it to you now, and hope that he will watch over you."* Now that I no longer can, I thought.

"I cannot take this," Genevieve protested. *"You should keep it to remember your mother by."*

"My memories of my mother live in my heart," I told her, *"where my memories of you will also live. I wish you to have it, to remind you of me."*

Ragnar finally finished talking. I put the chain around my neck and tucked Genevieve's cross inside my tunic. It was time now to think of other things. It was time for a debt to be paid.

When Ragnar returned to his seat at the center table, Hastein walked to the front of the platform. While the army sat idle in Paris waiting for the tribute to be delivered, he had occupied his time searching out the finest cloth, the richest leathers, and the best garment makers the Frankish town had to offer. He was wearing some of his new finery now, and looked resplendent. He'd even had a new belt and scabbard, decorated with intricate silver fittings, crafted for his favorite sword.

One article Hastein was wearing was not new. Around his sword arm he wore a thick band made of solid gold—the oath-ring of a godi.

I thought he looked more like a king than the Franks' King Charles had, and certainly more regal than Ragnar. He looked like a man who had been born to command; one whom others would naturally trust and wish to follow. This night, he would try to lead the hearts and the minds of the army.

"This is an opportunity the like of which we will not have again," he had explained to me. "Remember, you are not after just Snorre. Toke is the one you must ultimately destroy, and he is a very dangerous man, for he is a powerful chieftain whom many respect. This night, we will try to slay Toke's reputation. When the army disbands, its warriors will spread across the lands of the Danes, and beyond. We want them all to know of Toke's treachery and to carry the tale with them. If we are successful, wherever warriors from this army venture, Toke will find he has few friends. Men of courage and honor cannot abide the company of a

Nithing. He will be known for what he is, and it will be much harder for him to find allies."

Standing now at the front edge of the platform, looking out across the floor of the arena and the faces of the warriors seated there, Hastein held up his hands for silence. "I am Hastein," he began, "jarl over the lands around the Limfjord. Most of you know my name, if not my face.

"This is a night of celebration, as it should be. We feast this night to honor what we have achieved together, because on the morrow, we will part. We came together and formed this great army, and sailed to the land of our enemies, far from the safety of our homes. We have fought here together and have won many victories. But we have also seen many of our comrades find the ends of their fates here. Look around you, and be proud. This is a company of warriors who have won glory and honor, who deserve the songs and tales that will be told about our deeds here for years to come."

The arena erupted in cheers. When the noise died down, Hastein continued.

"You have heard many chieftains and our war-king, Ragnar, himself, praise you for what we have done here in the land of the Franks. I cannot speak fairer words about you, about our army's successes, than those already spoken this night. So I will not try. Instead, let me entertain you. Eat, drink, and enjoy yourselves while I tell you a tale of brave deeds and dark treachery, of bold warriors and evil, cowardly men—no, not men, less than that: Nithings. Let me be your skald this night, and entertain you while you feast." And so Hastein began his tale: the tale of Harald and Toke— and me.

"Once there were two brothers, as unlike as day and night. One was fair and brave, a warrior loved and admired by all. The other was dark and brooding. He was a berserk, feared by many.

"Their father was a mighty chieftain, a leader among the Danes. Ireland, England, Frankia—they all trembled with fear when his ships appeared. Eager his warriors were when battle loomed. And their fine silver-clad swords, gilded sword-belts, and arm-rings of gold and silver attested to their prowess and success."

I had not realized Hastein possessed such skill as a storyteller. He made these men sound like legendary heroes of old. Had I not known of whom he was speaking, I would not have recognized my father, nor his men. Though they were certainly doughty warriors, gold and silver arm-rings and gilded sword-belts had not been something commonly seen in my father's longhouse.

"The fair son accompanied his father on many distant raids and daring voyages, winning much renown," Hastein continued. "He was a loyal son and a brave comrade, and his father trusted and loved him above all others. The dark son, jealous and angered by the love his father showed his brother, left home to seek his own fate and fortune. In time, he became a renowned chieftain in his own right.

"The threads of life of all men, even the greatest, sooner or later are cut by the Norns, for no man lives forever. During a great raid against the English, in a fierce battle, the chieftain was struck down. Knowing his father was dying, the fair son brought him home. There, on his deathbed, the chieftain divided his lands and treasure. And he entrusted the care of his youngest son—one not yet old enough to have followed his father as a warrior—to his fair brother. 'Teach him well,' their dying father said. 'Help him become a warrior as fine and renowned as you.'"

I was very pleased at the way Hastein was telling this tale. I especially liked the way he omitted the fact that I had been a thrall in my father's household.

"Here is where this story truly begins," Hastein said. "For the division of the chieftain's possessions led to the deeds of courage and of treachery I will tell you of this night."

Hastein paused and reached his arm behind

him. Cullain, who'd been squatting behind Hastein's chair, stood and handed him a large silver cup filled with ale. Hastein drained it and handed the empty cup back to Cullain to be refilled before he continued.

"But first, I should put names to the men whose deeds I tell you of. For these men are not ancient heroes, known only in legends or in songs sung by skalds. These are warriors who have walked among us—whom some of you may know, or may have fought beside.

"The chieftain's name was Hrorik, son of Offa. Some of you may recall him as the leader of the first great raid against Dorestad, when that rich town was sacked and much treasure was won. I myself knew Hrorik well, and have fought beside him. Hrorik died early this year from a wound he received while fighting in England."

Up on the platform, Ragnar was staring at Hastein and frowning. Ivar, seated beside him, had a small grin on his face. Although Ragnar did not know what Hastein intended, Hastein had told Ivar of our plan, and had enlisted his help with it.

"The fair son," Hastein continued, "was named Harald. Again, I myself knew him; some of you may have, also. His skill with a sword was widely admired. And the name of his brother, the dark son, is Toke."

I had been watching Snorre, who was seated up on the raised platform. Until now, he'd been slouching back in his chair, laughing and talking with the chieftain beside him. He'd been paying no attention to what Hastein was saying. But at the sound of Toke's name, he sat up and began listening, a puzzled look on his face.

"When Toke learned of his father's death— Hrorik was, in truth, his foster father—he returned to the land of the Danes to discover what inheritance awaited him. He was enraged to learn that Hrorik had left him nothing. Most of Hrorik's lands and treasure had passed to his son Harald— all save one small estate on the Limfjord, in the north of Jutland, which Hrorik gave his younger son, whose name is Halfdan."

Ragnar's puzzled frown had turned to a scowl by now. He leaned forward across the table and spoke to Hastein in a voice loud enough to carry to where I sat, just beyond the edge of the platform. "What are you doing, Hastein? I thought you said you intended to entertain the army with a tale."

Hastein answered him in a low voice, "Do you think they are not entertained? We will see what happens. The best is yet to come."

Ragnar threw himself back in his chair, glancing restlessly from side to side. "I am entertained,

Father," Ivar told him. Ignoring them, Hastein continued.

"I met Halfdan earlier this year and took him into the crew of my ship, the *Gull*. His brother, Harald, taught him well. He is a formidable warrior who has fought well here in Frankia as part of our army. Though but a young man, he has already won much renown. Our war-king himself has honored Halfdan. He may be better known to you, the warriors of this army, by the name Strongbow."

Tore, who was seated on the ground beside Torvald, looked over at me. "The story the jarl is telling is about you," he said in a surprised voice.

"Your wits are as quick as ever," Torvald told him.

"There is more than one way to inherit wealth and lands," Hastein said. "Harald and Halfdan traveled north to the Limfjord to inspect the estate Halfdan had been left by their father. They were not expecting trouble, and were accompanied by only a few of Harald's housecarls. Toke followed them there with his entire retinue of warriors. He thought to win with murder the inheritance his foster father Hrorik had failed to leave him.

"Toke struck in secret in the night, no doubt hoping to slay Harald and Halfdan in their sleep. But his cowardly attempt at murder failed. And though badly outnumbered, Harald and Halfdan and their men beat off Toke's attack and barricaded themselves in the longhouse.

"Hoping to protect those who had no part in the fight, Harald secured a promise from Toke that the women, children, and thralls of the estate could leave the longhouse in safety before the next assault. Toke gave his oath—he pledged his honor—that they would not be harmed. But if an oath is sworn on the honor of a man who has none, it is meaningless."

As he was speaking, Hastein had stepped forward to the edge of the platform. He nodded down at me now and said, "You should hear from one who was there how Toke honored his oath. Tell us, Halfdan. Tell the noble warriors of this army what happened when the women, children, and thralls left the safety of the longhouse."

Hastein leaned down and extended his arm to me. We clasped wrists, and he pulled me up onto the platform.

I turned and looked out over the army of warriors seated on the fire-lit floor of the arena, a sea of faces that were now all staring at me, and said, in the loudest and clearest voice I could manage, "I will remember what happened that night for the rest of my life. I saw Toke step into view. He held a torch and called to the women and children. He urged them to leave the longhouse saying, 'Come this way to the light and safety.' They went to him, trusting in the promise he had given. Then, when all were beyond the reach of any aid we could give, Toke shouted to his men, 'Kill them all! There can be none alive to tell the tale.'"

Angry murmurs swept across the floor of the arena. "That is a grave accusation you have made," Hastein said.

"But it is true," I told him. "You are a godi. You are wearing the oath-ring. Let me hold it and I will swear upon it."

Hastein slipped the gold ring from his arm and held it out in front of him, clenched in his fist, and stated, "Do you swear to Thor, God of oaths, and of strength and honor, that you speak the truth?"

I clasped my hand over the other side of the ring and answered in a voice loud enough to carry out across the floor of the arena. "I swear. I give my oath, upon this unbroken ring and upon my honor, that all I say is true, and may Thor himself strike me dead if I lie. Toke and his men murdered innocent women, children, and thralls, after he swore an oath to my brother, Harald, that they would be safe. And there is more. After that dark deed was done, Toke and his men set fire to the longhouse, seeking to burn alive the warriors they could not best by force of arms.

"We tried to fight our way clear of the burning longhouse and reach the safety of the surrounding forest, but once in the open, we were too few, and Toke's warriors too many. In the end, only Harald and I were left. Harald died cutting a path clear through the surrounding warriors, so I could escape. 'Someone must survive to avenge us,' he told me. I did survive. And I have sworn to avenge the murderous deeds done that night."

Ragnar could restrain himself no longer. Pushing his chair back so violently that it fell over with a clatter, he stood and pounded his fist on the table.

"What are you doing, Hastein? What are you playing at, with this business of oaths and accusations? This is a feast. We are here to celebrate our army's victory. This is not a Thing."

Hastein had warned me Ragnar would be angry. Ivar had agreed. "This feast is Father's last chance to remind the warriors of our army what his leadership has won for them. He will not like you distracting them from that."

Hastein turned to Ragnar and told him, "You are right, Ragnar. This is not a Thing. And I am not bringing a lawsuit, nor is Halfdan. Not here, not now."

Turning back to the upturned faces of the army, all of whom by now were watching intently, Hastein said, "Why am I telling you this, my comrades? Why have I told you this tale tonight, one that as yet has no ending? It is because you have proven, by your deeds here in Frankia, that you are brave and honorable men. For the rest of your lives, you will be respected and honored for having fought and won here.

"But there is one among you, and perhaps more than one, who does not deserve that honor and respect. Some do not deserve to be a part of this company of men. Knowing that Halfdan escaped that night up on the Limfjord, knowing that one witness to his treachery had survived, Toke sent one of his most trusted followers to find Halfdan and slay him. He sent a man who had helped him kill the innocent women and children up on the Limfjord, and who had helped him slay Harald and his men—a man who had as much to gain by silencing our comrade Halfdan as Toke himself did.

"I have told you this tale, my comrades in arms, because there is a murderer among us—one who is guilty of Niddingsvaark. It is time to unveil him, so all here can know him and his master, Toke, for what they are."

While Hastein spoke these last words, I walked down the platform until I stood in front of where Snorre was sitting.

"I accuse you, Snorre!" I shouted. "You were

there that night. I accuse you of murder for helping Toke kill my brother Harald, and his men, and
the women and children and thralls of the farm. I
accuse you of joining this army and coming here to
Frankia, not to fight our enemies, but to try to
murder me. This night I will see you pay."

For a few moments, there was only silence. No
one in the arena spoke. Snorre himself looked
stunned, as if he was unable to comprehend what
had transpired. Then he regained his wits. With an
angry roar, he leaped to his feet and jerked his
sword from its scabbard. In an instant, Stig and
Svein were also on their feet. They seized Snorre's
arms, twisting them behind him, and knocked the
sword from his grasp.

Ragnar, who was still standing, shouted at
Hastein, "Look what you have done! Have you
forgotten that I have forbidden our warriors from
fighting each other while we are in Frankia?"

"The army disbands on the morrow, and we
sail for home," Hastein told him. "One duel this
night will do no harm."

"And think, Father," Ivar added, "this will add
to the tales men will tell about your campaign here
in Frankia. It will make the farewell feast you have
given this night one that will long be remembered.
Besides, you should think of our warriors, of what
they would want. Hastein promised to entertain

them. What better than a fine show of blood and death?"

I had walked back down the platform and stood before Ragnar. "I did not do this to anger you," I told him. "But bringing vengeance to those who killed my brother is my fate, and I will not shirk it. You told me not long ago that you were in my debt. I ask this now of you in return. Let me fight Snorre this night."

"You have planned this together, haven't you? All three of you," Ragnar growled. "You have been very unwise this night, young Halfdan. You had won much when you earned Ragnar Logbrod's gratitude. It was not a thing to be so lightly discarded."

While a runner went to Snorre's ship to fetch his weapons and armor—I had brought mine to the feast, knowing what was to come—our army's warriors relocated to the rows of stone benches overlooking the arena's floor. Judging from the volume of their voices and laughter, their spirits were high. Ivar had been right—they were definitely entertained by the prospect of watching a duel.

I, on the other hand, was feeling increasingly nervous. I hoped it did not show. In my impatience to strike some blow against Toke, had I made a terrible mistake? What had made me think I could best Snorre in a duel?

Torvald and Hastein were with me, helping me arm myself. I'd already pulled on my padded jerkin and mail brynie, but when I reached for my helm, Hastein stopped me.

"Not yet," he said. "Its weight will tire your neck and shoulders. Do not put it on until you need to. You must not waste any of your strength. You will need it all. A duel is unlike any other kind of fighting."

Hastein's remarks were no doubt supposed to be helpful, but they were having the opposite effect. My stomach was queasy—had I eaten a full meal, it would surely be coming back up—and I was feeling light-headed and short of breath. At this rate, by the time the duel began I would not be able to walk, much less fight.

"Have you ever fought a duel before?" Torvald asked, looking at me closely. I shook my head. "Hunh," he said. Then, after a long moment, as if he could come up with nothing else to say, he finally added, "Well, it is good to get your first one out of the way." I wondered if he was thinking it would likely also be my last.

"Remember, quickness is very important in a duel," Hastein said, continuing with his worrisome advice. "Few duels last long. Unlike in battle, you and your opponent have only each other to concern yourselves with. The smallest advantage can be decisive; the smallest mistake fatal. I myself do not like to use the shoulder strap on my shield when dueling. I have more speed and freedom of movement without it, though eventually it is more tiring."

Ivar sauntered up. "Hail, mighty Strongbow," he said. "You are quite the talk of the army this night. If the duel goes well, your reputation will be made. Of course, if Snorre kills you, the fine tale Hastein has taken so much trouble to spin will not have the right ending at all.

"But did Hastein leave some parts of the story out? I, too, knew Harald and knew of Hrorik. Now that I give some thought to the matter, I do not remember Harald ever mentioning a younger brother. And Snorre is telling all who will listen that you are a slave, or at least were born one."

I wondered if Hastein had foreseen this. I certainly had not.

"Is there nothing else you have to do now, Ivar?" Hastein asked.

Ivar ignored him and continued. "A slave who becomes a famous warrior and who pursues a vow of vengeance. The skalds will love this tale—if it does not end tonight."

Einar joined us. "I have been talking with some warriors who've spent much time in Dublin town in Ireland," he said. "Several of them claim to have seen Snorre fight duels before."

"What do they say?" Hastein asked.

"They are betting on *him*," he answered. That was encouraging to hear. What else could my comrades do to boost my spirits? "They say he fights with a great-axe, and that he wields it well."

Hastein frowned. "Interesting," he said. I thought *alarming* was more apt. "He certainly has the size to handle one, and with his long arms, it would give him quite a reach." Turning to me, he asked, "Have you ever fought against a great-axe before?"

"No," I said, shaking my head. It had been my father's favorite weapon, but when Harald had trained me, we never worked with axes. He did not fight with one.

"I myself have never seen one used in a duel before," Hastein said. "They can be deadly weapons in battle because of the great power of their blows, but most men think them too much slower than a sword to use in a duel. But Snorre is a big man. If he grips the axe near the end of its handle, be especially careful, for with its full length added to that of his own arms, he will be able to strike at you from beyond the reach of your sword. And you must be very careful how you parry his strikes with your shield. A great war-axe can easily shatter one." He was silent for a moment, thinking. "Are you comfortable fighting with a spear?" he asked.

At this point, the only thing I would have felt comfortable fighting with was my bow. But duels are fought hand to hand.

I nodded. Harald had trained me to fight with a spear.

"Good," Hastein said. "Use one tonight. At least with a spear, you can match his reach."

"Some of Snorre's men are already sneaking out of the arena and going to ready their ship," Einar volunteered. "I think they are concerned for their safety, regardless of the outcome of this duel. Jarl Hastein did a fine job of telling the tale."

Torvald clapped his hand on my shoulder. "There is Snorre," he told me. "It is time."

I strapped on my helm and picked up my spear and shield. Following Hastein's advice, I shortened the shield's strap and tucked it out of the way. Breathe, I told myself. Do not forget to breathe.

Einar clasped my shoulders with his hands and stared into my eyes. "Do not forget, my friend," he said. "Trust fate."

Hastein walked with me out onto the arena floor. Extra wood had been thrown on the fires scattered across it. They were blazing high now, lighting the ground on which Snorre and I would fight.

Snorre was waiting out in the center. I stopped a safe distance away. There were no courtesies to be observed in a fight such as this. We were here to kill each other.

"This will be a duel to the death!" Hastein shouted in a voice loud enough for all in the arena to hear. "No quarter will be asked, no quarter will be given." To me, he murmured, "May good luck be with you, Halfdan." He made the sign of the hammer with his fist and added, "Strength and honor." Then he turned and walked away.

"There are only the two of us now, boy," Snorre said. "Just you and me. You have nowhere to run, and no one to help you." He raised his shield and began moving toward me.

He led with his left foot, one step at a time, holding his shield centered in front of him and his axe hanging down loosely and angled slightly to the rear. He was holding it by the very end of its shaft, like Hastein had warned.

What were his weaknesses? There was the blind left eye, of course. That was obvious. But he held his head cocked slightly to the left to compensate, giving his right eye a more centered field of vision. Still, it was something to work with. I began circling to his left, backing as I did in time with his advance, to keep my distance from him. I was not ready to feint, to try to feel him out. I did not know how swiftly he could swing his axe.

Suddenly Snorre lunged forward with his left leg, swinging his axe in an overhead loop as he did. I jumped back far enough that he missed me altogether. Then I lunged forward after his axe had swung down past me, holding my shield angled out in front of my chest while I stabbed with my spear at his left leg.

I'd thought it would take him longer to recover from a missed blow, but he blocked my thrust easily with his shield and, at the same time, using his axe's momentum he whipped it around in a complete loop and smashed it down against my shield.

The impact almost knocked the grip from my hand. I scurried backward, glancing down at the face of my shield as I did. There was a deep gash across its face, just to the left of the iron boss. If another such blow landed close to the same spot, the planks would surely break.

Snorre's mouth twisted into what looked like a grim smile—although as scarred as his face was, it could have been a snarl—and he resumed his slow, steady advance. "It's different fighting man against man, isn't it, boy? It's not like with a bow." I glanced quickly behind me and realized he was trying to back me toward one of the bonfires.

I could not win this fight if I stayed on the defensive. Reversing my grip on my spear, I slid my hand farther back along its shaft, closer to the butt, and held it against my forearm to brace it. The spear felt heavy and awkward, holding it this far back of its balance point, but I needed the extra reach.

I flicked the spear head out toward Snorre's face in a series of quick, feinting jabs. He stopped advancing and raised his shield slightly, but did not overreact or give me any opening. He merely raised his axe, holding it cocked and ready, and waited to see what I would do next.

He is more experienced than me, I thought. And it shows. Snorre did not look frightened at all, not even anxious. My own heart was hammering in my chest. I took a deep breath and let it out slowly. Trust fate, trust fate, I thought, repeating Einar's words in my mind. If it is my fate to be a killer—to avenge Harald's death and Toke's treachery—then it will be Snorre's fate to die at my hands this night.

I needed to make him commit, one way or another. I needed him to raise his shield enough to block his vision for just a moment, or to strike at me or my spear with his axe. Either would suffice. I needed some kind of opening.

Suddenly Snorre roared out a wordless cry—an

old trick, but startling nonetheless—and lunged forward as he had in his initial attack, raising his axe to strike. I leaped back, stabbing out at his face with my spear. As soon as I did, I realized my mistake and tried to stop my thrust and jerk my weapon back.

When Snorre had leaped to attack, he had not actually swung his axe—not until after my thrust. He'd merely feinted with his shoulder, drawing me out. Then when I struck at his face, he whipped the axe down, chopping at my spear. The axe blade clanged against the iron socket of my spear's point and drove it downward, but did no damage. Had it hit the wooden shaft, it would have cut it through.

But now I was off balance and my weapon was out of position. Snorre lunged forward again, his arm cocked, the axe ready as I stumbled backward.

I could not safely retreat as swiftly as he was charging. He had me in his killing zone. His great-axe swung up, and when it began swooping down I pushed my shield up to meet it, trying to brace myself for the blow I knew would come.

The axe blade smashed through the already damaged planks, narrowly missing my wrist and showering me with splinters. Snorre wrenched his axe to the side, trying to jerk the shattered shield from my grasp. A triumphant look gleamed in his eye.

I let him have it. I let him pull the ruined shield from my hand and fling it aside. As he did, I thrust down hard with my spear, stabbing its long point completely through his left foot and into the ground.

He screamed. It was more like the howl of a wounded beast than the voice of a man. Most men would have fallen—the broad, sharp blade of the spear had cut through bone and tendon, almost severing the front portion of his foot.

But Snorre somehow remained standing, and flailed out wildly at me with his shield. The rim caught me in the face. The nose guard of my helm stopped the worst of the blow, but the edge of his shield gashed my brow and cheek open, and the blood that spurted from the wounds ran into my eyes, so I could not see. Stunned by the impact, I staggered back, releasing my grip on my spear and wiping frantically at my eyes with both hands to clear them. Then I remembered the axe.

Snorre shook my ruined shield free and swung a low, sweeping, off-balance blow at my legs. I threw myself backward. As the axe whooshed past in front of me, I hit the ground, rolled clear, and scrambled back to my feet.

Snorre dropped his own shield, freeing one hand, and used it to wrench my spear from his foot. He grunted with pain when he did, and blood spurted from the gaping wound. Again I marveled that he did not fall. Then, using my spear like a staff to help him balance, he began hobbling toward me.

Shaking my head to clear it, I retreated a few more steps, keeping safely out of his range. I could move far more swiftly than he now. Snorre stopped and leaned on the spear, panting and watching me.

Time was on my side now. Snorre was badly injured and would only get weaker. Unless I made a serious mistake, he was mine.

I slid my sword from its scabbard and drew my dagger with my left hand. It was the dagger Harald had given me on the night he had died.

"Snorre," I said, "there is only us now. Just you and me. Man to man. It is not like fighting with a crowd of Toke's men to support you, is it? It is not like killing women and children. There is nowhere you can run, and no one who will help you. I am going to kill you, Snorre. And you are just the first. Some day, I will kill Toke, too."

Whatever else Snorre was, he was not a coward. He tried to move forward to meet me, clutching the spear shaft tightly in his left hand, using it to take the weight off his maimed foot. He'd switched his stance, so his right leg was in front, supporting most of his weight, while he dragged his wounded foot behind, leaving a broad trail of blood. He let the axe's long handle slide down through his hand till he gripped it choked up high on the shaft, above the center. It was a much stronger grip, one that would allow shorter and quicker—though less powerful—blows.

I let him come closer, making him use up his strength. He did not have much left. The pain, and the blood pumping out of his foot, were draining it away, like water draining from a punctured waterskin.

When he drew into striking range, I sidestepped to his left and circled him quickly. As he tried to pivot and follow me, he put weight on his injured foot and gasped. I could see him momentarily lose his balance. I lunged in and thrust my sword's point toward his face, to see what he would do. He jerked the spear shaft sideways, batting the sword's blade aside.

That was something I could work with. I danced back and forth in front of him, feinting to the left and right. Snorre stood watching me, leaning on the spear, keeping it in front of his body like a shield, waiting. Then I threw a lunge at his face again.

It was a trick, a feint. Once more, he swung the

spear shaft across his body to block my sword's blade, but it wasn't there. I pulled it back, then snapped it forward again in a quick cut that hit his hand where it clutched the spear, cutting it nearly in half.

"That was for Harald," I said, but I was lying to Snorre and to myself. Killing him was for Harald. Dragging it out, cutting him to pieces, making him feel pain, was for me. I wanted someone to pay for all that I had suffered.

Snorre was breathing hard. He looked down at the gaping wound in his hand, then let the spear drop and spread his arms wide, exposing his chest.

"Finish it," he said.

As I stepped toward him and raised my sword, he threw himself forward, wrapping his wounded arm around me and raising his axe to bury it in my head. I caught the blow with my sword and held the axe above us. "This is for Harald," I repeated, and stabbed the long blade of my dagger into Snorre's throat. I backed away, ripping my knife free as I did. Snorre stood swaying for a moment, then sank to his knees. While I watched, the life faded from his one good eye and he toppled sideways onto the ground.

Hastein, Torvald, and Einar ran toward me across the sandy floor of the arena. Up in the benches, the warriors of our army were on their feet, chanting "Strongbow, Strongbow!"

"It is done," Hastein said, when he reached me and looked down at Snorre's body.

"No," I told him, shaking my head. "But it is begun."

LIST OF CHARACTERS

Adelaide	The abbess of the convent at the Abbey of St. Genevieve in the Frankish city of Paris where Genevieve, the daughter of Count Robert of Paris, lives.
Bertrada	The wife of Wulf, a Frankish sea-captain and merchant in the town of Ruda, or Rouen.
Bjorn Ironsides	A Viking chieftain who is one of the sons of Ragnar Logbrod, and one of the leaders of the Danish army attacking western Frankia.
Charles	King of the Western Kingdom of the Franks, which roughly corresponds in territory to modern France.
Clothilde	A Frankish woman who is the personal servant of Genevieve, the daughter of Count Robert of Paris.
Clovis	The first Christian King of the Franks, who ruled from A.D. 486 to 511, and built

the Church of St. Genevieve in Paris.

Cullain Jarl Hastein's personal servant, a former Irish monk captured and enslaved during a Viking raid on Ireland.

Derdriu An Irish noblewoman captured by the Danish chieftain Hrorik in a raid on Ireland, who became a slave in Hrorik's household and, as his concubine, bore him an illegitimate son named Halfdan.

Drogo A Frankish cavalry officer; a son of Count Robert and the brother of Genevieve.

Einar A warrior in the Danish army, a skilled woodsman, and a friend of Halfdan.

Genevieve A young Frankish noblewoman; the daughter of Count Robert of Paris.

Gunhild The second wife of the Danish chieftain Hrorik, and the mother, by a previous marriage, of Hrorik's foster son, Toke.

Gunthard A retainer of Count Robert assigned to escort Genevieve, Count Robert's daughter.

Halfdan The son of Hrorik, a Danish chieftain, and Derdriu, an Irish slave.

Harald The son of the Danish chieftain Hrorik by his first wife; Halfdan's half-brother.

Hastein A Danish jarl who befriends Halfdan, and who is one of the leaders of the Viking army attacking western Frankia.

Horik The king of the Danes.

Hrorik A Danish chieftain, known as Strong-Axe; the father of Halfdan, Harald, and Harald's twin sister, Sigrid, and the foster father of Toke, the son by a previous marriage of Hrorik's second wife, Gunhild.

Ivar the Boneless   A Viking chieftain who is one of the sons of Ragnar Logbrod, and one of the leaders of the Danish army attacking western Frankia.

Leonidas   A young Frankish cavalry officer; the cousin of Genevieve, and a nephew of Count Robert of Paris.

Odd   A crewman on Hastein's longship, the *Gull*, and a skilled archer.

Ragnar   The war leader of the Danish army attacking western Frankia, known by the nickname Logbrod, or "Hairy-Breeches."

Robert   A high-ranking Frankish nobleman; the count who rules over a number of towns and lands in the Western Kingdom of the Franks, including Paris; Genevieve's father.

Sigrid   The daughter of the Danish chieftain Hrorik by his first wife Helge; Harald's twin sister, and Halfdan's half-sister.

Snorre   A Danish warrior who is the second in command of the chieftain Toke.

Stenkil   A Danish warrior; the comrade of a man Halfdan killed.

Stig   A follower of Jarl Hastein, and the captain of the ship the *Serpent*.

Svein   A follower of Jarl Hastein, and the captain of the ship the *Sea Wolf*.

Toke   A Danish chieftain who is the son of Gunhild by her first marriage, the foster son of the Danish chieftain Hrorik, and the murderer of Harald, Halfdan's half-brother.

Tore   A crewman on Hastein's longship, the *Gull*, and the leader of the archers in the crew.

Torvald The helmsman on Hastein's longship, the *Gull*.

Wulf The captain of a Frankish merchant ship captured by the Danish fleet.

GLOSSARY

berserks: Warriors in Scandinavian society who were noted for their exceptional fierceness and fearlessness in battle, and for their moody, difficult dispositions in periods of peace. Ancient Scandinavian sagas sometimes describe berserks as possessing the supernatural ability to take on the form of bears or wolves or assume their powers in battle. Some modern scholars have suggested that the barely controllable warriors known as berserks may have suffered from mental illness, possibly manic depression or schizophrenia.

boss: The raised iron center on the front of a wooden shield, to which the planks of the shield were riveted, which provided extra protection over the hand grip on the back side.

brynie: A shirt of mail armor, made of thousands of small iron or steel rings linked together into a flexible garment.

Dorestad: A Frankish port and trading center located near the convergence of the Rhine and Lek Rivers, in the area now forming part of the Netherlands. Dorestad was one of the largest trade centers of early medieval Europe.

fletching: The three feathers at the back of an arrow, used to stabilize its flight.

Frankia: Also called Francia; the land of the Franks, roughly corresponding to most of modern France, Belgium, the Netherlands, and western Germany. By A.D. 845, the setting of *The Road to Vengeance*, the former Frankish Empire had split into three kingdoms: the Western Kingdom of the Franks, roughly corresponding to modern France; the Eastern Frankish Kingdom, stretching from the Rhine River eastward through the lands now comprising modern Germany; and the short-lived Middle Kingdom, which stretched from Frisia in the north to the Mediterranean coast of modern France, and also included parts of northern Italy.

fylgja: A beneficial spirit that attaches itself to a person and brings him or her good fortune. Some were visible and took the form of animals, often reflecting some aspect of the character or personality of the human they followed, such as a raven symbolizing wisdom, or a wolf ferocity. Others were invisible, but were generally considered to be female guardian spirits.

godi: A priest in pagan Viking-age Scandinavian society. The position of godi was usually held by a chieftain, and typically a godi would not only preside over religious festivals and sacrifices, but would also administer oaths, which were sworn on a large metal ring, usually made of iron or gold.

greaves: Armor, usually constructed of curved steel or bronze plates, worn to protect the lower leg from the knee to the ankle.

Hedeby: The largest town in ninth-century Denmark, and a major Viking-age trading center. Hedeby was located at the base of the Jutland peninsula on its eastern side, on a fjord jutting inland from the coast.

hnefatafl: "King's Table," a Viking board game of capture and evasion, where one player begins in the center of the board and tries to move his king to the outer edge, while the other player tries to block the king's escape and capture him.

housecarl: A warrior in the service of a chieftain or nobleman.

jarl: A very high-ranking chieftain in Viking-age Scandinavian society who ruled over a large area of land on behalf of the king. The word and concept "jarl" is the origin of the English "earl."

Jotunheim: In Viking mythology, the mountainous realm of the giants located between Midgard, the earthly home of men, and Asgard, the kingdom of the gods.

Jul: The Germanic pagan midwinter feast, known in England as Yule.

Jutland: The peninsula that forms the mainland of modern and ancient Denmark, named after the Jutes, one of the ancient Danish tribes.

Limfjord: A huge fjord that runs completely across the northern tip of the Jutland peninsula, providing a protected passage during the Viking period between the Baltic and North Seas.

longship: The long, narrow ship used for war by the peoples of Viking-age Scandinavia. Longships had shallow drafts, allowing them to be beached or to travel up rivers, and were designed to be propelled swiftly by either sail or by rowing. They were sometimes also called dragonships, because many longships had carved heads of dragons or other beasts decorating the stem-post at the bow of the ship.

Niddingsvaark: Acts of infamy; the dishonorable acts of a Nithing.

Niflheim: A vast wilderness of snow and ice that, according to the mythology of the Viking peoples, existed in the great void even before the earth was created. Niflheim is the home of the frost giants.

Nithing: Also Nidding; one who is not considered fully human because he has no honor.

nock: The notch cut in the rear of an arrow, into which the bowstring is placed to shoot it. Also the notches cut into the tips of a bow's limbs, in which the bowstring is secured to the bow.

Norns: Three ancient sisters who, according to pagan Scandinavian belief, sat together at the base of the world-tree and wove the fates of all men on their looms.

Odin: The Scandinavian God of death, war, wisdom, and poetry; the chieftain of the Gods.

Ruda: The Viking's name for Rouen, a Frankish town near the mouth of the Seine River.

runes: The alphabet used for writing in the ancient Scandinavian and Germanic languages. Runic letters, comprised of combinations of simple, straight strokes, were easy to carve into stone or wood.

scara: A unit of Frankish cavalry. Each scara was composed of several smaller units called cunei, each of which numbered from fifty to one hundred men.

skald: A poet.

Thing: A regional assembly held periodically in Viking-age Scandinavian countries where citizens of an area could present suits to be decided by vote, according to law. Lawsuits heard at Things led to what became, centuries later in English culture, the concept of trial by a jury of peers.

Thor: The pagan Scandinavian God of thunder and fertile harvests, and of oaths, strength, and honor—the virtues of a warrior. Thor was considered the mightiest warrior among the Scandinavian Gods.

Thor's hammer: A common piece of Viking Age jewelry, worn as good luck charm by both men and women, representing the magic hammer that was the favorite weapon of the God Thor.

thrall: A slave in Viking-age Scandinavian society.

Valhalla: The "Hall of the Slain," the great feast-hall of the God Odin, which was the home in the afterworld of brave warriors in pagan Scandinavian mythology.

Valkyries: Warrior maidens who served the God Odin and carried fallen warriors to his feast-hall, Valhalla, where they spent their days fighting and their nights feasting.

wergild: The amount that must be paid to make recompense for killing a man.

White Christ: The Vikings' name for the Christian God, believed to be a derogatory term implying cowardice, because he allowed himself to be captured and killed without fighting back against his captors.

HISTORICAL NOTES

The Danish campaign against the Franks in which Halfdan becomes a full-fledged warrior and wins his name is based on an actual Viking attack up the Seine River in the spring of A.D. 845, which was described in various contemporary Frankish sources, including several annals maintained by different Frankish monasteries. Each of the sources provides slightly different details about the campaign, but most agree that the Vikings' fleet made it as far up the Seine River as Paris, and all report that Charles the Bald, the king of the Western Kingdom of the Franks, ultimately paid a large sum—described in one account as a "bribe," and another as "tribute"—to the invading Viking army, to persuade it to leave his kingdom.

From careful comparison of the various contemporary sources that contain accounts of the expedition, the following additional details about the campaign are probably accurate: the Vikings' fleet numbered 120 ships; the Franks' King Charles responded to the Viking attack by dividing his army, sending part down each side of the Seine River; and the Vikings fought and resoundingly defeated one part of the divided Frankish army. After their victory, according to some sources, the Vikings killed 111 prisoners by hanging them. After defeating the Frankish army, the Viking army captured Paris in a surprise attack on Easter morning. The amount King Charles paid the Viking army to leave his kingdom was 7,000 pounds of silver—an incredible sum for that time period.

I have used these bare facts as the framework upon which to build the story in books two and three of the Strongbow Saga. The leaders of my fictional version of the Vikings' army—Ragnar Logbrod, his sons Ivar the Boneless and Bjorn Ironsides, and Hastein—are all based on actual Viking leaders of the latter half of the ninth century. One Frankish source, the Annals of Xanten, does identify Ragnar as the leader of the Viking fleet that attacked up the Seine in A.D. 845. I felt it plausible that on so major a campaign, Ragnar might well have been accompanied by his famous sons, Ivar and Bjorn, and Hastein could well have participated, too, because Bjorn and Hastein are known to have raided together on other occasions.

Hastein—sometimes called Hastings in English and Frankish sources—seems in particular to have been a colorful character. He is known to have harried the Atlantic coast of western Frankia, particularly Brittany, for many years. And together with Bjorn Ironsides, and possibly Ivar, he led a large-scale raiding tour of the Mediterranean that lasted from A.D. 859 until 862. Like the fictionalized Hastein who befriends Halfdan in the Strongbow Saga, he is known to have enjoyed using clever stratagems to win victory over his foes.

Genevieve, the young Frankish noblewoman who is captured by Halfdan, is a fictional character, as is Halfdan himself. However, her father, Count Robert, is based on an actual Frankish leader. Robert the Strong was a very powerful nobleman in western Frankia who ruled as count over a number of towns, including Angers, Blois, Tours, Autun, Auxere, Nevers, and—according to at least one source—Paris. Count Robert was killed fighting a force of Viking raiders in A.D. 866, but one of his sons, Odo, is a revered French hero who, as Count of Paris, led that city's successful defense against a year-long siege by a Viking army from A.D. 885 to 886.

During the late Roman Republic and the Roman Empire, Paris was a thriving city, one of the cultural and commercial centers of the Roman province of Gaul. The Roman city was built on the left (south) bank of the Seine River, on the top and sides of the large hill that later came to be known as Mount St. Genevieve. The large island in the Seine, now known as the Ile de la Cité, appears to have originally housed some sort of Roman regional administrative and possibly military headquarters. Around the year A.D. 280, after a period of barbarian raids that swept across Gaul, the island was fortified with a wall around its perimeter.

Although the city declined in population and importance during the period when Rome's vast empire was crumbling, after the Franks conquered Gaul and the Frankish King Clovis converted to Christianity, Paris regained some of its former glory. It was the capital of Frankia during the period when the Franks were ruled by the Merovingian dynasty, from roughly A.D. 486 until 752, and during the Merovingian period, its population is estimated to have reached as high as 20,000. However, the Frankish kings of the Carolingian dynasty, which began in A.D. 752, did not use Paris as their capital, and over the next hundred years the city's size and importance again declined.

By the year A.D. 845, Paris would still have borne a strong resemblance to its Roman-era predecessor. In addition to numerous smaller buildings and homes from the Roman period, the great forum, the center of every Roman city, still existed, although apparently some of its upper-level structures had been dismantled to provide a source of stone for later building projects, possibly including the defensive wall around the Ile de la Cité. The arena, one of the largest outside of Rome, was also still in existence. In fact, its lowest levels can still be seen in Paris today. As with the forum, by the ninth century, the upper levels of the arena had been dismantled to provide a source of stone for other structures, but the arena is known to have been partially restored around the year A.D. 577 by the Frankish King Chilperic I, who used it as a site for horse racing. The large Roman-era building now known as the Cluny baths, which in Roman times housed a massive Roman public bathhouse on the lower north slope of Mount St. Genevieve, still stands to this day in a remarkable state of preservation. It was used as the royal palace during the Merovingian era.

The Franks had put their own stamp on Paris by A.D. 845, however, and it is possible to identify some of the buildings of the period the Viking army would have encountered. After converting to

Christianity in A.D. 508, King Clovis built a large stone church on the top of Mount St. Genevieve. By A.D. 845, it had become the center of a convent, the Abbey of St. Genevieve. Similarly, the Church of St. Germain de Prés, built in A.D. 542 at the base of Mount St. Genevieve near the banks of the Seine, by A.D. 845 had become the center of a large and wealthy monastery, the Abbey of St. Germain. The Abbey of St. Denis was another large and important monastery located in Paris in the mid-ninth century. The town and surrounding countryside also contained a number of other churches and smaller monasteries built by the Franks. Because the city had not seen war or been looted for several hundred years, Paris was without a doubt a very rich prize when the Viking army captured it in A.D. 845.

My description in this book of the battle between the Viking and Frankish armies, which occurred when the Viking fleet moved upriver from Rouen, is entirely a work of fiction, because no details of the actual battle are known. However, I have based my descriptions of the tactics used by both sides on descriptions of various battles and skirmishes of the period. The Vikings, for example, are known to have often made heavy and effective use of archery fire, and the formation Ragnar uses in *The Road to Vengeance* is loosely based on descriptions of the formation used by Norwegian King Harald Hardrada against an English army containing a large force of cavalry in the battle of Stamford Bridge in A.D. 1066. Similarly, my description of the Frankish force as being composed entirely of mounted troops is based on the fact that by the mid-ninth century, the Franks had come to increasingly rely on cavalry when maneuvering in the field.

The Bretons, who play a major role in my fictional account of the battle, were a people of predominately Celtic origin who lived in the area of France along the southern Atlantic coast known as Brittany. Although they were not Franks, by the ninth century, the Bretons had somewhat reluctantly become subjects of the Frankish empire, and as such were required, on occasion, to contribute troops to fight for the king of western Frankia. The Bretons were noted for being skilled mounted warriors who fought protected by relatively heavy armor, armed with spears, javelins, and swords.

It is known that after the battle, the Viking army hanged 111 Frankish prisoners, although detailed descriptions of that action, and the reasons for it, have not been recorded. One modern historian has suggested that it was an act of intentional terror, an effort to demoralize the remainder of the Frankish army. A far more likely explanation is that the mass hanging was a religious sacrifice. The Vikings are known to have offered animal sacrifices to their Gods, and on rarer occasions to have sacrificed human victims as well. In their culture, great victories were sometimes marked by religious celebrations thanking the Gods, which included sacrificial offerings that were sometimes hung on trees. A description from the year A.D. 1070 of worship practices at the great pagan religious complex at Uppsala in Sweden, for example, describes huge periodic sacrifices where men, as well as numerous types of animals, were hung from the trees of a sacred grove surrounding the temple.

Readers who would like to learn more about the Vikings and Franks, their culture and history, and the world in which the Strongbow Saga is set, are urged to visit www.strongbowsaga.com, an educational website dedicated to the Vikings and their age.

Acknowledgments

Many people have been of great assistance in my work on the Strongbow Saga, but I would like to give my special thanks here to some of those who assisted in various ways with this particular book: my agent, Laura Rennert, whose belief in this project helped bring it into existence; my editors, Susan Rich and Patricia Ocampo, whose valuable insights and suggestions helped me hone the story's focus (and extra-special thanks to Patricia, for always having answers to my questions about the sometimes bewildering process of actually creating books from my words); my writer friends Luc Reid, Tom Pendergrass, and Laura Beyers, for acting as critical readers and helping me spot weaknesses in the story; to Luc also for designing and maintaining the Strongbow Saga websites; Michael Livingston, for invaluable help in tracking down Frankish sources; and, of course, my wife, Jeanette, for everything.